THE PLACE WILL COMFORT YOU

Stories

Naama Goldstein

SCRIBNER

New York   London   Toronto   Sydney

SCRIBNER
1230 Avenue of the Americas
New York, NY 10020

SCRIBNER and design are trademarks of
Macmillan Library Reference USA, Inc., used under license by
Simon & Schuster, the publisher of this work.

For information regarding special discounts for bulk purchases,
please contact Simon & Schuster Special Sales at:
1-800-456-6798 or business@simonandschuster.com.

Designed by Kyoko Watanabe

Set in Adobe Caslon

Manufactured in the United States of America

2   4   6   8   10   9   7   5   3   1

Library of Congress Cataloging-in-Publication Data
Goldstein, Naama, date.
The place will comfort you: stories/Naama Goldstein.
p. cm.
Contents: The conduct for consoling—The verse in the margins—Pickled
sprouts—A pillar of a cloud—The Roberto touch—Anatevka tender—
Barbary apes—The worker rests under the hero trees.
1. United States—Social life and customs—Fiction.
2. Israel—Social life and customs—Fiction. 3. Jewish youth—Fiction.
4. Jews—Fiction. I. Title.

PS3607.O485P55 2004
813'.6—dc22
2003068609

ISBN 978-1-4165-7867-3   ISBN 1-4165-7867-6

For Bobkin.

And he arrived at that place and passed the night there for the sun had gone; and he took a rock of that place and put it under his head and lay down in that place. And he dreamed, and behold, a ladder stood on the ground and its head reached skyward, and behold, angels of God ascending and descending on it.

GENESIS 28:11–12

CONTENTS

Part 1

OLIM (ASCENDING)

Part 2

veYORDIM (AND DESCENDING)

Part 1

OLIM (ASCENDING)

The Conduct for Consoling

THE CLOCK SHAPED like a headache pill says three-eleven.
For this I always look into P. Eliyahu Drugs, corner of Brenner and
Kibbutz Galuyot Street. I have my places where I like to look if
there is time when school is done so, halfway home, I check the
drugstore clock. The breath from me grays up the window, clears,
comes back and goes again. Inside a grandma argues at the counter.
Legs squeezed in brown bandages, she keeps sniffing a jar of medicine, then tries to give the pharmacist a turn. Each time he shoves
the jar away. He shakes his head and jabs his finger at her, makes his
mouth to shout. She sniffs the jar. He should, too. No, he will not.
I think he's going to win. The store is his. The clock is his. The time
is three-fourteen.

Leviticus: Write and memorize each offering in chapter 9.

Math: division.

History of Our State: questions, section 3 (The Dreyfus Libel).

At five o'clock on Lebanon TV comes on *Doug Henning's World
of Magic*. He only comes on once a year.

The pharmacist slaps at the register. The grandma wipes the air
like there's a chalkboard in between them. In the corner of my eye
somebody rushes from the sidewalk, pulls open P. Eliyahu's door.

The bell sings. Suddenly I can't see anymore what's with the argument. A face is squashed against the window from inside, blocking the view. Nose to my nose, eyes to my eyes: When I jump back the squashed face laughs. Around the twisted laugh the face is flat and white, but from that yellow hair I know exactly who it is. The long locks shift like satin ribbons with each move, except for a thick cowlick at the top, dull, stiff and blunt. The face unglues. The shop door opens out, again the bell. And it's the orphan, pushing into me, giving a small quick hug.

"Girl," the pharmacist shouts. "Blondie! For the final time I tell you children, come in here to buy, or—"

"Make exchanges! If you call yourself a store. Adler before you for just one example, Kupelnik by Central Station, Fania Elmaleh—" The door slams on the grandma's voice, and on the bell.

"You waited for me like I knew you would," the orphan says.

Someone tied sacks around the clusters in the date palms on this block. Across the way a street cat with a belly full of kittens crawls under the porch of Or Akiva Synagogue with the white peeling walls, the door tattered with notes announcing who has died, and who's been born, who's selling near-new things for not a lot, and who will tend children weeknights. A soldier blinking on a bus-stop bench gives up on being awake; his neck bends, his chin sinks to his chest. The orphan skips to him, touches his gun. His eyes spring open, someone's brother going far or coming back. She stands there watching him, hands linked behind her, ropy middle bulged. She's still in her school uniform. She doesn't have her book bag on. We didn't leave the school gates as a pair.

A yellow-bellied bird flies towards the swaddled dates. The soldier shuts his eyes.

We never walked together before and I was not waiting for her today.

e   s   o

I went consoling at the orphan's place a week ago. A cat gave her mother cancer, so she died. The orphan still has a father but she is orphaned from her mother and that's enough; she is an orphan. She was always something wrong and now there is a reason.

Three girls from the third grade got picked to do the shivah call. The homeroom teacher chose only top students, with top grades and clean pressed shirts, because she wanted us to represent the class. My last report card in Leviticus I got an *Almost Very Good Minus*, in History of Our State *Almost Very Good Plus*, in Math *Good Minus* which is a difficult subject for me, but English class, even though it's new this year, from the minute it ever started I was ahead. I can come up with more rhymes than anyone for Pin. They can learn all they want but I will always have more English words. I use them every day, to ask for honey on my toast, seconds of cereal, whether the socks I want are washed, who's locked up in the toilet, and to say good night, which half the time I say in Hebrew just as tired. I talk two languages without being taught. I know—I understand with the full feeling of living life—that you can be of one place and another, not at all the same. So does the Russian girl with the eyes slanted far apart, close to the surface of her Russian face. But Russian we don't have to take in school, nothing like *Doug Henning's World of Magic* comes from there, and the Russian girl did not get picked to go consoling. Only me and two more girls the homeroom teacher told the rules. There is a conduct for consoling and a conduct for the grief. We memorized our part.

Do not knock on a mourner's door, just open and walk in.

Don't say hello and not good-bye. Do not wait to be seated.

Ask for no assistance, offer none. Solicit no instructions. Your presence in itself is sustenance, judge whether more is needed on your own. Take care not to contribute to the burden. If the bereaved engages you in talk, don't laugh, keep the voice moderately pitched, nowhere near loud. Don't force the heavy topic. Wait for the mourner to address her loss, and don't remove the cloth from any mirror.

We found her family name on the mailboxes right away, but stood awhile in the building's entrance hall. A death notice was hanging on the Tenants' Council board, printed with letters in the holy type of prayer books. Each letter in itself was almost book-sized, shelved in a heavy black frame:

BY DIVINE PROVISION

DRORA EVVEN
WIFE AND MOTHER IN ISRAEL
5704–5737
MAY HER SOUL BE GATHERED IN LIFE'S SATCHEL

THE FUNERAL PROCEEDING MONDAY 29 ELUL
FROM OR HAGAR SYNAGOGUE
TO THE ETERNAL REST GROUNDS AT GEULA
FOLLOWING THE EARLY MORNING SERVICE

That had already happened. We didn't go. To see a mother carried high in a white shroud towards the grave, then covered by the earth, is not for children's eyes except an orphan's. Consoling anyone can do who learned the rules.

People were coming down the stairwell, talking. *Broken. Shouldn't know from such.* We looked, each at the other two, to see who could move first. The three of us were here to represent the class. We weren't friends otherwise. A sweaty hand squeaked along a near down banister. *The experience of my brother-in-law, what he witnessed after his young sister, I should say it was a place where the community, I won't besmirch, the west end of Neveh Keedma. She left five children with the man.*

Three fathers stood atop the first rise of white stairs. One had an attaché case, one large empty hands, and one a green net grocery satchel, half a loaf black bread caught in the mesh. They stopped their talk and changed their order to walk one behind the other. My two partners in consoling lined up, too. We started on the climb. Each of us passed each of the men. We still had on our uniforms from school. They were in their office clothes.

I thought it would be dark in the apartment. It was light. When we walked in immediately I saw the cat, a red one with gold eyes, hunched in the shade of a consoler's folding chair, nose searching from the gap between two legs in army pants. The father sat on what would be a sofa if the cushions weren't all pulled out, so he was lower to the ground just like the teacher said, his sweater rent just like the teacher said, ruined on purpose, one rough tear over the heart. His face was such a way I couldn't look. In front of him were plates with rolls and hummus, eggplant spread and herring and some cakes, and in a pitcher raspberry squash. Nothing was touched except the fish. Grownups moved slowly or stood still. The cat sprang, landing neatly by a slice of marble cake. A man's hand picked the animal up by the neck. The cat made a quick journey through the air, stood where it fell, then walked off in a hurry, rubbing all along the papered wall. It held its striped red tail like a lamppost, looking back once at all the people in its place. We followed, to the orphan's room.

She was sitting on the tiles, next to a blanket. We got down, too, me on the corner of the blanket when we ran out of floor. We waited, like the teacher said, with not a word of greeting, not a word of pleasantry, no talk, nothing to tax the scant reserves of the bereaved. She started talking right away, but to her cat.

"Here. Here here. Here."

The cat came closer and the orphan made a grab. She was wearing a gigantic housedress, so her lap looked like a field of pansies grown over two sticks, on which now stood a cat. She held the animal tight; even though the cat had led us here, it seemed to have another place in mind. But soon it slumped and lay there, front paws pointed towards the orphan's navel. Now she bowed and pressed her forehead to the furry one. Her hair became a covering to both of them, the two heads overflowed by yellow shine, streaming down from that ugly tuftlike liquid from a tap. I saw the cat's eye narrow till it closed. The bigger human eye kept staring, wide and blue. Finally the lashes batted, thick as bristles on a brush. The orphan drew up straight, her hair just hers again, her eyes on us.

"Small eyes is happy," she said. "Closed is in the clouds. I know about cats. Do you have a cat?" We waited to see who would answer first. Until this day we had never been to where the orphan lives. "Zeessie loves a guest," she said.

The orphan before being an orphan came to birthdays uninvited and brought stupid gifts. Half a pencil or a notebook with the pages used and then erased. She'd push to be the first in every game. She'd laugh too hard and at wrong times. Whenever she would lose a contest, every single time it was no fair. She'd argue even with the grownups, until someone stuck a favor bag in her hand early, so she'd go. With or without, she always leaves last.

She dragged the animal up from her lap and showed it all around. Its weight stretched out the downy armpits so we could see their suede, the hind legs dangling over every lap of ours, in turn and then around again. The velvety toes spread apart like chicken toes, the claws popped out, each lap wiggled back, and every time the orphan laughed and tossed her hair.

"That's what she does!" she said again and again. "She wants to feel something under her. Here, Zeessie. No, here, Zeessie." I thought someone should say something. But could your first word to an orphan be, Stop? I knew it could not.

After a while someone came and whispered, "Quiet, girls. Remember where you are." We couldn't say it was the orphan who forgot.

She set the cat beside her on the blanket, which was baby-sized, knitted in loopy pastel checks that I could feel through my skirt. The cat took a step towards the door, but stopped, stepped back, looked at a swelled fold in the blanket and gave it thought. Again the paws reached, toes together now, reaching by choice to test the wrinkle, and make sure, and one more time, and so it stayed there, pawing at the blanket, like a digging for something, but slow and loving, pawing, rumbling, shoulders rising, falling, head sunk down, pointed end nuzzling.

"She thinks it's going to give her milk," the orphan said. "Watch," she said, and tugged a corner so the fold became a flickering snake. The cat's head snapped awake. With round gold eyes, it watched the snake. The orphan tugged again, the cat slapped. The orphan yanked, the cat glared and bit in.

The orphan said, "I've been to your home, and to your home, and to your one," and it wasn't any lie. The cat spat out the blanket and rolled over on its back. The fur was of a different kind below, the palest yellow-brown, thick as a heat-spell cloud.

Outside the front door opened, people whispered. The door shut again. A kettle started whistling; someone stopped it right away.

The orphan said, "I like your home the best."

To me.

She said, "Who made your little birthday cakes, sprinkled on top of every single cake with number eights in balls of silver many times like in a jewel box of eights?"

I said, "My mother, but I sprinkled," and I almost put my hand flat to my mouth, hearing I let it slip about her loss. I shouldn't have said Mother. I should have said something else. "The silver is safe to eat," I said.

"In that amount and only once or twice a year it won't catch up for a long time," the orphan said. "So let's say you and her next month can help me with my party. But do nines."

How would I have known the orphan was older than me? She never had a birthday party before. I thought, her mother didn't let.

What kind of mother wouldn't let her child celebrate her birth? A mother of that kind you wouldn't want. You would be wishing for a new one a long time. I didn't feel anymore like speaking of my mother. I thanked HaShem our God I didn't have a cat. They said in school a cat can kill your mother with disease, plus anyone who stays the night, and I said, Like I didn't know.

The orphan said, "Americans make better cake than what we do here."

I felt so shy with happiness, I smiled at my knees. This year on Our Many Cultures of Good Taste Day almost all my gingerbread men ended up one-legged in the trash. Everyone thought they would be chocolate. The year before I brought a loaf of mac and cheddar cheese and someone said, because of this your legs are fat. On Our Many Cultures of Good Taste Day suddenly the best thing to be is Yemeni or Moroccan, and I'm not.

"Tell me the recipe," the orphan said. She pushed the cat, both of them sidling up, the blanket bunching towards me. The animal was busy licking its own chest, and didn't look up. The orphan tossed her hair. A strand whipped close. "Two buckets melted chocolate," she said. "Right? Or three. Twenty-five eggs, only the yolks. Everything sweet and wet as much as possible, the flour sifted fifty times so it fluffs up to full apartness. Nuts. You should have put in nuts. In mine we'll put in nuts. Otherwise everything the same, including favor bags, with red clowns on the front and back, drawstrings to close them, inside every one a singing water whistle, bird shape, red or blue. A two-tone toffee, four big pretzels." Every favor that I had she knew, and every one she wanted. "Sourballs, three, none a color of another, double-joke Bazooka, a nougat banana."

One of my partners in consoling got up on her feet, and stood in her school uniform.

The orphan didn't see. Only a dirty little heel popped out from beneath the pansy field, then ducked in again. "And we should keep all the same games," she said. And she remembered, each one by its rules and name plus how it went that day, from when I tried to pin the donkey tail on Grandfather of blessed memory in his old silver frame, to when I stumped every last guest with my Life Story quiz. From when my team jumped up and down because my soldier cousin said he'd be our mummy, to when I was a hundred percent right it wasn't fair; we had the same amount of time and length of paper as the other teams, sure, but we had more to wrap. She said, "When your mother said to wait for all your guests to be served cake before you stuck the fork in yours, and you knew on your birthday you don't have to? You pulled the anger right out of your face. Almost immediately you really couldn't see, good and quick."

The girl in her school uniform stepped forward. It was a Friday. The teacher said not to stay long. We had a duty to console. We also had a duty to get home before the Sabbath Queen and clean our home for her, and bathe.

"Your mother is beautiful," the orphan said. "Your TV's huge. Your father's smart."

The girl opened her mouth and took a breath. "The Place will comfort you," she said, "among all the mourners of Zion and Jerusalem," just like the teacher said. You cannot utter from your mouth the real name of God, but you can talk about His Place, from which comes consolation for our gravest trials.

Now my second partner in consoling stood.

"Those ruffle socks you wore," the orphan said, "with roses on the ankles out of lace. I love them. There was food enough for a whole zoo. Your parents aren't cheap. Your towels smell good."

"The Place will comfort you," the second one said, "among all the mourners of Zion and Jerusalem." And both my partners stepped around, and out, without good-bye, just like the teacher said.

I was surprised that I was left there on my own. I was surprised I didn't mind them leaving. They weren't my friends but they were something like me, pretty good students with not too wrinkled shirts. Us three were picked to represent the class. Not the class president, and not the most pretty, not the precisest dodgeball slammer, not the singing daughter of the cantor. First up the stairs had been the Parsi who uses oil on her hair and lets no one touch. The first to speak the parting consolation was a bucktooth with three bucktooth sisters. Me, the orphan was excited to see.

"I like your dinner plates with the blue edge," she said. She also liked our rocking chair. She also liked my bed. I knew then how it would be to watch a program on TV about a me which everybody wants to be.

All of a sudden I jumped to my feet. Something had been wrong and I only knew now. A wet warmth scraping me. My palm and fingertips and knuckles and between. The cat looked up at me, the pink tip of her tongue poking out. She drew it in.

The orphan said, "You touched your feet before you came here, don't say that you didn't! She can taste them. You have feet all over you. If not she'd only lick the nooks. Why'd you touch your feet?"

I said, "I have to get back home on time or I'll be dead." I almost died right there for saying Dead. The orphan looked insulted, but, thank God, it wasn't what I said. It wasn't even her that was insulted, but the cat.

"That isn't what you do with cats," she said. "You can't jump up all of a sudden. Look how hurt her feelings are. You scratch them first. You tell them next time they can come along."

I squatted where I was and reached my fingers to the cat. I told myself, The left, the left, so I'd remember which hand I should wash.

"Under her chin."

The cat stretched out her neck.

"Slower."

She squinted her gold eyes.

"Now tell her."

"Next time you can come."

Zeessie kept stretching up her chin. She smiled, shut-eyed, lips like edges of a clam shell coming open, sharp pearls glinting. Her breath was liver and old cheese. Red hairs stuck to my hand.

I hurried through the living room, sneaking my eyes to the TV and mirror and glass cabinet doors, all covered, like the teacher said, every reflection hidden in a time not suitable for looking at your own shape in this world. Our solemn thoughts must dwell on that which has no shape. We all knew what this meant. The warning passed around: The mother's soul! The mother undeparted, who was waiting in her home behind each sheet. Either she waited everywhere at the same time, or else she knew which sheet your fingers itched to lift. There she would be. As soon as one thin sliver of reflective surface flickered back at life, she'd travel on the ray, glide down the tilted plane of suffering and drop at our feet to crawl among them, hunting for the cat.

I blew the fur off me, wiped my hand on my school skirt and saw more hairs stuck there. I turned around. The orphan watched me from the hallway. Standing in her mother's pansy dress, she cradled the cat, the red tail lashing back and forth. A sofa cushion tripped me. Two hops sideways kept me on my feet, two extra skips ahead kept me going. I had to go on moving or I'd fall, with nothing to grab at but sheets.

I shouted, "Thank you for the hospitality, good-bye," like gracious houseguests should. But I forgot that what I was, was a consoler.

There is a conduct for consolers and there's one for whom we visit, but I forgot my part when I ran out, so no one in the house of mourning said any words back. Someone closed the door behind me. I ran the whole way down. New visitors heaved themselves up.

Early today the teacher in Leviticus maybe forgot this was the orphan's first day back. Because right in the middle of the verse she stopped and, as if this were a day like any day, yelled at the orphan, "So I take it that your endless jabber is in fact supremely useful in the shaping of Mankind, otherwise who could fathom why HaShem our God Himself is obligated to suspend his all-knowing Instruction—" And so on and so forth, fire in her eyes and smoke shooting from her nostrils.

The orphan scraped her chair back. Tiles screeched. Tears tumbled from her eyes like diamonds. Hair flew out like golden spokes around that dingy tuft.

She yowled, "Who can concentrate when it's so dull with you? Dull, dull!" she screamed. "Dull!" like some big discovery. Which it was, to the teacher. "Your voice," the orphan said, "is like cold boiled rice for every single meal, every day. Lists! Lists! The pieces of the animal to cut, the pieces of the animal to burn, the pieces and the pieces and the pieces! Can't you tell a story? Tell a story maybe once! We liked Mrs. Shuvali better!" That's who taught us Exodus last year.

Bang. You could hear her crying extra loud out in the hall. That's how she's always been. Only the speech before was new, and the reason for howling.

The teacher pulled the kerchief on her head a little lower to her eyebrows, bowed and read aloud about the fire from HaShem our God that came forth and consumed all of the offerings of chapter 9. " 'And when the people saw.' " She looked up from the book, across her high, green desk, eyes flooded full of privacy, beneath the silver-threaded cotton covering her head. " 'They rose in song and fell.' "

I liked to hear about this happening. I knew this part would finally come. She told it well. The orphan's howling in the hallway faded and was gone.

She never came back to the lesson, or the rest of that whole school day. It was only in the time after school that I saw her again. I wasn't used to seeing her in this time.

Under the date sacks hanging from the palms, over the oat grit on the pavement by the donkeyfeed shop, left at Hannah Szenes. The Bee Gees squeal from the Gruner Corner record store. I don't know why they have to sing like that. The orphan isn't curious.

"You like *them*?" she says.

"Where did you go after you ran out of Leviticus? What did you do up until now?"

She says, "I had a conversation with the principal."

"What did she say to you?"

"She said," the orphan says, "that she would see I wasn't treated such a treatment in her school again. She knows the mayor and the prime minister."

"Guess what! I know what they're singing in that store. I could tell you the words."

"I know them. Ahh, ahh, ahh. Tayna lie."

"That isn't how. Should I tell you? They come from where I came."

She says, "Americans are fat."

I thought she liked Americans. I thought she loved our cakes.

She says, "On you it looks nice. You're full-figured but it's how you're meant to be. You're an exception, plus you have some color in your skin, and where's your accent full of spit? Don't have one, why? Because you count like you're from here. Let's go."

This hurts my feelings. Then it fixes them a little, then it makes me angry, proud, and grateful, till I'm left annoyed. One thing I know for sure is that I have a complicated answer to get out: "Like *you* don't have a history of passage?"

"I was born here."

"Sure, you. But what about—?" I know how the rest of it goes, my mother gave it to me, we practiced long. But that boy in summer camp could not have been an orphan. To an orphan you don't talk about his parents, or his parents' parents, any kind of parent. A mother is a parent. It is not for you to turn their thoughts upon their loss.

The record seller leans out of his store. "The Brothers Gibb are not American." We run away from him.

At the distance where he couldn't leave his store so long, I stop. The orphan streaks on, and I am alone again for a good time. Or not so good at first, because approaching every turn I pray to our God HaShem she won't be there. I am not used to her in this time. She's unfamiliar to me here. I like her better at the other edge of a great many others in our uniform, within a fence.

In all my worry I can't stop to check the crack in the old beadle's wall. I cannot hear the conversation of the balance-sitting boys, high on the sidewalk safety rails, spitting their shells, today of pumpkin seeds. But when I see my playground I stop praying. This is always my last place.

I know the busy times and slow inside the low stone border, for the short slide and the tall. I knew the gutter of the water fountain would be almost dry now, the bees flown. I see at least one face I recognize here every time I go, not necessarily such that I have to say hello. I knew, this time of day, this time of year, the Arab women would be shaking down the olive trees. And there they are, in dresses over pants, beating the gray-green branches, olives hailing down a little lighter than yesterday.

Oval green marbles hit the tarp and roll into the wrinkles. This is not their playground, but the mayor must have said okay. They're in no rush. They drive in from their village for the olives in the morning and they leave before the crowd. The top of the tall slide is the best place to sit and watch and think about the shapes and clothes of country Arab women.

Yellow stripes whip before the ladder rungs, gold strands lashing my fingers as they reach to climb: the orphan, jumping from behind a bush, blocking the slide. "Keep walking," she says. "Don't be scared."

"I'm going up the slide."

"Run."

"Usually I use the slide"

"Usually, fine. Today there are Arabs."

"I know them."

"You can't know Arabs."

"They wear skirts over pants. They pick olives."

"Did you know they were looking at you?"

I didn't.

"Did you know they're talking?" She grabs both my shoulders to stop me from turning around. "Are you crazy?"

"Who says they're talking about me?"

She looks at me with kindness. "Go."

"Who says they don't like me?"

"They would like to spill your blood."

"They're picking olives."

"Exactly. You were going to watch."

"So?"

"They don't want you to watch."

"Why?"

"Because they're picking olives."

"Like I said before!"

"Which aren't theirs."

"They asked the mayor."

"They hate our mayor. They hate to ask."

"He said okay. They came last year and yesterday."

"There is no *time* for this!" the orphan yells. "One is heading over with her stick! Act normal. It's two. It's three now! What is the fastest way home?"

Hand in hand, we run around the slide, over the path to where it softens by the water fountain, then off, between two baby cypresses and over the low border. The orphan follows every move I make along the shortcut that I found when Crazy Petersburgski, from the house without its panes and door, zigzagged through traffic and stepped up behind me. From our porch, I saw him pass the opening in our hedge, continue down a block, then blaze a trail through the weedyard of his house, his hands still moving with his shouting at the air. Some days he doesn't.

This time, when the orphan and I lean out from the seventh floor, we see nothing but my key chain swinging from my neck plus, lower down, the roaming little sisters from the arguing apartment.

"We should spit on them," the orphan says.

"Should not." I hold her wild blue eye just long enough. I live here. I have seen the mother of the girls throw sheets of newspaper for them to move their bowels onto, on the street. They do it. I understand from this it is a rule with them that, once you're out, you can't come in. I don't need trouble with this type.

The orphan pushes a thin shoulder into me, so now her smile is my only view. "Wow, scary! Right?" she says. "We ran hard."

"Can someone pick you up?"

She grabs a rail of the porch. "I never had my lunch," she says. "I missed the cafeteria break. Like I could stay after what happened in Leviticus? She didn't give me any choice." Her voice begins to fade. "I could collapse and faint." Her neck grows soft. "There's a condition that I have," she says. "I get too hungry, I can die."

In the kitchen she heads immediately for the stove, kneels, and glues her face to the cold glass. "Where's your cake?"

"We don't keep it there."

"Then where?"

"Nowhere. It's the middle of the week and no one's birthday."

I know for a fact all she can see are two bare racks, but you would think the glass looks out on the sparkling sea. It does not. I know this from across the room. I know it just the same once I'm beside her, tiles against my knees.

"None?" she says. "Nowhere? Nothing?"

"If we had any it wouldn't be here."

She keeps staring in. No, she is looking at my image. In the see-through mirror, all of our differences are two: the first our hair, dim gold streaming by a black-brown cloud, and the second our shoulders, mine saddled with my bookbag straps, hers bare. The rest is twinned: pink shirts, pink-collared necks, a face next to another, egg-shaped both, eye-stained, the details blurred but sharper than the room around. The oven rungs show clearest through the areas of dark.

"Then where?" she says.

"Where it won't spoil."

"So? An oven between bakings is good. Cool, very dry."

"There isn't the right level of concern for hygiene in this country. You should keep it in the fridge wrapped up in plastic."

"Says who?"

"My mother." I push away the floor and stand. I can't not say *my mother* in *my home*. Anyway, the orphan isn't bothered. She hops up. Her mood is much stronger than a minute ago. We're still facing the oven, but she's looking at the tin-handed timer clock.

She bats her lashes. "When does she come home?"

"At the end of her work."

"And makes dinner?"

I cannot carry on with such talk, when I know this: It is one hour and ten minutes until *Doug Henning's World of Magic*. If I don't do my homework, there'll be no TV at all.

"Right now is homework time."

She says, "Maybe for you."

At the far end of the kitchen counter I touch a cabinet door. The door sinks in. The swiveling pantry spins and shows its shelves. I tell the orphan to take what she wants, then turn the bend around the breakfast island, choose a stool, slip off my bag, unbuckle it, and let all my supplies slide out.

I organize the pile, last to first, open my pencil case, find one pointed, line it up beside where I will stack my documents. These documents, translucent, glossed, embroidered with the teacher's hand and spaces framed for mine in purple mimeograph ink, slip smoothly off my binder prongs. I take a deep breath of the sharp, head-clearing smell, and I am ready. This is my work station. The pages go in their decided place.

50, remainder 1.

86. 4.

32. 9.

16.

In History of Our State you must take care to respond in full answers, which contain the question.

1. The unjust punishment of Captain Alfred Dreyfus by the French was five years exile on Devil's Island in prison clothes with the guards saying we will keep you here for life, the judge told us to, but first in front of everyone they tore his decorations that he earned off of his captain's uniform and broke his weapon and the onlookers all shouted for the blood of Jews and launched a hunting season and the least but personally painful thing was that he also had to give back the Captain's uniform, down to the army-issue underwear and socks, for life, even after he was ultimately cleared.

2. The real traitor was Esterhazy.

3. His disguise in flight was to shave off his mustache.

4. A subsequent fact for history's consideration is the death of the Captain's granddaughter, Madeleine, in Auschwitz.

5. Herzl's grand vision was that he understood the matter of the climates and the crops.

And here I am, done with two subjects out of three, with time to spare, enough room to expand into the part I left for last. The purple script of the instructions balances, top of the page, above the columns:

Complete and memorize.

This must be done in stages. First, the look into Leviticus and the transcription, every *Offering* matched with corresponding *Substances* and *Method*. Later comes the recitation, but the first phase is the work I love, the words I transfer very fine, the spectacle they carry strange. This is the worship as we practiced it for the first time, in desert passage.

Sin offering.
Peace-offering.
Wave-offering.
A bull-calf. An ox. A ram.
Oil. Incense.
Meal of grain.

A drawer rolls open. Cutlery chimes.

The fat and the kidneys and the lobe of the liver.

The drawer rolls shut.

Breasts and right thigh.
Inwards and legs.

A plastic plate scrapes lightly across the counter.

Washed and made smoke.
Smeared with blood at the base and corners.

The orphan crows out of the quiet, and the luster of the verses is made dust. "You seen this?"

Her narrow back is turned to me across the breakfast island, a shoulder laboring, sleek mane shifting with that one lock an exception. She has set up her own station in the neighborhood of the sink. As far as I can see, she is supplied with our tub of chocolate sandwich spread, our loaf of bread, much shortened, and our toothiest big-handled knife, which I hear crunching. The teeth don't show, only the handle. The blade is shoved down. The orphan steps back, fingers around the wood. Then, finger after finger, she lets go, and waves her empty hand. Yet the knife stands. The blade is buried in the marble. She has stabbed our kitchen counter.

I move all at once like the army, down from my stool, around the island, across the floor: "Stop!" Even though it's already done. Done, there before she found it. I know that crack. This is a feature of our kitchen and she didn't put it in.

"Should I take it out?"

"Take it out."

She jerks the handle one way and the other, and free. Stone meal has stuck to the chocolate-greased metal, up to a point. She says, "Deep as this."

"You made it worse."

"With such a thin knife?"

"Metal beats rock."

"So metal made the crack?"

"My mother, with a pot."

"Why?"

"She took it off the fire, ran, dropped it on the counter and leaped back."

The orphan finds the stain before I point it out, how could she not, a beet-red splatter on the ceiling, a wildly flaming planet, droplets violently striving everywhere. "I like borscht," she says. "With sour cream and pepper. Why did she do it?"

"Pressure cookers make her nervous."

"So why did she use one?"

"To save time."

"Did she get hurt?"

"I told you she leaped back."

"You saw?"

"I heard."

"And then?"

"I came."

"And saw?"

"Her hands shaking. She was sitting on the floor."

"Dropped?"

"Legs straight ahead."

"And no one helped?"

"She didn't want at first but then she let. My father took her hands."

"What did he say?"

"I don't remember."

"What did she say back?"

"'God damn that pot.'"

"With you there?"

"They didn't see me. That's not her usual language."

"Did she take it back?"

"She didn't say one more word. She looked like she had found him after a terrible, long trip."

"Show me the pot."

"I can't." I put out a hand and she gives back our knife. "My father threw it out. It was archaic and a hazard. Better technology is just around the corner."

"I could have told you that," she says, again gazing up. Her chin is bearded with a dab of chocolate. She slips her fingers through her hair; they meet up at the crown, over the damaged patch, to feel it gently, then come apart. "For a whole week I didn't dream," the orphan says. "Last night I did. I bit right through a windowpane. Inside was light and outside dark. I bit a hole right through the middle of the glass, black in the middle of the shine, the shape of my mouth. It didn't hurt, it didn't not hurt, I didn't feel any blood running."

I don't see what this has to do with anything right now. "We have a big assignment in Leviticus."

"I don't." She keeps on staring at the stain, but glassy-eyed, bored sick.

"The teacher gave it after you got up and went."

She says, "Gave you. But I'm exempt."

"You have chocolate on your chin."

"So?"

"You should wash it."

She says, "Let's watch TV."

I almost laugh at her. Nothing can tempt me before five o'clock today. He comes on only once a year. I smile. "Only after home-work. That's my mother's rules."

The orphan finger-pats her tough, blunt lock. "Maybe for you."

"What happened there?"

She spins around to push the lid back on the chocolate. "Finish your boring work," she says. "If you finished we'd have time."

"It isn't boring." I lay the knife in the sink. She hands me the soft-sided tub, which I return to its home in the pantry.

"Boring." She licks her thumb, presses it onto the breadboard, then pecks off the coating of crumbs. "This year there's no more story," she says through speckled lips.

"There is."

"No."

"Yes. What do you call the people in the desert? Exodus they got away and headed out, right? The tabernacle was built to practice for the Future Temple? This year they are learning how to worship in it and they get to try. In chapter 9 they have a test. What happens?"

She lifts the loaf and squeezes it like an accordion. I grab the bread and box it.

"If you'd have stayed in class you would know. They get it right! They offer everything correctly. A fire comes forth from HaShem and eats the offerings. And all the people rise in song and fall, because they got it right."

She says, "So why'd they fall?"

"That's just the bowing."

"You said fall."

"That word in the Torah just means bow. A sudden bow that looks like falling. From the reverence."

She says, "For such a easy word as fall you have to learn a expla-nation? I feel sorry for you that you're not exempt."

The fragrance of the mimeographs wafts over the air. A trapped fly struggles in a tiny burst; this is the nature of the sound which says the clock's tin hand is straining in a tricky nock, and out.

"Go watch TV."

"For real? What if she walks in?"

"The rules are just for me."

Her sandals slap over our tiles, then are muffled by our carpet. The television knob clicks smartly and releases seltzer noise. The fizz acts up in six new ways, then smoothes into the trill and prance and festive kindergarten teacher's voice of an Arabic commercial meant for kids. The orphan has chosen Lebanon TV. Next come Loony Toons, two, rich and quick, carnival ruckus on each side of a chase. Big deal. It's nothing I can't watch on the National Channel, later, an extra row of printed exclamations coursing below, Hebrew flowing above the Arabic. *You see how tables turn, my lucky duck!*

Though I smooth the pages of Leviticus back at my work station, my thoughts stay on translation. Why do we translate the Toons for Arabs, along with us, but they translate only for themselves? Because Israel has Arabs living in her, but the Arab countries, no Israelis. Also they wouldn't like to do a favor for the children of our nation. And we? Do we translate every program for the Arabs? How could I truly know? I would have to watch every single show on the National Channel, all day. No mother would allow it. But the answer doesn't matter when I don't need translation in the first place, since I understand the Toons as they are said: *Tha-tha, that's all—*

The ending is cut short. The orphan has switched somewhere else, a sterner place, Jordan TV. A string orchestra slices its rows with slanting notes while a kingly voice keens. The orphan turns this up. The singer and strings complete their job, slow down, and stop. A newer Arabic music gallops in, and just as quickly halts.

Ladies and gentlemen, good afternoon to you, a welcoming voice says, but not in Arabic. No. Otherwise, explain how I know what he just said. The greeting may have come out in their sounds, but that is our language, here. Hebrew is what he's speaking, with an Arab accent. Jordan is talking so we'll understand. An enemy reaches out.

The orphan has pushed our rocking chair from its belongful spot. The curved base rocks over the smashed nap of our carpet, in front of our TV. The screen is showing a man who I can see is Arab, polite and serious in a pinstripe suit behind a desk. The number on the dial says it's Jordan, but I recognize every word.

In a secret address broadcast to the Israeli cabinet today, United States president, Jimmy Carter, vowed to withdraw all aid within a fortnight if no reforms are seen in Israel's policy of gross coercion and brute force.

The orphan is laughing and clapping her hands. "Oh, good one," she says. "Very clever. Try a little harder, liar. Lying Arab liar."

"Who is he talking to?"

"Who do you think? Me and you."

"Why? What's happening? What are they going to do?"

"Like you never saw this before?"

"What was it that he said? What did it mean?"

"It isn't true," she says. "He is a liar for a living." She makes room for me on her chair, but doesn't stop the rocking. I must catch the rhythm fast and jump at the chance. She grabs me as I land.

Last week in Belgrade, Maccabi Tel Aviv's basketball team claimed the European Championship cup.

"That's true," I say. "We did win."

"Stop bunging up the rocking," she says. "Do like me. Pay attention."

Probes into stimulant abuse by runtish point guard Motti Aroesti have been quashed, the newsman says, *by American Jewish financiers of the competition.*

"Lie," she says.

"The part I understood was true."

A poll suppressed by the Israeli censor demonstrates that the over-whelming majority of Jews collected from the Arab countries and trans-planted in Palestine since the inception of the Zionist experiment would like to be collected again, and put back. The European Jewish ruling class

alone stands in the way of a movement of return to lands where this now
sorely disenfranchised group had previously been perfectly happy, typi-
cally affluent and influential.

"No one wants to go back! We all like it here!"

"Who's talking to you?" the orphan says.

"Him, no? You said."

"I also told you he's a liar. Anything he says is the opposite of
true. If he says go away, stay put. He says you're weak, you're just
that strong. Me and her watched it every day before dinner. Lost
means won. News equals propaganda."

I don't know of such a thing. The man delivering it shuffles his
notes. "He said we won. We did."

"You don't understand how it works," she says. "Make sure not
to eat up what's coming next. The strongest lie will always use
sights and actors. What look like stumps are really tied up in the
pants or sleeve. Any pus is mustard."

The television blinks away the man. His voice speaks on.

In today's objective third party report, a Belgian camera crew turns its
equipment. The screen looks out on an alley, narrow, unpaved,
unloved, spangled with water-filled footprints in mud. *One refugee*
family, uprooted and banished from a village of antiquity which was sub-
sequently occupied and renamed. A knock-kneed child appears, splash-
ing away from us over the mud, barefooted, a boy in shorts. His
hands are joined behind his neck, clasping the handles of a grocery
satchel which rides on his back. His back is stooped in a manner for
carrying what is heavy. The net shows through only a stack of flat
bread loaves, bouncing against the thickness of a book bag. This last
thing is the weight.

"He's learning how to be a murderer," the orphan says. "Next
year his mother will take him to your playground at the crowded
time. He'll blow up your slide. Where are you going?"

This is the matter which God commanded you, Do.

Take ye a he-goat for a sin offering and a bull-calf and lamb, a year old and unblemished to raise up in fire. And an ox and a ram for a peace offering to consecrate before HaShem, and a grain-meal offering mingled with oil.

Today HaShem will be apparent to you.

"There's hidden salt in chocolate spread," the orphan says, crossing the room. "You sit. Where's your drinks?" The fridge door suction gives. She finds the grapefruit squash, the ice, a cup.

"Grain meal. Oil."

"What?" she says. She brings her drink over to my station. "Did you want—?" she whispers. "No. Shh."

"Mingled with oil." How truly thirstily her juice goes down. *"Mingled."* She's just as eager for the empty cup. She makes her lips long and draws out the shrinking ice. Water shines on her chin. Ice clacks behind her teeth. *"Oil. Meal of grain."*

She spits the ice back out. "You already said that."

"Aren't you missing your show?"

"It's over. I came to be with you."

"I'm learning by heart."

She looks at my station. "And what else after?"

"Nothing."

"Only this and then you're free? You're almost done!"

"I'm having a hard time."

"Finish! Be done!"

"The copying I liked but nothing sticks."

She takes the mimeographed columns from my hands and breathes their purple scent, for a long time. When she comes up, the sun of good ideas lights her sky-blue eyes. She says, "You need a hands-on exercise."

And these are the things which the orphan says, get:

Cream of wheat. Soy oil.

Sliced salami. Plum jam.

Corkscrew noodles in sauce.

"Anything else red?" she says, rummaging through the fridge. She finds the ketchup in the door. "What else?"

"A paper towel for each mess."

"What else?"

"For the fire we'll just make noise."

She says, "We'll figure it out as we go."

Never was homework so alive.

Red on the corners of the counter. Red at the base. This I will not forget. Grain meal whispering while pouring, as she waves cold cuts in the air. (She likes the way I can control the sandy stream. She nods. "You should fill your hands of it," she says.) The sensation of the meal grains passed in the thousands, hand to hand. (She drapes the cold cuts on her shoulders like a pair of epaulettes. "Now hold still.") The grains sopping the weight of drops and cleaving to each other, then to the creases of the palms. ("Mingle," she says, twisting the oil cap.)

We mingle it until our fingers turn the coarse dough gray. Our hands had looked perfectly clean.

We push the matter into different shapes, then scoop and pound it into a sturdier stock and start over with an animal theme. We try again with the idea of a whole landscape, which needs a base. Salami is a natural choice. Fish sticks make good trees. Some of the plums in the jam are entirely whole, only shrunk and hollow. One contains part of a pit.

Now, when the clock's tin hand shudders, it's no longer punishment to me. I don't fill with the early sorrow of my favorite show coming and passing, unseen because unearned. The time draws close and I have earned the time. The sound of struggle is a prize.

The solid foods come away easily. The sauces must be given a quick wipe. The meal-dough clings in the crack.

"It's a good match," the orphan says.

We pat some more in, lick our fingers, smooth the edges, level the ridge. This day proceeds from good to best. My mother will be extraordinarily pleased.

The orphan says we should correct the ceiling, too.

She climbs up on the counter, stands with one shoe on each side of what is no longer a crack. She stretches her thin neck. "Go get some bleach. You have some on the spinning shelf that's on the dryer."

She leaps down, runs off on a separate path. I return with bleach, she with a toilet brush and my father's spare glasses. Both she hands to me. She takes the chemical. Under the kitchen sink my mother keeps a pair of rubber gloves. We each get one. She puts the stopper in the sink and pours the bleach inside, closing her eyes. I shield mine with the glasses while pushing off my shoes. She stays down while I go up. She dips, I scrub.

"A little more," she says. "A little more." Until a key turns in the door. Immediately I jump down to the floor and hide the brush. Exactly how the job was done shouldn't be what my mother sees first; I hang my gaze on the improvement we've begun. Where the stain was there is still a stain, except not beet-red anymore. It's blue. The orphan dunks her gloved hand in the sink and pulls the stopper. Bleach gurgles away.

My mother is surprised. First thing she does is get confused, which brings in her a dreamy look. A lot of moods try out her face. Something is different, she can tell. She can't tell what, or what to do.

She says, "It's strongest here," then drops her purse and slaps her forehead, bellowing to wake the prophets in the hills, if they know English. "You get over here!" She yanks my father's glasses off, sniffs them, drops them. One lens cracks. "Go! Keep going. Move. Run!"

She chases after, a grown lady, not a person who moves fast. This is emergency behavior. Soon I'm naked in a bathtub, on my knees, my mother pulls my head down by the hair to save my eyes, hosed water flushes over me, the current walling off her shouts. We have come to a time like others I have known. The roughness of the treatment shows her fear for me. The fear is how much I am loved.

The pipes squeak. We're both coughing.

"Go open every window in the house. Stop! Use your—oy a broch—your head. First put pajamas on your skin."

I'm in my bedroom wearing just a pair of panties when the orphan tiptoes up. "What does she think of what we fixed?"

"They itch?" my mother shouts, her voice approaching. "Don't you touch them. Pop 'em wide and let the tears come." Standing in the door she sees the orphan. "Oh." She switches language: "Ah. Sweetness, back in school so soon?"

"It's my first day in school a orphan," says the orphan.

My mother lifts off, adrift again, but now her dream is fogged with tears. A smile cuts through, for the orphan. For me there is only a scolding: "Did you offer your friend a drink?"

The orphan shakes her head. Their silhouettes merge in the hall-way as my mother leaves instructions, walking off. She says to finish covering up, and not forget to open everything. Both I accomplish swiftly, even with a towel knotted on my head. Still, by the time I've thrown open my way to the kitchen, the orphan has shoved my station aside. She has planted herself on my stool. Where my documents lie stands a new glass of squash. In the place of my pencil, my father's cracked glasses peer from a plate. My mother digs at the counter with a knife.

She and the orphan both are turned away from me, quiet, absorbed, my mother in her task, the orphan in my mother. A sorrow greater than my own does not exist. I see the clock.

"It started!"

The orphan turns to peer at me, pink tongue slipped in the glass. There is no time to wallow in an ugly sight. The show is a room away.

The sound and motion are delayed only by a twist of the power knob, and a channel switch:

Doug Henning is surprised. He doesn't handle the emotion like my mother. The magician wears expressions like he wears his clothes, a suit of starlight and skintightness. On the stage beside him rises a great cage. An elephant shuffles inside. The shimmer of a lake-wide cloth floats down just at the high point of a gesture from the animal. A dark trunk waving drowns. Doug Henning's broad teeth flash. This year's ambition is clear, and what a notion! What a thing to do! And what a place to allow it. This is where I came from.

"Remember," says Doug Henning. "The utter glory of the world! The utter wonder of it, is totally available to—"

Poof, stillness and dark. One dot of light hangs in the middle of the screen.

"Is it not obvious you've sacrificed the privilege?" My mother has cut off the show.

"No. No! Check my homework!"

"Your achievements in my kitchen I already saw. Your reckless self-endangerment I won't address. Not yet. The property destruction. Your uniform in ruins. I noticed perfectly good fish sticks in the garbage. Plum jam was consciously applied to my cabinet doors."

"It was the orphan." A yellow head pokes from the kitchen doorway. "Her. She made me do it."

"You ask a friend home, you're responsible."

"I didn't ask! She came all of a sudden from the pharmacy."

"Okay. Before we get absurd."

"You can't! You can't you can't you can't you can't!"

"Why's that?"

"He comes on only once a year."

"In other words he'll come again."

"Who knows? What if not? Or what if he comes over there, but we don't get him here? The first time I don't think we got him. He's not from local programming. He's from the States. Like me."

She says, "That man is a Canadian."

The television crackles off spare electricity.

"Sweetness!" my mother says, but not to me. The orphan comes, still chocolate-smeared. My mother takes the towel off my head and with it wipes that dirty face. An orphan squints with pleasure while a mother lets her daughter's eyes drip tears. "Your friend would like to see you safely off." The orphan mentions dinner. "Next time we'll plan for it."

The elevator sinks. I count each floor by every jolt as we fall, eyes on the door. The orphan breathes behind.

Six. Five.

"You look gorgeous," she says.

Four.

"Really cute. It's like no style anyone's seen yet, like of a real star. You'll get loads of attention. You'll feel very proud. But people will be jealous, and for that you will have to be strong."

Two. I whirl around to face the mirror and the news catches up. Gold yellow stains me like a melted crown. Sorrow comes gushing up again, cascading over me. She rushes to dive in with an embrace but I keep her out. I finger-wag, telling her this: "I only came to represent the class!"

"I know you came!" she says. "That day the people brought good things. For dinner I had marble cake, the best I ever had. Did you get a piece? Did you taste the herring?"

"You lie." I realize this now. "How many best cakes can there be? So about me helping with your party: I will not. Just celebrate as usual with that shit-breath cat."

The words are fuller of my feelings than what usually gets out, but she is so crammed full of hers that mine don't make a stir. She only tweaks a dainty portion of her cowlick. "Zeessie washes herself eighty more times a day than you do," she says, "if you wash yourself once."

Ground. Though I hold the door open she stays inside.

She says, "Wasn't that fun with homework? We could think of more activities like that. Remember how I helped you all the way home? How we ran! We're good friends. If we made a mistake today tomorrow we'll make it right."

"*You* made it."

She keeps harvesting that tuft, busily pulling nothing up. "You never said stop."

"I can't see my own head! You can. You didn't say one word. Why? *That* was your mistake. You make mistakes on purpose. You think no one will figure it out." She only looks at me, her hand continuing to work. I have given her something to think about. Here's more: "Your father's broken. The way you're going you'll break him worse. Your mother caught her sickness off your cat."

Hairs snap. She flicks them, radiant and short, quick fallers, in the air between us. Wordless, she walks out.

The next day is full of troubles from its earliest thought. A sun hat will cover it best. The weather worries me. It's not so sunny. Questions will come, and how to explain this: My mother has written a note to show the office. The hat stays on indoors.

But the trouble I expect is never first to come. The orphan sits on the stoop outside my lobby. Beside her rests a plastic crate, gray, capped with a board of wood which is secured with rope. She pushes herself to her feet. She comes behind me, helps my book bag off, and slips it onto her bare back.

"What kind of sandwich did your mother make today?" she says. "Salami? Jam." She bends and hoists the crate, as well, joggling it to reckon with a moving load. Gold eyes peer through the slats.

Who will decide the destinations between home and school and back? The orphan takes too big a part in her own scheduling. Like she won't do the same in mine? She leaves the group without a parent or permission. Last spring, Amalya Blatt had an appointment for a cavity at noon, and saw the orphan on the sizing bench at Ivgi Shoes, alone, being measured. On a field trip to Nili Street, she snuck into the bakery and bought napoleon cake for a smile. And, summer break, I think I saw her in another city. I was traveling with my summer camp to see the ships in Haifa. On the docks a girl like me sat on a milk crate, thin legs folded Eastern-style, skirt tucked like a diaper. A patent leather lady's purse was hanging down her side, nobody watching her as she played dress-up in the shadow of the cranes, while men in foreign sailing clothes arrived and went.

A blue-green truck rolls past. It pauses at the stop sign on the corner, flashing left, left. Women sit in the open bed, cloth covering most of the heads. The olive pickers, hiding their contempt. The orphan ducks behind too thin a trunk.

Why go on? I should have abided by the conduct in the grieving home. I could have completed the assignment with the lawful words.

The truck turns. Children of other buildings run out in uniforms of different schools.

"Sometimes she's with me all day long," the orphan says.

She sidesteps the ficus and starts to go, her crate leading the way, my schoolbag following.

"Would you have guessed?" she says. "I never told anyone till you. We'll leave her in the bomb shelter. At break we'll sit with her, I'll open up the crate and for the first five minutes she'll stay close. We'll take our shoes off. She will lick every single toe. You're going to get to know her really close. Cats are tigers. I can work her into it and out of it. I know her a long time." She hands the crate to me. The heavy load does not like being passed.

The orphan dips her hand into her collar.

In the locket she pulls out, young Zeessie looks more like a fawn. The face is miniature, but the eyes and ears full-grown. The red furred torso is stocky, the legs tapered and long, lengthening as she stretches up out of a catnap on a washcloth, spine strained like a bow, hamstrings taut. Pointed head the arrow, baby eyes the shine, she's ready, aiming to advance her education in the world.

The orphan clicks the locket shut. It doesn't look fake. The metal is handsome in all its stages, as much where she has polished it as where she has neglected. I did not think the orphan would be carrying a thing so good.

The Verse in the Margins

THIS YEAR'S EARRINGS were reprehensible.

"You remove those, you remove those immediately, and take also the opportunity to go to the rest room and wipe that paint off your lips, all of it comes off. Also your eyes."

The girl rose and left Mr. Durchschlag's classroom.

Under normal circumstances, he liked to think the girls could find in him a father figure. No, he did not think that, so why should a man even in his thoughts to himself settle on an inadequate coinage? Not a father but an uncle figure they found in him, relatively young, kind, though of an acerbic wit, someone from whom a growing girl could exact her daily toll of male attention without risking a holdup. He was a larger presence to tussle with at no risk. These girls had no concept of the risk, of the urges they were so eager to summon from the aggregate of this world's men. Imagine such earrings as the girl had been wearing before he had sent her out, out! Such ostentation, as if the ear were a rack in the window of a toy shop. If only she understood she advertised not goods but a transaction. However such a transaction she should not consider. How then could he explain what his students would understand only when, as wives, they had to adjust, eyes closed with forbear-

37

ance, or, God forbid, when it was too late, which was to say too soon for a little girl? Dealing with these girls' immodesty, their twinkles of metal and jewel or—let him remember where and when he was—plastic, clouds of perfume, gales of laughter, their raids into the meditations of their neighbor, he had no choice but to shed his benignity completely because he was disgusted with how constantly they wanted in.

"Shhh, sha!"

The rising chaos of female voices subsided in declining ripples. Front center by an empty partner seat, Orna Magouri covered her face with both her hands. Across the narrow aisle Mali Shemtov smoothed the pages of her book.

They all commuted here. Perhaps this contributed to the mood of hovering dissolve, the girls so far from home, and moreover placed on crumbly turf here in the dunes of Tel Shamai, to which they flocked from the inner lowlands and the coastal plain, from the cities of Rosh Ha'Ayin, Givat Shmuel, Holon, and Netanya, some even from his native Bnei Brak, to gather here, in one building in an undeveloped area outside Tel Aviv. The sea pulsed near, scenting the air but invisible from the road below the tufted sandy headland. A hotel stood in the distance, a glass-plated tower with no hint of stone, its base hidden upshore but the head seeming to peek up towards the school, as though the waves were less a hold on the imagination than what stood higher and farther inland, in a low maze of corridors, he and they, teacher and students, in a vocational school for religious girls.

Here, on this loose-earthed margin of the country, the girls convened. Their parents paid a deeply subsidized tuition in return for an unusual offer, that their daughters be taught a worldly trade without compromising the work of their Creator—ostensibly. Disadvantaged, the main category of the girls enrolled was called, but what the term commonly referred to was the least of their problems. Didn't the mere act of birth threaten an overdraft at the bank and an underdraft of the mind? The girls' most serious shortage was neither financial nor academic. For whether a Tami's or a Shoshi's father mixed cement or cake batter made no difference when the real concern was that in no case was he a Jew learned in the commandments and strict in their fulfillment, so forget about his daughter. And how to furnish his Etti or his Dalya and her failing grades with an income upon graduation should weigh immeasurably less heavy on the conscience of a Mr. Edri or Araki or Shimon than the wholesale degradation of the Jewry of the Islamic countries here in the Jewish state.

He could smell their cookery at the mere thought of them, as if before these musings carrying him off he hadn't been standing in a classroom full of fractious and less-fractious girls, but rather had been climbing the stairs to his apartment, near to dinnertime, when suddenly the door of Rahamim Medina and Medina's wife on the third floor had opened: chicken, lemon and tomato and—what were all the other accents? Spice wisdom such households held on to; their grip on God's teachings was feebler. When their immigrant forefathers in, you could still say in some circles, the backward countries, Yemen, Iraq, et cetera, had been summoned here by the exultance and grief howls of the State's birth days, barely had the newcomers brushed grains of Holy Soil from their longing lips and wiped tears of redemption from their eyes, when Prime Minister Ben Gurion had farmed off their children to labor with the Zionists in agricultural cooperatives. The offspring molded into the new local breed while the immigrant forebears were left to squat in tent cities. Young hands dispossessed of holy books, stuffed with shovels, mouths taught to praise radishes and not the Lord above.

And here their granddaughters sat today, descendants of those few young newcomers whose faith was not altogether lopped off along with their apron strings and sidelocks, who would commemorate their thinned but extant loyalty in a moniker: Traditional. Well, so at least not Secular, at least not "Free," as the bulk of this regathered nation so shamelessly announced themselves. But also nowhere near Reverent, as he and his fold pledged their souls and their days, not even Observant, as did the rather less committed in their knitted skullcaps and short sleeves and motley fabrics off the same rack as the "Free." Traditional. As if they bore the foremost loyalty to their tradition makers, to mortals rather than their Maker and His law. How could God's legacy have been so swiftly reduced in the seed of scholars and commentators and physicians to kings? But also silversmiths and poets and spice mixers, embroidering songsters. He believed that this precisely was their problem, Babel crafts, too many towers, striving in too many directions: a tremor and it all fell apart, and lo. Where now was their sky unto which they had reached? But if God's worship could degrade to almost nothing, awe on the other hand could not. Reverence kept smoldering in them, dimly, so they sent their daughters here.

To him. The professions that girls learned here they might pick up elsewhere. His discipline they would not. But did he delude himself? What really could the girls glean from their teacher of Mishnaic Law, their welcomer to the first thickness of rabbinical interpretation, to the day richly ordered in accordance with God's word? Of such devoutness as his they couldn't conceive, such interaction with the holy, action by action prescribed in worship: the fiber of his clothes, the most recent laving of his hands, the bodily thoughts of which he cleared his mind, the precise distance at which he stood from a female. They would see nothing of it, only this: a pale man of the European Jewry, less effusive than their fathers, less undulating in conversational pitch, a figure identical to and identified with so many others in his neighborhood whose name would mean to them just his sort of person. He in particular was built squarish but trim, fast-moving in his black suit, black hair well clipped beneath black skullcap, beard black also, fully black with not one bristle gray.

A man in monochrome trappings, this they saw, but first a man, and rare at that, one of three in the whole building, the others being the janitor, an old shuffler, and the principal, pock-faced. And so despite his stringent image in black and white, these girls regarded him with dilated eye and flaccid jaw as if he were a pop star. Did he enjoy at least the influence of a pop star on his fans? Recall the earrings, despite everything he said. Thick glazed rounds of plastic in garish colors like sucking candy, the size of them like candy also. A machine spits these earrings out molten and maybe some Arab glues on the posts with which a young unmarried Jewish girl skewers her lobes. Even tiny pearls on a young unmarried girl, however, the smallest chip of gem, what was the need? Why wanton damage to the tissue? And in return for what? How could he but hate this year's gobs of glistening plastic, dazzle bought so cheap?

And when, as today, the earrings called his attention to organs which previously had been notable for function rather than form— that was to say, when a good girl and a listener suddenly became a displayer—this sickened him most of all. The girl in question had worn the very same pair for the first time yesterday, which he had thought the last time, too. For she was not like the others, not by lineage, not in upbringing or character. He had not expected in her a conformity so swift and stubborn. Did the girl take him for an ass? No, she was acting in defiance. Yet only three months ago an exemplary child. On the fifteenth day of the month of Shvat he had brought the class dried fruit in celebration of the Renewal of Trees, and she alone amid the garbling gigglers had mouthed the grace before and after just as if fruit could be eaten only thus.

She had appeared just before the Renewal, new herself this year in his tenth-grade Mishna class, moreover new to the country, a startled face in the front row of the Graphics track home-room, as the vice principal Mrs. Adeena Plyer had told him to expect: began the year in a better school, couldn't keep up with the language, liked to draw pictures. So here was the girl to match the profile, but he would have recognized this Shifra even had every one of the girls in the class been new to him. Immediately it was apparent to him she had sat at the head of the class not to command his attention so much as to exclude the other girls from her selective field of vision. She could only be appalled by their wild gesticulation and trumpeting voices, this pale girl with a tender fetal quality to her pale skin, such skin as might erupt with prickly heat at the slightest adult touch, and flaxen-haired, perhaps of the Hassids of Hungary, though to Israel she had come by way of Sydney. How such pallor could have survived the hot sun of Australia he didn't know. Perhaps until her family had landed in the safety of the Holy Land the child had been secreted in her mother's pouch. In her mother's pouch. Later that day Mrs. Adeena Plyer also would appreciate the joke after of course a little added commentary on his part and a literal explanation to the janitor. Kangaroo! The very word was humorous, strange, straining the jaw with the deep palate sounds doubled. He had made it his business, all jokes aside, to thank the vice principal for admitting such a student into the school. May such a student, he had told Mrs. Adeena Plyer, be the rule here and not the exception. In her dress the girl didn't follow the strictures of his Bnei Brak set, but though she wore no stockings, her skirt came well below the knees, and though her shirtsleeves bared her elbows, she left only her collar button open; here you called that modesty. And the girl had besides such an awareness of propriety, such a touching shyness, a humble girl, in her quiet, quiet voice and broken Hebrew, catching herself for poise, catching herself for language. Hers was such a delicacy as might be taken for melancholy, having the same unobtrusive waft, like a refrigerated carnation from the florist's.

Then, less than three months after her arrival, yesterday, the earrings.

Well, he had told himself when they affrighted his eye—hanging beside the hinges of her jaws like shields of pitiable inadequacy, and lurid, lurid—the girl was diffident, he had told himself, but still a girl, concerned with the opinion of her peers. She could not make her voice heard in their din, so had to find another way to be loud. However, the blood that would rush into her cheeks each time he lauded her midot—the word *dimensions* in the ancient Hebrew of the law interpreters, he might remind the tittering girls, in this context indicated the measures of conduct exclusively—convinced him that his estimation of her would hold, ultimately, more sway than theirs. No need to exercise harsh authority. A single private talk, in the public sphere for decency's sake, would do.

So he had held his tongue until recess. After the bell he had taken a stroll through the yard and found her sitting on a manhole cover, gnawing voraciously on Yemeni fried dough dotted with pepper paste. He settled the right distance from her, across four amot's length of spiny turf, tipped his head and winked to signal, in case she couldn't see, that from behind his beard a smile greeted her. He pulled his wallet out of his back pocket, warmed it between both hands, then took out what he wanted. Working his fingers as if snapping to a tune, he flipped his famous medal in the air, over and over, the whirling brass sparking in the sun.

"What did you trade away for that, Shifra?"

Shifra had stopped chewing. Until now, it seemed, she hadn't gathered that he'd sat down to address her. But why else would he sit in her vicinity, though facing slightly away, to provide a man and woman release from thrall?

She stared across the four amot in terror, the color rising, indeed, in her crammed cheeks.

"Food you're allowed to barter," he told her. "Food is no problem, Shifra. Eat. I'll talk."

She resumed her chewing, her eyes remaining fixed upon the medal. He inhaled in a brief luxuriance at the chance for lasting impact, raised his eyes towards the dunes beyond the fence, nibbled on his whiskers.

"A week ago I wanted to buy my wife for Shabbat to put on the table some white carnations," he began. That he had wanted to buy his wife carnations for Shabbat was true, if not last week then in a time he still recalled. Particulars were of no consequence when he told the story by way of a parable. His wife came to mind naturally. In Shifra he had seen something of Elisheva Durchschlag, mother of his six girls, two of them twins, and God willing any day now maybe a boy. Elisheva possessed wrists so slim he might surround them twice with his own fingers if fingers were ropes. The blue veins inside her wrists were misted over by white skin, but the tendons always bulged as his did only when he clenched exasperated fists. The roots of her thumbs were prone to cramps. Repeatedly he told her she must let the girls peel the potatoes and stitch the hems, but she always forgot which were the damaging tasks. To little Shifra on her island of cement he would get across. "At the florist's," he told her, "my eyes darkened. True, in the refrigerator behind the glass they had a bucket of white carnations, carnations which HaShem had created white as the neck of a swan, pure white. So did I buy my wife a bunch? No! No. And why? 'Certainly I have white carnations!' the florist woman says to me when I walk through the door. 'I have white carnations better than white carnations. Something special.' Shifra," Mr. Durchschlag said, "when I saw these special carnations I shuddered. Instead of pure white, their petals were streaked with a terrible purple that in nature doesn't exist. But the florist was very proud. 'I soak their stems in dyed water,' she tells me. I looked in the bucket and it was true. The poison chemical had run through the veins of the pure flower and now the petals, instead of being pure and modest as HaShem our God created them, were streaked with an ugly garish color like, you'll excuse me, the painted cheeks of professional women."

Shifra's own cheeks drained. He worried that she would not only throw out the earrings, the color of concord grape juice mixed in cream, but also lacerate her earlobes so that the piercings might scab shut. By now she had finished her fried dough. She reached for her ears. He smiled again to nurse her fear and close the chapter. She had learned her lesson. He even let her hold his medal, his trademark in the classroom and the established reward. This she accepted and held for examination in one open palm, the earrings clenched in the other. She turned it over once.

Ordinarily the medal saw only the filtered light of the classroom. In the daylight he'd noticed tarnish which had eluded Elisheva's last polish, a fine ridge crusted around an olive leaf and a wedge between the etched legs of the Gimmel last in his surname. He had wished to scour the medal at once, with a rough twig lying near his knee in the grass. At his request, just as the bell had shrilled, Shifra had tossed the medal back, in order that their fingers might not touch.

How could she have sat in his class again today with her book open to the Mishna, wearing those earrings, and not only those earrings, but the face tinted now, too? Less so, granted, than many of the other girls, but a step in the wrong direction, her lips smeared today, more with grease than color, glossy like a drooling infant's. So he had addressed her again, but now with an audience of her peers.

"Shifra!"

Gentleness had gotten him nowhere and worse. The moist inside of her lower eyelid was somehow lined with blue; how? How? What pointed instrument did they insert so perilously close to the eyeball? To hazard blindness in the hope of capturing lust's eye.

She licked a finger, inclined her head, and flipped a page of her Mishna book. A quick sharp breath, painted eyes on the text: "'A bull who has gored . . .'"

"No!"

She tried again, laboring to chisel and desiccate the sound of the letter Resh, bloated and sodden with her strange accent. She produced only a gluey, Russian-sounding trill. "Who has gorrred . . ."

"No! No and no!"

Quickly, she peered into the book of the girl beside her.

"Rest assured you know where you should read," he said to her. "Rest assured that's not the problem. But where you yourself should be, I think in this regard you are confused. Because when you took the bus to Tel Shamai, evidently you meant to disembark a stop earlier closer to the sea where such an appearance as yours is profitable." So, in no uncertain terms.

Never before had he invoked this plainly the prostitutes who had been roaming these dunes since long before the school's existence. Whenever he was obliged to provide his professional address to some bureaucrat or another he was certain to catch a snicker at his expense, the relish all the greater because of his reverent garb. Today with this brazen defiance the girl had pushed him beyond the subtlety of his usual allusions. An unbecoming red bloomed across Shifra's cheeks, and once he had advised her to repair to the rest room and adjust her appearance, she had arisen and left the classroom.

And never returned.

Seventeen minutes had gone by. Clearly he had managed to keep the lesson on track; the girls' eyes were all riveted on their books. He could see only the round crowns of their skulls, and eyelids veiled with fringes of hair. With a beckon of his finger, he summoned Yaffa Pirozadeh, a dark dwarfish girl attentive in class but uninspired in exams. Without disturbing the other girls, he instructed her to investigate.

Yaffa returned alone.

"I can't find her, HaMoreh."

He could have sworn there had been no kohl on this one's eyelids when she first left the room but it would not do to make a farce of the situation by sending her out again. In his early teaching days the girls could have duped him into diluting their numbers until the population swell in the corridors would become known to the administration. No more. For years now his rule was to no longer kick anyone out, nor would he allow girls anymore private departures from the class. He made it known on the first day of every school year: Take care of your outside business before class or after. No exceptions, until today. In the first few weeks he would find an opportunity to introduce the medal and the experience of his service, he would establish his clout and finished. After this his authority never failed long. So, never again a loitering girl outside his class door, and, behold! No more needling from the office. No: *Should the administration be concerned?* Nor: *Was is possible order was falling apart? And could the administration* (as represented always in such matters by the heavily deodorized Mrs. Adeena Plyer) *on the other hand remain confident that Mr. Durchschlag was able to suspend his standards of observance to conform to the realities of this student body? Furthermore, religious as he knew the administration was if certainly not of his camp, had it not made adequately clear to Mr. Durchschlag the institutional gratitude for his learned example? On the other hand had the administration not accurately represented his intended pupils as, in many ways, unlike his chosen society in Bnei Brak? Was there a question of compatibility?*

He knew where he stood. There was no kohl on Yaffa Pirozadeh's eyelids. The girl was swarthy. The color was no doubt epidermal pigmentation, which among her people was often pronounced in the area of the sockets. Not that he would dwell on female features to confirm, and he didn't need to. This fact of taxonomy he had learned as a younger man in service during the Yom Kippur War, a member of the Holy Society of Burial, the voluntary servants of last honors to God's image, washers of bodies and gatherers of parts. Any Jew's parts, regardless of their level of worship in life, would be treated in death with the most reverent care. And so it was that in divergence from most men in his community, some of the reverent, including himself, in effect enlisted with the secular ranks of the army. The first of the fallen soldiers he had prepared had been whole. The only oddity had been that the boy was very purplish-brown around the eyes. However, because of beginner's overpreparation, Mr. Durchschlag's imagination, pressed down too tight, had sprung at a touch. He was handling a victim of the Syrian torture masters, he decided, upon which thought everything became the blackened eyes. The pummeled eyes. The agonized leave-taking in the company of hate, tears for this world receding, glazed eyes of animal suffering, organs of sight pulped blind, life in the end forgotten to pain as the poor boy would have known no prayers. What would he find under the boy's clothes? At a regrettably impressionable age Mr. Durchschlag had read in the secular paper, over a shoulder in the bus, about the Syrian methods, including the wiring and electrocution of genitals. On that occasion he had fathomed the abuser's glee, his avid matchmaking of shame with agony.

He found himself unable to remove the boy's clothes, only staring, instead, at the eyes. Finally he had broken away to seek a substance of camouflage in consideration of the relatives identifying the photo. In his panic he had asked the cook for some flour. It was then he had learned that to his squadron mates the dead man had been known as Shiners Aboudrahem. "You think the corpse wants cosmetics? Rabbi," the cook said—to this ignoramus anyone in a beard and a black suit was ordained—"his whole family looks like that, Rabbi. Maybe in the Yeshiva you need more of a variety of Jews, a little color. Take a look at me. Look at my knuckles. Not all of us are Lithuanian stock." Does a reverent Yeshiva boy not take the bus with every other sort of person or go to the shouk for a kilo of loquats in season? He knew of what the world was made; he had merely sunk into the depths of a detail. After the first body he came to witness actual defacements he could fathom neither as the fruit of vicious human fancy nor as the handiwork of decay. Gradually he had built up an immunity.

A roomful of girls in powder-blue uniform blouses goggled at Mr. Durchschlag over open Mishna books. One figure stood out, transfixed by the text. Sadly, only Shulee Bouzaglo, a girl born with a bullhorn for a throat, not quiet in learning but rather fueling before the next blast. Sure enough, her arm shot up at the very same time that her mouth gaped and blared out in contention with the sages, may their memory be blessed, who had in her opinion erred in condemning to butchery the shor mu'ahd, the confirmed gorer, when the innocent bull was only doing what his nature decreed. He needed only calmer treatment from birth and a better fence. She drew back her hand to rub vigorously at one of her eyes, given to sties.

"When it's you who has been gored, Shulee," he said, "then I recommend you bring your protest to the sages in person." The girl's hand froze over her irritated eye. "You want your vision tested, Shulee? I don't happen to have a chart but I'll tell you an exam wouldn't hurt." He yanked off his black suit jacket, remaining in white shirtsleeves. "For now, along with everyone in this room you will read the next two Mishnayot along with the commentary, in complete silence, and write an independent synopsis no briefer than four pages, in two drafts without consultation. I will be directly outside the classroom and I do not need to see your faces to recognize whose voice I hear. I regard this as a necessary exercise. Whenever your dedication wanes, write the following in reduced letters on the margin, with full punctuation." He turned to the board, pinched up a stub of chalk, and struck the sections of the psalm verse into being. "Happy is the man who puts his trust in God, and does not turn to dazzlings and diversions of deceit." He dropped the chalk in its moat. "End of verse. This must be executed in pencil. After inspection we will rub it out from the work. You and I both will find the frequency of the occurrence in the margins instructive. Half a grade increase for this term if you can ascribe the source."

Pages began to riffle. Mr. Durchschlag left the classroom, closing the door behind him.

The school corridors were wide, built after an American design with the money of American benefactresses whose league, as the administration was wont to mention in faculty meetings, financed also shelters for beaten wives and learning institutes for the congenitally impaired. He did not know how they could work this architectural style into cramped Israeli cities. In the dunes of Tel Shamai there was the space for such expansiveness. As windows were limited to the classrooms, the corridor was cool, the light gray. Sweat wormed down his ribs and chilled him. He stepped towards the end of the corridor. The sound of a recorded piano clanged through one of the doors he passed. The girls of the secretarial track accompanied the plodding music with a dogged percussion of typewriters.

The next door was the girls' toilet. In the whole building there was only one such room for his use, and why would there be more for a mere three men? Nonetheless the trek every time he required the facilities between lessons was a waste of his time and in such a spacious school accommodations could have been made. To girls who tried his rule and asked to leave class in the middle, always requesting to drink as if this were more proper, he liked to say, "Anyway the water will pass through you right away." He might offer the blushers a conciliatory wink, but there would be no leaving. With every unclish wink of his to every blush of theirs the world revolved more steadily, the proper ratio of this to that restored. If only they would understand once and for all that the attention they could endure they already had. Women liked intimations and there the affection stopped. Didn't the blushing mark the threshold of their tolerance? He tried and tried to explain but how could he usefully do so while restraining the topic? This predatory appearance they assumed when in fact they were the quarry. Again and again he invoked the dangers before them, again and again and again, and again. But for now he should try to understand why he must check the bathroom. Unimaginable that he should set foot in such a place. And why should he? He had broken his rule and sent a girl out. After her he had sent another who had returned alleging an outside faced alone. Would Yaffa Pirozadeh lie? No. But even by this school's standards she was no genius. She would not have taken a truly thorough look. He peered behind him, down the corridor. He looked to both his sides. He tilted his ear towards the silent toilet. A sweet smell of artificial peaches sifted through the door, such artificiality as could engulf any other odor and introduce it to a human nostril like hidden medicine.

"Shifra," he whispered. The peach smell whispered back.

He took one step through the door. The toilet air was cold and damp, the peach scent a fine fatty mist. The men's room beside the principal's office was never perfumed, but assuredly the pains taken to mask who knew what fumes in this privy were due merely to the utter magnitude of users.

"Shifra," he said. An old sweating pipe along the wall beside him broke into a wounded whine which at first he thought animal, grabbing a porcelain sink to steady himself. Immediately he let go and wiped his palms on his trousers. He had an educator's duty to be here but no need to touch. With the tip of his shoe he nudged open every stall door. In the last cubicle a gray puddle on the tiles in front of the commode reflected white light from a high window. Having exhausted the options here and not found the girl, he found himself for some reason relaxing. This was a toilet, a toilet like any other and he had to go. He unzipped his black trousers, planted each black shoe on a dry bank of the luminous puddle, tipped his hips forward and urinated into the toilet. The contents of the female refuse can were a passing thought, the can itself no more than a marred silver cylinder in the periphery of his vision. Who cared? The eye-ache of studying what stood outside the focal field was punishing, and anyway nothing could be truly seen like that, only blurs of ugly color and simplified shapes. When he shut his strained eyes he stumbled into the puddle, wetting a shoe and a cuff of his black trousers, with what? Girls by their positioning had control; the puddle could be nothing but relatively untainted septic tank seepage, untainted, that was, until he had been made to lose his footing in mid-elimination. He kicked the base of the commode and left at once, without flushing or lowering the seat, only laving a hand under a dripping faucet and grabbing a coarse paper towel to wipe. Halfway down the hall he stood and recited voicelessly the proper sanctification.

Blessed are you, Adonai our God, King of the world, who formed man wisely, and created in him perforations upon perforations, hollows upon hollows.

The tinny sound of the piano swelled when the secretarial classroom door swung open. A girl in blue passed him on her way to the toilet. He stuffed the paper towel into his back trouser pocket, confident she wouldn't recognize what he was mouthing when their repertoire of prayer here was so grossly abridged.

It is apparent and known before Your Honor-throne, that should one of them become ruptured or one become blocked, it would be impossible to exist and stand before you.

She leaned in, mistakenly attending, trying to determine: a rebuke, a directive, a pleasantry? He closed his eyes to her. One did not move until the blessing was done.

Blessed are you, Adonai, healer of all flesh and wondrous originator.

When he was done he was pleased to find that the girl had understood her lack of relevance and left. He returned to class.

The Mishna classroom hissed with the scratching of pens. He smacked his palms together and every head jerked up.

"Agreeable," he said. "Worthy. The class will continue this good work extended to include the following three Mishnayot as well, the synopsis amounting altogether to no less than six pages. In the meantime I will confer with Shifra, who is awaiting me now in Mrs. Adeena Plyer's office. Each class member will continue her work in complete silence unless she desires to join me and Mrs. Adeena Plyer in a conference of her own. Conversely, the writer of the most serious essay will be permitted to retain the medal for the rest of the day, assuming responsibility and some sharing."

Back in the dim corridor Mr. Durchschlag pulled at the lobe of his left ear, a little too hard, and broke into a brisk stride, sweeping every corner with his eyes, leaning in by every door and, hearing lessons in progress, moving on. Any silent door he opened. In one room Mrs. Zeidish the textile design teacher was holding an exam, but she was knitting a cocoa-colored baby boot and did not notice him, or the door slowly shutting again.

When he had inspected every alcove and recess from the top flight to the ground level, Mr. Durchschlag approached the graphic arts display cases at the entrance to the school. He pressed both his palms against the glass. He watched the hand-shaped fog contort and disappear. Not disappear. Faint, oily imprints hovered over advertisements for fictitious products executed in clashing colors.

He would have to alert the principal to the situation. Girl missing. He pushed his forehead and nose against the cool glass. What he had said to the girl he had said to open her eyes and sometimes to open the eyes of the insensate acrid vapors are required. When one has lost her wits sometimes only a slap brings her to. The earrings were repulsive. Granted, she wasn't the most scandalously errant, also already an accomplished student well-regarded by the faculty, a neat painter apparently, a daughter to educated parents. The greater the urgency, then, to extricate her at once from the ill-chosen path.

Thirty-five girls had heard what he had said, gabbers and squawkers, one word of his unleashing forty. He should speak to the child. If she was nowhere in the building she must have gone into the dunes. As timid as she was, she wouldn't have strayed far from the road. He would find her. He would bring her back with her purple earrings. From now on, Shifra'leh, maybe a little paint on the face if so much you want to be like your friends, but no lollypops stuck through the ears, agreed? Agreed. The sorts that visited these dunes, though, their intentions on the fringe. He must find her right away or it could be a tragedy to her future.

"You need an Akamol for your headache, Mr. Durchschlag?"

With one hand Meshulam Banai, the janitor, who had emerged from the ground-level rest room, pushed a giant garbage canister across the lobby floor, the scrape of heavy plastic against stone tile masking the echo of his Moroccan accent. The *Girls* plaque of the rest room kept rattling on loose screws as the door, swinging heavily on its two-way hinges, gradually lost momentum. With his free hand the janitor dug into the pocket of his sagging brown trousers and by the time he had reached the graphic arts display cases, he had extracted a linty white pill, which he offered to Mr. Durchschlag upon a black-whorled pointer finger.

"Take it, take," Meshulam said. "I got more in my other pocket and a whole box in my closet. With four hundred girls clucking all day long you have to take precautions, not to mention the chemicals they use to set the dyes in the textiles give me sinuses and pressure on the chest. Make saliva in your mouth, you won't need water." Meshulam pulled a spray bottle from his belt, bespattered the display case with white foam, and wiped away Mr. Durchschlag's prints. When Mr. Durchschlag swallowed the pill, Meshulam reached over and thumped his shoulder, then slipped his hand below the small of Mr. Durchschlag's back, dove swiftly into his back pocket, and produced the crumpled brown paper towel.

"That I should get rid of this for you?"

The thin smell of artificial peaches insinuated itself into Mr. Durchschlag's nostrils. The man was as attuned to him as to a spill on the floor. He was hoping to sop up a conversation. Mr. Durchschlag could not expend the time. "It's yours," he said.

Meshulam tossed the paper into the barrel and used a long-handled dustpan to compact the garbage, which released in the process a complicated smell, overwhelming that of peaches. Mr. Durchschlag disguised his distaste with a cough.

"Is it working on you?" Meshulam said.

Mr. Durchschlag looked quickly away from the barrel. He must disengage. Something in his demeanor was indicating interest to the old man.

"I can give you another one if it's not working on you," Meshulam said, digging a hand into his trouser pocket again to find a second pill.

To judge by this Meshulam's expectations, his primitive faith in medicine had medicinal value in itself. In that case Mr. Durchschlag would authenticate this faith and the man would be satisfied and go away. "There! It began," Mr. Durchschlag said. "No need for a second dose. Quick action."

Meshulam let his pocket be and pressed down the garbage again. He examined the bottom of the dustpan and peeled off something thick that he let drop into the barrel. Next he began picking at a residual clingage. It seemed that no matter how Mr. Durchschlag strove to present himself as a finished project, the man would find another one near.

"The students aren't waiting?" Meshulam said.

"The students?"

"Your students in your class that you teach, they aren't waiting for their teacher to teach them?"

"The girls are taking a test," Mr. Durchschlag said.

"They won't copy?"

"They're taking the test on the honor system."

"If you want I can check they won't copy."

"You have my full admiration for your fine work in area maintenance," Mr. Durchschlag said. "I'll thank you to leave the teaching to me. I trust the girls."

"The principal allows this new system testing since when?" Meshulam said. "They had a meeting and I didn't hear? It's no problem for me to check," he said. "My next stop is the toilets room upstairs."

The men observed each other.

"Listen, Meshulam." Mr. Durchschlag pressed his fingers into the janitor's upper arm, which was large and layered, soft but underneath inflexible with muscle. The man liked to eat but had been mopping many years. "You are a religious man, Meshulam, true?"

"Banish the evil eye." Meshulam spit into the barrel. Mr. Durchschlag removed his hand. "Of course, yes, with God's help, a believing man. Every Shabbat eve, healthy or sick, at the synagogue. They already asked me when they hired, ten years before they hired you." He inhaled to continue. "Adeena was maybe only a young bride," he said, "but even then no problem for her to ask the questions, questions she always has but for sixteen years never again that."

He had finished. "Tell me then," Mr. Durchschlag said. "The way the girls dress in this school, Mr. Banai, do you think it's becoming?"

"Some girls more than others. A man sees but he also remembers his age and his position and the family at home."

Mr. Durchschlag moved to massage his temples, but caught himself before he would incite another bid for medication. The message hadn't crossed yet but it would. He tented his raised palms in a contemplative gesture with which he prodded the space between himself and the janitor. "There it is in your own words," he said. "You shouldn't have to *see*. Do you see? And how well our teachings provide, for if they were followed to the full you would in fact not see. What I mean to tell you is that here you find yourself compelled to strive beyond your job description."

For a moment the man looked startled but in a flash he chose relief and took on a jocular aspect. "What, Adeena gave me the wrong numbers? Sixteen years I'm cleaning some rooms twice?" He slapped the side of the barrel like the rump of an animal and laughed. "I have no complaints," he said, becoming serious. "In nine years they retire me with pension. My work respects me."

"And likewise I, Meshulam," Mr. Durchschlag said, welling indeed with a poignant charity towards the man. "But, Meshulam. I speak not of the job assigned to you by our esteemed vice principal, Mrs. Adeena Plyer, but of your duty as a member of the sacred congregation of the Holy One, blessed be He. Your duty as a Jew, a Jew and a man."

Meshulam Banai stared at Mr. Durchschlag. Mr. Durchschlag stared back and nodded.

"Modesty of dress and modesty of voice, by these measures a woman protects a man. That is her job. Her very fortification keeps a man advised of his, let's call it, potentiality. It is a partnership. Now, ask yourself: If one partner shirks her duty, who is to blame when the whole business falls apart?"

Meshulam wrapped an arm around the barrel and hugged it to his hip. "Rabbi," he said, tightening his grip on the long-handled dustpan. "With all due respect, Rabbi, these are young religious girls."

"Religious. Religious?" Mr. Durchschlag underscored each repetition of the word with a wallop of the garbage barrel rim. "Religious?" His next question in store had been did Meshulam have a daughter, a daughter-in-law, a niece, a granddaughter? They would have named their female kin and reached a convergence in their viewpoints regarding strong words in crucial times. Meshulam would have helped him comb the dunes and recover the girl.

But now he saw that the tortuosity of argumentation required to lead this character towards the first glimmers of insight would require such an expenditure of time as would altogether preclude the finding of the girl intact.

"Meshulam, if you think I am ordained, Meshulam, if you think I am ordained to the rabbinate simply because of my clothing, just because of the hair sprouting from my face am I a rabbi, then you are liable to be the tail to any bearded head and you are more a pagan than a Jew. You are a primitive." Mr. Durchschlag stopped hitting the rim of Meshulam's barrel and rubbed his smarting palm on his pants. "You will not, Meshulam," he said, "you will not, however, interfere with my educational methods. You will not so much as touch the door which stands between you and my girls whom I am testing on their honor. Go wipe women's toilets."

Shoving open the lobby doors, Mr. Durchschlag shouted to the janitor that he was going out to recite the afternoon prayers in the open air. His thin soles banged over the concrete pavement of the enclosed front yard. The heavy gate was chained for safety, so he scaled it, catching his pants cuff on one of the pointed posts as he came down the other side, barely escaping injury. He clung to the gate as he slid down it. For a moment after his feet had touched the asphalt he remained in this embrace. Then he let go and ran. He had taken only a few bounds outside when the black pavement dove under the gray sands and disappeared.

It would be easier to walk on the road but he could not risk being seen. The sands sucked at his footsteps and slowed him as he climbed over the first dune. Standing in the cleft between it and the next he could see nothing but ungenerous soil, pebbled, briery. When he looked down he saw that even he blended in. His black trousers had paled, his white shirt darkened. He resumed his climbing, scaling the next rise. He would tell his wife they had sent him on a field day. She would wash his clothes tonight, press them, starch his collar, and drape the garments, restored, over his chair for the next morning. He would like an egg sandwich for tomorrow's lunch. He must mention that before she had fixed yellow cheese and margarine again.

His thighs ached from the battle with the sands. On the fourth or fifth peak he stopped again to look around. The sky was whitened with the glare of a late spring sun. He wiped the sweat from his forehead, and his hand came away damp and gritty. He could hear the sea, still distant. He could smell it, seaweed and tar. He was an idiot for thinking he could find her. Through the window of a bus the dunes did not disclose their sprawl as they began to, now. But she would keep to the road. She wouldn't dare stray very far off the road. He moved on, wresting his feet again and again from the hungry sand, keeping his eyes trained on the road, which exposed itself between the dunes in black wedges glistening with illusory puddles. The sound of the sea rose to a dull headachy rumble, or else his own blood pounded in his ears.

When a hand touched his shoulder, he fell. A bale of brambles pierced the soft skin behind his knees through his trousers. Shards of seashells cut his palms.

"Shifra," he said.

"I can be a Shifra," said the woman. "Whatever you want, Rabbi. I can wear my skirt like a kerchief on my head. I'll say a blessing. I remember lots from Grandma. Want to hear one?"

Mr. Durchschlag looked up and directly looked down again because her shimmering skirt hijacked the eye with a green bird-feather shimmer, which evanesced to reveal everything else. Where her thighs would rub together walking a prickly pink rash had erupted. Above the rash the skin was smooth as a boiled egg.

His wounded palms burned. They required attention.

Too close to his, her feet, in thin-strapped sandals, were planted far apart but not firmly, on high heels in a constant teeter, as if the dunes were the sea and she on a raft upon it. He looked away from her buckling toes and their dark red nails. He turned over his hands and plucked the shells and pebbles out. When he tried to rise, brambles bit his bleeding palms and he lost his balance again, but the woman squatted and caught him under the pits of his arms, pulling him up with demon strength. They stood face-to-face.

"Don't touch," he said. In the sun her scent rose like a smoke-screen of sickly incense, quavering and fruity.

"All right," the woman said. "I'll even move away a little, you'll get used to me first." She stepped back. The smell subsided somewhat. Her blouse was turquoise and only a tube of fabric with no sleeves, her shoulders crisped with freckles. "See, I'm keeping my hands to myself," she said, folding her arms over her chest, tucking her fingers into her bald armpits. "I'm a very obedient girl," she said.

"No touching the Rabbi." She let her splayed fingers rake her breasts as her arms came unfolded. She gasped and rolled her eyes. "More?" she said. "Fifty shekels."

"You misunderstand," Mr. Durchschlag said.

"No problem," she said. "It's all a big misunderstanding. All my idea. It'll be completely against your will. Fifty, Rabbi, then anything you don't want. Come on. Why always all the hemming with your type? You're here. I'm here. Let's go."

"Listen to me, please, lady," Mr. Durchschlag said. "I am out here only to look for a young schoolgirl."

"And you found one. It's just the fashion to dress up like ladies early on, for you. Why should I wait? I want you now. My little body needs your love. My baby head needs you to tell it what to do." She stuck a finger in her mouth and sucked on it. He stared, uncomprehending. Baby? His youngest came to mind, Suri Malka, a pudgy wobble, fat cheeks rosy in that rapt, expectant face with which all girls begin. But what he saw before him now was a woman of twenty-five or so, large-pored, patches of pale makeup daubed beneath eyes torn open in a look of demented stupefaction. Her earlobes were elongated, their perforations drawn into notches by bronze hoops, the sun illuminating the blood in the surrounding membrane. All at once her wet finger dragged down her lower lip, trailing over her chin, her chest, her stomach. She reached under her skirt, her eyes growing even larger. "Ooh," she said. "What a little baby-girl find *here?*"

"Enough!" Mr. Durchschlag smacked his wounded hands together, welcoming the mind-clearing agony. He turned to walk away.

Instantly the woman was before him once more, savage fragments of her again intruding, like a clawed paw into a burrow, a gnashing snout. Her shoes shifted from heel to heel. "Forty shekels," she said. He tried to dodge her and stumbled. The woman extended her arms but showed him her palms in deference when he regained balance. "Thirty-five," she said. "To come this far was hard enough for someone like you. Don't let yourself down."

Mr. Durchschlag turned his back to her and remained still. At least he'd spare his eyes the sight.

"Thirty," she said. "Thirty and that's it. For a better bargain go south of the hotel but when she's done with you make sure to take a bath in bleach."

He didn't respond. Why should he negotiate with her for his freedom? And what sort of freedom if by the time she was persuaded to let him go, his memory would be infiltrated by the furious parodic desperation in her voice, which would go on and on? The batty spite. The trumpeted knowingness of his supposed want, of the moment approaching when he would deposit with her the evidence she sought, of a reverent man stooping low outside his sphere.

"What's your budget?" she said. "We'll figure out the service."

If he paid her to leave him he will have paid a prostitute. He would know this for the rest of his life. Bad enough he had even spoken to one, as little as he had. He couldn't help but think that if there had been an opportunity to avoid this encounter, he had missed it early on.

"I can give you new ideas," she said.

He must scold her immediately at his sharpest or soon she would describe her mechanics. But what were even his roughest words compared to her daily dealings? How to overcome her? If it weren't for the proscription against touching any woman save one's wife, he would strike her and be done. She had chosen a life of violation but why must she violate his? He would strike her out. But she had assaulted the purity of his thought, not his life. If no life was at risk, the decree could not be overruled.

Unless he considered Shifra, lost in depraved surroundings. Three years ago a body had been found here, an elderly tourist robbed and dumped, a grandmother outside the watch of her community. American of course, an old Jew, and from what city, in what neighborhood and whose congregation, where the members simply carried on with their business when a woman wandered off to a wild remove? An elderly lady unprotected overseas. It emerged finally that she had been murdered by women, a pair. He had not kept his ear open to more foul details. The principle was enough: A woman traveling alone invites aberration, end of verse.

He couldn't give up. For Shifra's sake he must strike the whore down, not with intent to injure, not to relish, only strike out and proceed as planned. First he must be sure he wouldn't delay his search further. The professional had mentioned a colleague nearby. What if there were many, organized to charge up from the seashore in their heels? But he went too far. More likely, a pander would pounce out from between the dunes, wielding brass knuckles.

"Are we alone?" he asked.

The woman tried to step around and face him. He turned where he stood.

He heard her let out a harsh breath. "Just you and me. I keep a secret."

He twisted partway towards her. He began to see a glaring, opalescent stain in the far margin of his vision, her skirt. "You don't have nearby an overseer? A manager?"

"What do you want with a pimp?" she said. She craned to see his face, and he adjusted his stance in accordance, away.

"So you don't have one?"

"What do you have in mind?" she said.

"I'm wondering. I've never frequented these parts before. I'm not well versed. You said yourself that you could give me ideas."

"A pimp," she said slowly, "knows when to stay put, and when to show up."

"I notice you're not answering the question," Mr. Durchschlag said. "I notice more than a hint of evasion." He joined his palms, lightly this time.

His gesture was cut short when the woman's shape snatched itself out of sight and, just as quickly, his arms were pinned behind his back. Something rammed at the backs of his knees. His legs buckled. He was pushed down onto his stomach, his arms still held behind him. He hacked on sand. Someone was sitting on his legs. He heard a brief metallic spring, and the sensitive skin of his back raised an alarm against a needlelike sharpness, a fearful sharpness.

"What did you want to pull on me, you shit?" The woman's spittle moistened the inside of his ear. "I know exactly where your kidneys are. You need them? Right here's my pimp, understand? My pimp takes care of me. My pimp won't put up with the rough stuff and never takes a cut. Not from me. Cutting in general we like. I know where your kidneys are. You're small. Small was the first thing I saw after holy. Small holy man. You never show your big bastard to the world and you won't get to show him to me. I'm not interested. I'm never interested."

"I was only going to push you down," he said.

At this she slit his shirt to the collar, letting the blade sear a fine fiery line all along his spine. Her weight rose from his knees. She spit on the sand beside his cheek.

"Stay absolutely quiet," she said. "I have to think. You'll help me. Think what we should do with you. Let's decide." After this she said nothing for a long time.

A cloud evidently passed before the sun. The glare abated, then intensified. The ocean seemed to dash its waves upon the nearby shore with greater might but at increasingly irregular intervals. Each assault came sooner or later than he predicted, tearing into the silence. Finally his nerves had had enough. She couldn't be thinking at such length.

But of course she had never meant to think. She had simply left. Mr. Durchschlag pushed himself up onto all fours, grains of sand nipping their way into his raw palms. Nothing shoved him down again, so he righted himself and sat heavily, facing west. She had left recently. The sands remained unsettled. Her chemical fruit smell clung to each lingering mote, the haze descending over him. He had reached near the lip of the headland. He had seen the vileness of that woman but hadn't noticed this. Now, through the blur, he saw the blue sea sparkling, and the sallow filth-specked beach. The dust sank and let through the smells of the ocean. Perfume gave way to seaweed, salt and rust, beach refuse. Strongest was the scent of his own blood. A warm wind played at the exposed skin of his back. The cut was shallow, but long and still oozing, stinging badly at a touch, worse where he couldn't reach. When he wiped his hands on the rear of his trousers, he felt only his knitted muscles through the fabric. His wallet was gone.

In his front pocket, maybe? He patted himself. Of course not. Gone. His wallet for years.

Today in the wallet had been thirty-two shekels, and as always a spare key to the flat, his papers, and a stamp-sized piece of parchment minutely inscribed with the Prayer for the Way: . . . *and preserve us from the hand of every foe and lurker.* . . . Had he walked seventy amot and two-thirds, without praying, from the margins of what constituted built-up ground? The school? An unwitting breach. He would recite the prayer when he headed back. One had to be standing to recite.

The image of his wallet would not leave him. Gone? Black, polished, and embossed to resemble reptile skin. The heft and texture in his palm, never again? The wallet had cost him fourteen lira and seventy-six agorot years before inflation had forced the change of currency to shekels. A young unwedded Yeshiva boy, he had brought it down from seventeen-fifty at a shouk stall. A few stalls down he had rewarded himself with as many loquats as what he'd saved would fetch, pale orange loquats plentiful in season and then nothing until the next, when again he could roll the hard smooth pits between the tongue and palate once the teeth have burst the mild flesh and pulped it.

With age the black hide had fissured between the fake scales, so that now the simulation was more convincing. Last year one of his twins had picked off three scales in the right corner of the zippered change compartment, leaving gouges for which he had excoriated her. Initially he had hated the feature of a change compartment. He could remember a time when his thumb would recoil from the extra pouch as if the property weren't his, as if he had picked up the wallet of another. A young unwedded boy, he had tried to detach the change compartment from the rest with a paring knife. A change compartment made a wallet a purse. He had succeeded only in scarring the hide. Now his fingers sought the old scars, even the recent, daughter-inflicted ones. He had grown attached to the extra feature, liking the safety of the zipper, though of course he never used it to keep change. The pouch now bore the impression of an outsized coin, but it was only that of his medal, which had found its proper place there, protected on his waking person always. No more. His medal, his dignity, forever lost to a slut.

What would he give the girl with the most serious essay when he returned? As a teacher he always followed through. But what had been promised was lost. What substitute? His clothes were the color of sack, the shirt cut and bloodstained. A thorny vine could have ripped it, ripped the surface of his skin. His jacket awaited him back in class. He could cover the damage and prepare his wife. But would Elisheva believe he had gone out on a field trip with the students when it had been years since he had agreed to do so? Pale, brittle Elisheva with a big bump through the middle, expanding like her distance.

A great wave hurled itself ashore, and then another. He pressed the heels of his palms onto his ears so for once he might hear his own guiding thoughts. Sand chafed his earlobes. He let his arms fall and hang limp. The sea whooshed and roared. She wouldn't believe him.

One time and one time only Mr. Durchschlag had agreed to

escort his students on the annual school trip. Every year since, he had refused. He disagreed with the administration's policy of allowing the girls to wear trousers for the length of the event. Scorpions and snakes may wait along the path, true, and thorns like razor wire cross it. So let them take the girls where there are no snakes and scorpions and thorns like razor wire. Girls! Girls, not soldiers. A nice trip to the zoo. One time and one time only he had agreed and, though a mistake, though never to be repeated, the trip had had a groundbreaking impact on discipline in his classes. On the occasion of the trip he had shown the girls his medal for the first time.

He had agreed to go because he had been a new hire and hadn't known the policy, couldn't have imagined it in a religious school. On the day of the trip they had slung a gun over his shoulder and beckoned him onto a bus loaded with girls clothed in men's garments. He had protested, of course he had protested. But Mrs. Adeena Plyer had said that with him or without him they would have to go. The parents had all paid, the hostel beds had been reserved, the driver held a contract. If in the Judaea desert the girls should fall victim to such a catastrophe as an armed chaperon could have fended off, be it on his head.

Then, without a blink of the eye, she had allowed the girls to sing with men present on the bus, both he and the driver. It had been clear from the wear and fit of many of the girls' trousers, from their indifference to their limbs delineated in the public eye, that the garments hadn't been reserved for the annual trip. The landscapes of the trip he couldn't remember at all. Two girls dehydrated, one busridden with pains disclosed only to the females. He had been a young man then, with only the first two daughters, hoping for a boy soon with whom to study the holy writ, to journey through the branching laws and not the complex mist of sweats that filled the bus.

Why this fate? Why had he ended up surrounded with the female progeny of compromised Jews? Not by choice. New to teaching, he had tried to secure a position at a Yeshiva, then at some of the devout boys' schools, then reverent girls' schools in Bnei Brak, with no success until Tel Shamai. Perhaps his scholarly record at the Yeshiva hadn't been stellar, perhaps he did not come close to the levels of absorption which might approach the rapture of those hallowed days when God spoke directly to His sons. Perhaps even in those days he wouldn't have been favored. But to the task that finally was revealed as his lot he applied himself with good intent. He arrived furnished with the strategy of scented erasers in a bag as incentives to participation. And participate they did, but wrongly. Every day Mrs. Adeena Plyer complained about the noise. The girls would clamor for the scented nubs and he would submit in return for brief quiet. When he implored them to attend and forge their link in the Jewish chain the girls rolled their eyes at him, chewing gum.

On the second day of the annual school trip, after spending the night in a hostel room, alone in the company of the cold gun to which he had allotted the top bunk, as howls of jackals drilled through the night, Mr. Durchschlag had fallen asleep on the bus and dreamed he was a girl.

His last wakeful sensation had been the window rattling against his cheek. Later he understood that the smells, to which he had grown inured, had crept up on him again in his slumber. In his dream the cloud of female odor in the bus emanated from his own body. His flesh was swelling in new places. He felt brassiere cups pressing. Young breasts they must have been, intent on every subtlety of pressure, knowledge hungry. He had become breathless. A soft wind slipped under his elbows as if he wore short sleeves, a cool current lapping at his shoulders, slipping under them to breathe a thrilling chill onto damp hairs, then swirling between his thighs as if he were entubed in a skirt, out of which the breeze curled back and emerged ripened, reinvented as a sour animal spoor that set in motion a response in him to open wide, somehow, the whole of him widen like a yawn, expanding, ravenous, gulping. When the bus had lurched up an incline he awakened to his jaw hanging slack. He snapped it shut.

In a front passenger seat Mrs. Adeena Plyer and the girls' homeroom teacher had been asleep, the two girls seated across smiling at the bus driver who had smiled back through the rearview mirror. One of the girls offered the driver a sucking candy and he took it.

An orphan child, Mr. Durchschlag had felt himself then, stranded, without recourse. His ribs bore down upon his heart, outside the window nothing but desert sands. What to do except reach out and hold the girl across the aisle from him? If only he could, the two of them would have pressed together like twin sisters in a world of sisters, the closest of the close, yet of pure intent. Instead he had taken out his wallet.

Unzipping the scarred change compartment, he had pulled out his medal. The brass plating caught the light as he twisted it beside the window.

"Mr. Durchschlag," the girl, now he couldn't remember who, had yelled over the noise of the engine, "do you have more chocolate coins maybe?"

He corrected her.

"A medal?" she said. Other heads turned his way. "For what a medal, Mr. Durchschlag?"

He held the medal closer to her and let her read the inscription: *To Shahya Durchschlag, our esteem. Company Seven.*

The girl flattened her hand to receive the medal, which he let drop to be scrutinized, first by her, then all around. He watched it travel from the fingers of one girl to the next, the etched olive leaves and the letters of his name catching the dazzle of the day.

"I'll tell you, girls," he said, "about my time in the military."

"But men like you, they don't go to the army," the girl, or else another girl, said. "Don't you get exemptions and stay in Yeshiva instead?"

"To study the laws and protect us all in the eye of God. Who then is exempting whom? And why is such scant notice paid to men like myself, who serve on both fronts?"

"You served in the army?" She squinted at the medal, the olive branch curved in a familiar way, but the Israeli Defense Force symbol absent its sword.

"I served the army," Mr. Durchschlag said. "As a member of the Holy Society, I was stationed with this particular border patrol troop and in their station I received the fallen. The boys all chipped in for a medal, custom-made. A private gesture, hence not the full emblem. They recognized the voluntary risk. And you? Before every Independence Day you thank the armed forces for your lives. The Holy Society you don't thank. We're equally exposed, dangling over death itself to secure your position in the lap of safety."

The switch in their perspective had been visible, as tangible as the luster of imminent tears. Only a teacher was privileged to witness these rare moments of concentrated growth. For the first time, he warmly treasured his job.

"You buried the dead?" the girl asked.

"I prepared them for burial. I also took the pictures."

"The pictures?"

"The pictures," Mr. Durchschlag said. "For the family to identify."

By then half the bus had become his audience, a warm desert wind nuzzling his nape.

"Mr. Durchschlag," a girl whispered. "They show the family a picture of a dead face?"

Mr. Durchschlag smiled at her. "The family think the face is of a living man because we open the eyes and because, here." He leaned forward, further than allowed by law just this one time because of the tricky balance on the jostled bus, and spread his thumb and pointer finger as far as he could. With his fingers he framed the girl's jaws as if to caress her, but stopped short of touching. "This is a professional secret." Eyes all around him widened.

"We pinch the jaw at a very particular point, and the corpse grins." Withdrawing his hand, he demonstrated on himself, baring his teeth. "His own mother is convinced he is alive."

The girls stared at him. Two or three tried the maneuver on themselves without success. He showed them again, afterwards turning his palm this way and that, twisting it like a key while they gazed upon it. The medal kept passing around, the bus groaning.

After the annual school trip, Mr. Durchschlag discovered that Mrs. Adeena Plyer the vice principal had lied. The trip could not have proceeded legally without an armed escort. Had he chosen to remain behind, the girls would not have been in danger because they could never have left the school. But disciplinary difficulties did end after the trip, with his switching from erasers to the medal. Classes passed through and changed over. The new girls learned the meaning of the medal from the girls before them, and its potency prevailed.

In the dunes of Tel Shamai Mr. Durchschlag rose and turned his back to the sea. His time slot in the class had closed. By now the teacher to follow the Mishnaic studies would have discovered the girls abandoned, or else Meshulam Banai would have made a stink. The students would be queried, an administrative interest in pedagogical idiosyncrasies newly whetted. *She wore what? And he said what? No doubt the first time he said such a thing. Not the first time?* If the story of the medal were to come out, Mr. Durchschlag would deny it. What medal, what ill-selected reminiscence, and according to who? Girls gab and gossip. He turned out the undirtied linings of his pockets in a motion to convince the hand once and for all, no wallet, none, gone, and neither would he find his girl.

Pickled Sprouts

IN FIFTH GRADE comes the call to duty, and a new layer in the uniform. A white apron will protect the pink school blouse and the gray skirt, a tiara of white cotton will secure the head. You've never eaten in the cafeteria, but just like everyone you will prepare the food when your turn arrives.

It's part of the curriculum. But of the coarsening in your hair you have not been forewarned. The auburn baby-silk predominates still, yes, but tougher, darker stuff is threading through. There is talk of blood, the knowledge always secondhand, not from the source. Her?

Her. All down her legs.

In two years you will see firsthand what makes pants-wetters of grown girls. For the meantime, there are myths, the slide show in the darkened classroom tells you.

"'There are myths,'" the nurse reads what is beamed onto the back side of a map. She says, "Don't you believe them. For example, when you're in your Period, you can absolutely feel free to cook and bake as usual. There is absolutely no need for concern that everything you touch will botch the recipe. Girls, here we see just one example of a bubbeh myseh. Of a granny tale. A granny tale." She employs repetition for a placating effect; the second time you're less afraid although her voice does not grow softer. She's a healer with occasional bad news. On the first Thursday of each month glass dowels frisk your scalp for lice. They leave cool trails; cool oozes lovely towards the ears but sometimes at the end there is a note. "You haven't heard it yet, better that it should come from me instead of someone it so happens you believe."

She welcomes questions. Few are forthcoming. Someone says she heard that if you take a steaming bath, that stops the, stops it.

False, the nurse says, and to always check bathwater temperature before immersion, baths being our nation's fourth most common cause of moderate-to-serious burns. "All yours," she finally says.

The Homeland teacher shuts the class door. White-shod footsteps clop away. The map is flipped: a ram's horn curves along the blue Mediterranean. Back in fourth grade the wide trumpeting end was carved away and reaffixed on its wrong side, to Egypt. That was the year in which the schoolyard filled with prophets in pink shirts and pleated midiskirts. That was the year, they said, marking the start of the disastrous shrinking which would push us to the sea. The principal is doing what she can to stave it off: New-issue maps show the green scar, but the school map has not been changed. At home the downstairs neighbors' girl still plays that band of Swedes singing their bounteous intentions for the world in awkward English.

"But the second round of founders soon failed, too," the Homeland teacher says, "because of basing their economy on bergamot."

You think of the truncated horn on the new maps, without the Sinai just a mouthpiece kissing Lebanon, a gaunt neck craning against Syria and Jordan. Warm wind would stammer through, unamplified.

Shouts spatter the schoolyard with a spectrum of accents. Faces and limbs paint blurs of brown and tan and pink against the background of concrete. You're pale and you have a pale sound. Your parents came here from elsewhere and say they brought you with them, a history you don't broadcast in your public life.

Your mother likes to send you to the grocery with lists; she says you need occasions to speak up and, to this end, the lists are always subtly revised. From all your whining, all the begging off before each shopping trip, she says, no one would ever guess that you are practically a native. Where's the bluntness? Where's the extroversion? *What* is the big deal?

When your father and I brought you here, she says, oh boy. We didn't even speak the language. Transitioning on that scope, she says, it takes conviction and persistence. You will call things the wrong name, you won't know how to argue like the locals, you'll be found amusing, so? You can't afford to dwell. You forge ahead. You give yourself a push. So, go! And if he gives the wrong percentage fat this time, say something, say it twice. Out. Now!

She won't acknowledge this is all her fault. Because of coffee. It's your job to buy it, to influence, with varying success, the proper quantity, the right amount of change. But you are not allowed to drink it. Your mother says it stunts the growth. In your mind there is no question that it does the opposite. To wit, the children here all drink it, and they are sharp and harried as grownups, no one in sight as permanently stunned as you. It is as if you were raised somewhere very different, then put down here. You drink milk. You speak soft and slow. You sneaked a taste of coffee just last week, and it's too late. The harshness! You've been raised on mac and cheese.

An eastern current lowers a fine mesh of desert particles over the schoolyard. You trip up on an early stage of Chinese jump rope, once again assume the static role, supporting the elastic with your ankles. The other end is looped around a chair because you like to keep the players down to two.

Shlomtzee hops through three stages without snagging. "You up for cafeteria duty soon?" she says, and graduates to the next level. You slither the elastic to your waist.

"Do I know? What letter are we up to in the roster? Tet, right?"

"Yud."

"Already? Like I care." Of greater pertinence to you is whether one must eat the fare once one has done the work. "They give you eggs a lot?" you ask her. Shlomtzee owns a meal-plan card. "Hard-boiled? Soft-boiled?"

"Sure. Either one."

"Poached is just as bad, and fried with runny yolks or omelets not mixed-up enough, that slippery white. Disgusting." You move the rope up to your armpits. "She ever give you three-bean salad?"

"Yes."

"Sour pickles?"

"Yes."

"But only if you want, right? Anything with vinegar they can't make you eat. It tastes like nail polish. That stuff's on the side. She make you eat that? She really crazy in the head?" Everyone knows about the cook. Everyone could be wrong.

Shlomtzee weaves the white elastic with her gray-kneed legs. "Be sick the week your turn is up. Get better on a Friday. Friday is without exception schnitzel."

"I can taste the vinegar in ketchup."

"Ketchup's optional." She completes the stage successfully, and starts as if from the beginning—the elastic fully lowered—but with added complications in the steps. Shlomtzee Ateeya didn't used to be your type, a bolter and a brayer. Her mouth opens so wide it might unhinge her face and stick limbs from a recent growth spurt finish off the look. But she is winding down.

The fifth grade marks the start of a peculiar decline. It seems the shrill girls, like balloons, are caving in to circumferential pressures. Then again, some of the softer girls are growing tense. You have earned unprecedented black marks in the roster. You've been reprimanded, twice kicked out of class, and once sent to the office, each time for garbling answers through a mouth stuffed full of food. It started with you simply getting hungry earlier, but now you gobble on the sly on principle. Shlomtzee does, too, but isn't caught. She never brings her own snacks, being on the meal plan. You're the supplier. Food is how you two got close.

Your first exchange: Prophets class. "Give," she whispers. You've been assigned to the same desk and she has picked up on your habits.

You give, break bread over plump knees and drop it on her bony ones. Then she is whispering again, sputtering crumbs. "What kind of sandwich you call this?"

You grab a pencil and dig its point into the margins of Joshua, II, where at the moment you believe they're still fighting on the way to Canaan. You add this: MARGARINE. QUIET.

The Prophets teacher turns the focus of the class to the two girls in back, who, she explains, are grappling with a matter clearly so important that it can't wait until break. "Perhaps they'd like to share the insight with the rest of us," she speculates.

"They wouldn't."

Again Shlomtzee sputters, this time at your wit. The teacher hasn't heard you but her interest in you grows. She nears, discovers you eroding Joshua with your eraser and counsels you to kiss the holy text, secure the remnants of your sandwich back within their bag, recite the Grace After a Meal, with feeling, and leave the room.

Despite such interferences, the feasting carries on. In days to come, there are your strawberry jam sandwiches, every last strawberry picked off, your crackers, nice and limp after a morning tucked in plastic wrap with cheese, your sponge cake, your cold boiled potatoes. The two of you stuff your craws like single-minded hatchlings, drowning out the lessons with your grinding jaws. You eat such baby food, says Shlomtzee, as she crams another bite. The question of her adding to the spread never comes up, thank God. Mornings, your treats help mask her bitter coffee breath, afternoons they cover cafeteria traces, smelly portents of your fate.

Your letter approaches: Yud, Caf, Lamed, and you're it. You have set foot inside the cafeteria only for school rallies in bad weather. You have never seen the crazy cook.

"Tell me today's dish."

On a Wednesday, at the end of lunch, Shlomtzee emerges from that place, her uniform exuding sourness. The last of the Yud surnames was called today.

"Spaghetti in sauce."

"The sauce on top or mixed through?"

"Of course mixed through. How else can the spaghettis go all orange?"

You offer her a bite of ripe banana, too odorous for classroom eating. She accepts it, furtive even now, and rightly so. There is no eating in the yard; it isn't cultured, it isn't clean. The Civil Defense man at the gate, someone's granddad with a rifle, a hankie on his head against the sun, he doesn't care, but there are the Health Monitors, sixth-graders who will tell on you. As their reward, they get to tote the first-aid kits on field trips. They are in congress with the nurse and carry out her law. They launch surprise inspections. Hand towel folded in thirds? Sandwich hygienically wrapped? Place mat clean? Hands washed? Fingernails trimmed? You bite them! (Ten points off.) Say grace before and after.

"Who heard of such a thing, spaghettis plain? Even for you!" Shlomtzee received a bad grade on a pop-quiz in geometry today. You let her finish up the fruit.

The two of you traverse the concrete yard towards the classrooms. Bell time nears. Sixth-graders are a pink and gray fortification, hip to hip against the fence. Their gazes sweep the boys' school, across the street. You count the bra-strapped backs and ridicule—you're not sure what. But Shlomtzee isn't game today.

"My baby brother Elkhanan eats spicier than you."

You squeeze the bruised banana peel in your fist. "You don't like my food maybe don't eat it from now on."

"I eat it out of interest," Shlomtzee says. Black hair is pulled so taut across her scalp, her eyes are stretched, the frizz bunched in two puffs, a new look for this year. "You better learn to eat some real food," she says. "Your turn is coming up next week." Gold rings with garnet chips loop through her ears, and also new is a pink plastic belt, the pearly heart-shaped buckle in perpetual migration. It's on her back now. "You don't lick your plate clean by the end of lunch, what she won't do!"

"She won't do anything."

"As if."

"You seen it?"

"Everybody knows."

"I'm saying no. I'm going to say no," you say. "You all eat garbage like you have to and all the time it's just a myth that she goes crazy. No one's seen it. No one's seen it happen."

"Garbage, you and what you eat!" Her arms crook back with such a snap, that for a moment you consider the new hairstyle and accessories stand not for budding ladylikeness but a hazardous excess of energy, a mounting rage.

"I got some wafers."

"Give!"

Next thing, she's got a handful of banana-peel tentacles, and you are bounding off, she after you, but only for a spell before she catches herself, tosses you an adult scowl, and heads for class. Her luminous belt buckle rides on her left hip.

You do have wafers, in your pocket, so you work on them yourself, chomping and kicking through the dirt behind the classrooms, balancing along the edges of the bomb shelter, till a Health Monitor appears. You dodge her, but not soon enough. She screams she's going to report you. You run for your life, and in the process slice your thigh on a torn fence link.

Back in the classroom you must treat the bleeding cut with spit, and by the time you get home it's inflamed. So is your mother, prophesying lockjaw and demanding to know why in God's name you did not involve the nurse. The scar will stay, old as you get, scythe-shaped, paler than pale, forever threatening to fade.

There is a problem with a thing you have been given.

Walking home on Monday, you approach the new falafel stand with its long sign: TAWILI AND SON OUT OF THIS WORLD SELF SERVE. Shlomtzee gulps the smells of fermentation and eyes the goods in the steel tubs. The vendor hands out slit-top pitas, which the clientele packs with crisped chickpea balls, sauced eggs, diced salad, fries and Turkish eggplant, hummus, hilbeh, zkhoug, harissa, a kaleidoscope of condiments. Some patrons understand self-service in a way the vendor didn't intend. They clutch their pitas, eat the stuffing out, then step over for refills.

Tawili or his son flails a tongs behind the counter, shouting. "Get out of my eyes!"

You hold your breath, step over trampled cucumber cubes, turmeric-yellow stains of amba relish, pepper paste and cabbage on the pavement. The smells thin out as you walk on. Shlomtzee makes loving eyes at pigeons and at people you don't know. In gym today she jumped the longest in the long jump. She is buoyant, bouncing with each step. You slip your book bag off one shoulder and undo the buckle.

"Look what my mother's doing to me now." The thing inside has crushed your notebooks out of shape.

Shlomtzee is dumbstruck. She stops short.

You elucidate: "A lunch box."

"A lunch *box*?"

"A box for lunch." As soon as you turned the corner on your block this morning, you concealed it, tin and painted red, with hinges and a clasp. A birthday gift.

"A box? For lunch?"

"My mother put some money in the mail and they sent it."

"Who keeps their lunch in metal safes?" Here, those who bring food from home carry synthetic leather bags hanging by straps around their necks, maybe a Minnie lookalike stitched on, a knock-off Daisy Duck. The practice begins as soon as the teacher is no longer one who makes sandwiches. Those who elect to carry on with institutional feeding carry meal cards instead. Their lunches are hot and on a plate and subsidized as needed. "For tools, maybe," Shlomtzee says. "Is it for tools? Looks like a toolbox."

"My mother said when she was little she had one just like this."

"No! For children, metal boxes? Where? Not in our country."

"It keeps your food in better shape. That's what she says. It's sturdy."

"Where'd they send it from?"

"From Pittsburgh."

"That's what country she comes from?"

"Yes."

"You, too?"

"No. Here."

"So tell her no one else does."

"Like I didn't."

"It's stupid-looking," Shlomtzee says.

You know it. It's a problem, though your mother called it a solution. Just the thing to stand up even to your level of abuse, she said. No seams to fray, no strap to twirl to death, no zipper to untooth.

A problem. A resilient one, a well-constructed mark of shame. Shlomtzee averts her eyes. You seal your bag. You walk on to a bus stop shelter, where you pause to wait with Shlomtzee for her transportation. Settling on the bench, you kick the air with both your feet, you drop the book bag and what's in it to the pavement. Maybe you'll forget it there.

"Today," says Shlomtzee, "the cook gave us chicken soup. With noodles. Chicken soup you like."

"Strained."

"One girl from fourth grade," she says. "Her father drives her every day to school."

"So what?"

"He drives her in a garbage truck."

You make embarrassed faces at each other, cringe and simper, shake your heads for the poor kid till you feel better about things, almost contented, generous, finding how good to spend your own disgrace on others.

"Also!" Shlomtzee comes off festive now. "I'll tell you what. The terrorists are stupid."

"They're retarded." Public service ads on television demonstrate how watermelons, loaves of bread, dolls, if split open, may reveal ugly coils, fuses, clocks. Touch nothing you find on the street. Depart at once from the vicinity. Alert a grownup. "Stupid because why?"

"Look up." The two of you twist back your necks, your legs continuing to kick and dangle under the roof of corrugated metal shading you from the white sun. "If they were smart they'd rig up bombs on top of every bus stop. Who would see them there?" She rises.

You, too. Single-file, you stalk around the bus stop, trying for a full view of the roof. A grandma wheels her groceries by. She, also, cranes her neck.

"You lost a ball?" she says. "You shouldn't play on the street with a ball."

Shlomtzee and you plod with bent knees, pushing imaginary groceries, with rolling eyes, a mushy smacking of the lips. You prowl around the shelter a bit longer and sit back down.

"You're right," you say. "You wouldn't even notice any bomb up there at all."

"They're stupid," Shlomtzee says, but this time hushed, because you both see, suddenly, that once you've thought a thing, the world has thought it, and now what have you done.

In the gym changing room there is increasing prowess at dressing through and under layers, never entirely disrobing. Backs are turned, appearances transformed through narrow openings. Shlomtzee hides nothing, hasn't yet had a thing to hide. But there today are swelling nipples, pushing at her ribbed boys' undershirt. She seems oblivious. You are privately appalled.

You're drawing gym pants over good, straight hips when the teacher comes in with a note. The cook awaits, she says. Your turn is up.

"It's not. We're still on Caf with two to go: Cohen, Catabi. I'm not till the day after tomorrow!"

Well, today's girl is out sick; tomorrow's girl is present but disqualified by a productive cough.

You cough, producing nothing.

Grab your bag, the teacher says.

"The Tuesday dish," you whisper as you're ushered out. "Quick!"

Shlomtzee, lost inside her regulation gym shirt, doesn't respond.

The hair goes back; every last strand is kept in place with rubber bands and bobby pins she offers from a yogurt cup. Your head is crowned with starched white cotton and a whiff of bleach, your waist cinched in an apron which she double-knots behind.

Enormous whisks and spatulas hang side by side with colanders and pots the size of kettledrums; a touch would start a racket like a band of cymbalists. Everything is scoured steel and white enamel.

Everything is oversized. There is no package on the shelves that you could carry. Behind the kitchen door, you wash down with the pink school soap.

She says to scrub especially the nails.

The cook is pinafored, the fabric peach with light blue stripes. She looks like someone's grandma, although lovelier, by far, than any grandmother you know. Her skin is candlewax, of a dull sheen, the cheeks, the slim bridge of the nose, see-through although not, changeable seeming. Low on the forehead arc heroic pencil strokes, twins, each the perfection of a brow for just one day; above them glows a purple flame caged in a hair net. She doesn't smile. She doesn't look crazy either, only contained; human brown irises hooded in lids, although waxen, of skin. There is no need to be afraid.

Call her Miss Altbroit, please.

She says you're baking fish today, and fixing vegetables, to go with. To you fish tastes like nothing to be eaten, and of vegetables, only potatoes and cucumbers without the seeds, provided there's no bitterness. Miss Altbroit speaks with an accent. You are interested to know if you must eat in the mess hall with the others.

Beyond the kitchen wall the cafeteria floor sprawls, a flat field of tile planted with tables in rows. The tabletops are laminated with pale green Formica like your classroom desks, but rising much taller, and extending much farther.

"Vus?" she says, as she hands you a sieve. "Such a soft speaker, this."

You ask again.

"Oh," she says. "No. No. No. No."

You hold the sieve, firm-fingered. Everyone till now inferred a mandate where there is none, pressure in a place of calm, insanity where there is only nurturance. The cook pours scrupulously measured quantities of flour, salt, some pepper and some sandy-colored spice. She could proportion all of it by sight, she says, but would you learn like that? "No," she says, crystal clear in her instruction. You can see you two will understand each other well. She shows you how to dredge the fish. You replicate the action perfectly, you know, because Miss Altbroit says so as she flays a stick of margarine.

She wields it like a crayon, drawing streaks across a baking sheet the size of seven pavement slabs. "Such a good worker, all the more, deserves good treatment." She lifts the greased sheet, reveals a dry one beneath, sets the first behind you, gets to work on the next. "That you should have to wait who worked so hard? No. This is policy. The work is done, the workers eat." Her eyes narrow, and the effect is disconcerting. You perceive this is a smile, less its lower half. Though she moves briskly and with maximum efficiency around the giant kitchen, her voice floats like scattering steam.

"Not to touch with organisms from the halibut," she says when you're done dredging. "Wash with soap."

You rush to the dispenser, squeeze the pump. Medicinal pink fumes correct the odor of the sea.

The scent of baking fish isn't as awful as the raw, but when your nose suspends reports you are relieved. You peel potatoes, pausing to shake parings from your wrists. The damp cuffs fall into a deep black pail. Miss Altbroit is cutting up tomatoes. She uses a little gadget, which she has let you hold and test, to gouge out the hard green cicatrices. When you handed her tool back, you saw her coded forearm, flickerings of blue-green ink, and tried not to brush it with your blank one. She hums once in a while. Otherwise, only the gentle sounds of blades.

By now you would have been out of Gym and in Mathematics; from straining the limbs to the same in the brain. Miss Altbroit isn't crazy, you don't think. You will explain about your taste and she will say, That she should have to eat who doesn't like? No! This is policy. She is a reasonable woman.

She drops red chunks onto a mountain of cubed cucumbers and purple cabbage in a steel tub.

"We call this vegetable salad," she says. "Correct?"

"Correct, Miss Altbroit."

"Vus?"

"Vegetable salad, Miss Altbroit."

"This is a quiet and respectful one," she tells the salad. "We need like her more children in our country."

She takes the peeled potatoes from you, drops them in a vat of boiling water, hands you a knife. You work on the tomatoes together. The juice bites at your bitten nails.

"A tomato is no vegetable," she says. "It is a fruit. You knew this?"

You did not.

Naturally not, she says, when most adults don't know what goes into their mouths, how would a child? As for her, it is her job to know. "What makes a fruit a fruit?"

You're no authority.

"Being the ripened ovary of a seed plant. Which, an ovary, is—"

"The nurse already said." Once is enough.

"So, what a thing to put into a vegetable salad? Fruit." She laughs, you're fairly sure, a strange idea of a laugh. She wouldn't earn a big part in the annual school play.

The cloudy, steaming water is poured off the hot potatoes; into the vat you and Miss Altbroit add some milk, some salt, five sticks of margarine, crush it all up with coil mashers. The tables are set, bread baskets put out. There are seeds like black ants in the slices.

"Now," she says, "food for the workers." She puts a slice of bread on a blue plate. "Self-service," she says, and passes the plate on to you, and then a huge metal spoon. She holds your serving wrist and guides, as if you're blind. You scoop up mashed potatoes, her arid forearm against yours. "And fish for protein," she says. "And for the vitamins the salad. Always for a growing girl some salad." Surprisingly, you choose the biggest piece of fish, and take not one, but two heaping spoonfuls of the salad. "With good appetite," she says, half-closes her hooded eyes, smiles her lacking smile, lets go.

Small, cubed vegetables can be swallowed like pills. The food goes down in slow-traveling lumps. With the breath held, flavor can be censored to salty, bitter, sour and so forth. But before long, you'll have to breathe. You tuck bits of fish into forkfuls of mash, and that helps. Miss Altbroit eats with the thoroughness and industry of her kitchen work and does not seem to see you there, with her, at the table in the back of the school kitchen. And then, she does.

"You're my best worker, so far. I'm telling you it's not often I come across a girl so civilized. The children here, ah." With her fork she chases her last cube of cucumber. "What is this culture from? This pushing and the shoving." She wipes her plate immaculate with her bread, chews, swallows. "Like you I was a good, quiet girl, I had respect, there were ways. They're gone. What's gone is gone."

Her eyes rest on you while you render the food swallowable, chewing gently, trying not to extrude flavor, but also not to choke.

"More of anything?" she says. "No? Smart girl. Seconds should wait until you're done. I tell these girls," she says. "Appreciate, don't just assume, but in your case I see you understand. Someone has raised you to be prudent with your portions."

She draws a breath, fills up her chest and empties it, nods at you, seems to want you to observe her closely, and you're helpless in the face of this permission. Spun-glass hair contained by netting, penciled-in replacement brows, a face of wax. Lips open and lips shut. The cook accompanies your meal with a story.

Miss Altbroit isn't a good teller, no enthusiasm for the subject. The boredom in her voice means she cannot believe, even of you, even of such a worker, such a quiet and respectful kitchen hand and such an eater, that you'll take her in. She is right. You've heard this one. You've heard it in museums, by monuments, in History class, in Literature. And in the school gymnasium, a lectern draped with a black cloth, a candle lit, an old man talking. In the back rows, giggling. (Shhh! Shame!) Note, though: They have always told the story to the group, not just to you. It's not a story just for you; it's not a story for one child on her own to swallow. She should know this. She *does* know; that's why so flavorless. She cannot stop herself, but tries to spare you all the same. You feel only an increasing sense of fullness, full to bloat, so that you almost welcome, suddenly, a piquancy.

"My legs!" she says, her flat voice effervescing, eyes a little predatory, winsome, flirting. "It was always such a struggle with my weight, but they became so slim, especially I thought the calves, which until then—" She fades out shyly like a girl, half-closing her eyes. Then back to offerings more familiar in this kind of story: ghetto, trains, camp, wire, gas. But, listen now: The Liberators! This you savor. This will wrap things up as they should be wrapped up, dessert.

"Russians," the cook says, without the fanfare you'd expect. "Russian soldiers they were," she says. Trains, she says again. But this time it's a good word, a stouthearted word, humane, delivering the slender, starving girls with their fine legs.

She says the soldiers forced them in the aisles. "Forced us," she repeats. She looks to you for some response. "Each one of them chose one of us," she says. "Or more than one of them chose the same one of us, you understand?" she asks. "They shared. Now if you slept you spared yourself the precise details of, but on the other hand if somehow you could not awaken then your influence upon duration, as it were. You understand?"

Not yet, no. You insist no. No.

You nod.

"The only place that's safe for us is here," she says. She clears away your tableware, now that your plate is empty, and your palate stunned. "But look," she says. She plucks at the black net binding her hair. "What am I, senile? To forget the special treat." She beckons with her coded forearm.

Pudding? A nice piece of cake? You follow.

"Ay!" she says, reproaching herself still. "Of all the girls, my champion kitchen hand deserves a taste." She halts, facing a door you hadn't noticed, plastered with a poster of the seven blessed crops. She tells you you're her guest and, so, that you should turn the handle. It gives easily. She urges you to advance in. She tugs a chain. A yellow light illuminates the deepest pantry in the world.

The shelves lining the sides are whale's ribs. The many rounded organs blur together in the dimness, but it's clear that they go on and on and that they're pickle jars. Some of the glass is clean, some crusted. Vegetables of every kind float in the shadowy solutions, and fruit, too, now you know. Those are fruit.

"The recipe is mine that I developed," says Miss Altbroit. "See can you guess the secret in the brine."

She takes down a jar of pygmy cabbage heads, dark khaki-green, bobbing in yellow liquid, softly flapping their disintegrating outer leaves. "Everything was so mild," she says, "and what the meal was really missing we forgot. Some zing. How about these? Are you familiar? Brussels sprouts. Or there are baby eggplants, pearl onions, okra, cherry tomatoes, anything and everything. Even boiled eggs. Walk to the end."

After she seats you back at the table, brings a glass of milk, sits opposite you, peering; after Miss Altbroit's awkward, fingertip pats on your shoulders, more like a tap-tapping to awaken than a consoling touch; after she tells you there was no need to cry, she never makes anyone eat what they don't like, only what's on their plate, that she's no monster; after all this, you are the server, eyes dry but pinched-feeling, apron only a little stained, nauseous stirrings below your waist from the uncustomary lunch. Girls in pink and gray walk up to the steam table. You serve, with Miss Altbroit prescribing the balance. When this is done, you stand behind the kitchen door and watch the cook patrol the tables. And there's Shlomtzee, her stretched eyes upon you as she squirts a jet of bottled lemon juice onto a helping of baked fish.

Soldiers have taken over the school, good soldiers, our soldiers, and all the girls are evacuated to the boys' yard across the way.

At this time yesterday you were flipping halibut in flour. Now the girls' schoolyard is overrun with olive-drab, the boys' with pink, what a day, what a day, your kind of day. Girls kick an abandoned ball around the dusty soccer court until the teachers indicate that this must stop. Skirts are flying, it's unseemly. It's disruptive to the boys, who are in session. Their windows show vague shapes of blue-clad torsos, skullcapped heads. The sixth-grade girls maintain precarious poise.

Then the normal order is reinstated. Soldiers hold up traffic as you're herded back to school.

The Civil Defense man with the hankie on his head stands at the gate, his chair surrendered to Miss Altbroit. He holds a glass of water to her lips, presses his big, old man's hand on her shoulder, murmurs in a language of old folks. Miss Altbroit strums at the black netting on her hair. The nurse comes with a pill.

It's over. "Done," the Prophets teacher says in class. You must all settle down if you expect an explanation.

A Suspicious Object was found in the cafeteria pickle pantry, she says. As it turned out, an antiquated toolbox, which would indicate a workman's oversight predating all of us here, even poor Miss Altbroit. To resume: the siege on Jericho.

"You left it there on purpose," Shlomtzee says.

"Says who?" You stretch your legs along the bus-stop bench and flex your toes inside your shoes. The stiffness of the day's last lesson leaves your muscles easily, as smoothly as choked tears flow into spite and opportunity. "Maybe you also know who told them to let crazies next to children?"

Shlomtzee slides down the pole. The ridged roof shudders. "Was your mom mad that the army blew it up?"

"What do you think? It wasn't cheap. I have to do the dishes for a month."

The bus will arrive soon and take Shlomtzee home. In sixth grade she will wear a bra. Sometimes in gym she'll be exempted. You will find another friend.

"It was stupid-looking," Shlomtzee says. "What do you need a thing like that." She settles down beside you, centers her belt buckle, smoothes her uniform blouse and her gray school skirt. The skirt is houndstooth, to be accurate, minutely broken-checked with black and white. The eye tires and cheats.

Over the course of months and years you'll find your palate coarsening. Progressively you'll seek out flavors more and more assaulting.

But today you eat white bread. You let it soften to a porridge on your tongue. You wait. No one is here but you and Shlomtzee, four legs kicking, perfectly coordinated in a rhythm so placating, even the growl of the approaching bus lulls like a baby mumbling her own song, in no one's tongue, with no one's memories.

A Pillar of a Cloud

✥

THE COUSIN OF A third cousin twice removed from the granddaughter of our paternal great-grandmother's niece's nephew's son. The doorbell chimes. American relatives set foot in Zion and they all expect to be put up. They bring us presents, so all right.

But look at this one. Is it the peephole warping her? The doorbell chimes again and no one asks who it is. We can see, the elevator hatch glowing behind her as she stands outside our new Pladelet.

Plada equals steel; delet, door. The marriage of the two delivered our Pladelet, registered trademark, just a week ago. Slogan: "Ma aht doh'eget? Yesh Pladelet!"—"What are you worried? Got Pladelet!" The door is a hit and deservedly so. This has been a vastly satisfying week of entrances and exits. Either way the sweep of the transition is majestic, heavy, slow. The closing is best. The door is sucked in with a passionate kiss, upon which the bolts pop out, and plug themselves in every side, floor, jambs and top. The owner's manual shows them in X-ray view, a blast-resistant grid. Since the Mavo Dirot attack sales have shot up. Had that mother been this secure, so would have been her kids. There are five of us children here, and twelve bars all told, all controlled by one key. The key has no teeth; it has pocks.

The peephole we hadn't thought much about. We've had those before; it seemed the same as any other. But is not. According to this view the individual outside is built by the example of a dollop of whipped cream, everything settling from a point. Doesn't the object closest to the lens loom largest as a rule, the face? Perhaps the manual addresses this. We would go read up, except that our mother has ears in her head. She has heard the bell, several times. Someone must open. It's a question of who.

"I did last time."

"He should."

"She hasn't opened in a year!"

What's at stake here? We're not timid. But you never know the nature of these greetings, sudden intimacies with residents of unknown cities, strangers, as a rule better to do than us, but in terrible need, big-handed, broad-fingered. Children aren't asked, they're just enfolded.

The dilemma is resolved in a most shocking way. The cousin tries the door handle herself and reveals us where we stand.

"Well, hi! I thought I heard shy little voices. Oh my God."

The peephole lied, it seems for our protection. Though stout, she's normally proportioned, but she is homely in the most offensive way. She has taken our face and mismanaged it.

Behold the family gums. In us they're a touch indiscreet, nothing disciplined smiling can't swathe. But in her! The top lip flares up like a skirt. We study our shoes and the stone chips and shells in the tiles. Some enjoy a funhouse mirror, we do not.

It is a face we trace, in foreign documents, to Vienna. Uncle Isser in Ramot retains a brittle invoice for our name, bought from the Emperor Joseph, no returns or refunds, the initiative the seller's, the purchase mandatory. Klein was what we could afford or we'd have taken Gross. Until then we had been in the eye of fewer folks. We had kept to two circles, first-name basis and Titled, the former limited to kin and community, the latter to outside bringers of good or bad, Shayndl with the brilliant son or Gertrude the beggar, the Coalman and the Beast of Prey.

In our possession from an earlier passage are the pages of the Book of Numbers, providing the first-known mention of our first-known forerunner, Calev ben Yefuneh (chapter 13, verse 6), who would have glared upon his weak-kneed fellow scouts to Canaan through our own black-olive irises, beetling our heavy brows and flickering our sooty lashes in high spleen. The fiery red hair, we have surmised, was a Hungarian acquisition, later, from an ardent episode among the Hassids of Satmar. The beautiful Avreml may have passed to us, as well, the milky skin given to sunburn, the dancing crowds of golden freckles. We have been told that our good looks are dramatic. We've been told we stand out.

One hundred and twenty years ago, under fear of erasure, we steeled our expression and parted with the savage nobles of the European woods, seeking the new state of peace and self-dominion.

Here is where the split occurs: On the way to Palestine, certain features stop for a refresher on Ellis Island—and defect. They never rejoin us. Moreover, while in Palestine our complexion yellows with malaria and knots with battle scars, on Coney Island, in Newark, on the East Side, their face begins to alter in the low heat of the melting pot. Witness the cousin, with her double version of our chin.

"Lemme see," she says, agog, as if we are the curious-looking ones. "*You* must be, no. You. I had it down pat on the plane."

Again she displays the private regions of her teeth. The eyes, however, remain guarded.

The eyes.

HaShem above, what has she done to the family eyes? On us they are less than serenely wide-set; we have a naturally focused look. But hers are so little! This makes the face look so wide! A chimp would feel as we do upon encountering her first orangutan. It isn't nice to recognize the kinship in something so patently strange. Oh, those eyes. How easily a look of hyperfocus shrinks to fear, and back again. Too many versions all at once, ours reflecting back at us, transparent, on the glass of her bifocals. What does she have to fear?

"You. No, you," she says. "Uhh, wait. I was expecting girl girl boy, but what I'm seeing is girl boy boy—and boy, yeah, that is definitely it. In either case, the oldest's name I know is—Crud, crud, I give up. We've had a snapshot of you on our fridge since, well, forever. But you all pulled a fast one on me, am I right? You grew up and you're more. I need an update."

They all say this: It's wonderful to know they always have a home here, and family. Our mother welcomes them. Her young ones aren't as receptive, are more dismayed by the disruption of routines, the blurring of turf, and that a guest always gets first dibs on the shower. The presents help warm us.

The first guest we remember was a father of another cousin, a child he brought with its mother, the wife. They would not eat our breakfast cereal. The brand name is Boker Tov, which is to say, Good Morning. The units are cylinders, irregularly cut, the color tan, the consistency sturdy. The stuff was too hard on the relatives' jaws and the flavor, they said, was like dust. They bought boxes of imported Frosted Flakes locally at an inflated price. Because of the price they asked that we reserve it for our cousin, Melanie.

They came with gifts! The packs of purple bubble gum lasted us two weeks. The elasticity! The perfume! And a formula that has overcome the bitterness at the end. The wads were reusable. Also they bore long manufactured cakes sealed in plastic, one for each: a perfect uniformity of crumb, an extravagant astringency of cocoa cunningly subverted with a layer of sweet white fat. The whole of it placing no demand at all upon the teeth—a science of contentment. This branch of thought is well developed here, we had all felt, until then. The Devil Dogs dissolved against our palates, our worries bathed in chocolate awe. In appreciation of our uncle's contributions we took only a modest lien of the Frosted Flakes when the relatives were climbing to the Zealots' suicide fort of Masada in a cable car.

Tension ensued between the mothers. The American aunt, planted in our kitchen, wagged a depleted box of Frosted Flakes at our Imma. Why, said the American, why infringe? When yours are perfectly accustomed to the local stuff. It gratified us that our mother, who normally demands a stoicism on our part, a making do, in this case held her ground on our behalf. They could not hoard stock in our pantry and deny us. Our mother questioned us when they had gone, we hung our little heads. She said no more. She set her teatime sugar bowl beside our Boker Tov the next day's morning. Our hearts ached.

The uncle's family disliked our beds: span too narrow, mattresses too thin, no boxsprings? They moved to a five-star coastal hotel in Tel Aviv. Despite the strained relations they took us out to dinner at a touristy Chinese on the Marina—heavenly, everything deboned, the chairs tall-backed and soft, the music wordless. They let us look out at our sea through their tinted hotel panes and take in lungfuls of the frosted Sheraton air. A couple from a far-flung branch arrived only last month. They were no-tears shampoo and a jar of Fluff.

So what will this one be? For one, she's been at least an hour on our sofa sipping orange squash and chatting with our mother while her suitcase remains latched. We mixed the juice. We fetched a plate of lemon wafers, sat, attended to the adult talk without undue disruption. The sun descends. The tiles have left our bottoms numb. The older folks are bent on tracing family lines.

Often the datum doesn't jibe. Our mother will be under the

impression someone is long dead, or a convert. The cousin will correct her, no, alive and Jew, just hasn't kept in touch with the Israeli branch. The subject drops its anchor longest by one Cecil Kenneth Lyons, who now lives in Costa Rica with eleven pygmy hens. Our Imma finds the facts hard to digest. In Costa Rica? Operates an airtram through a cloud forest. The hens he considers his family, humble, he finds, hardworking and generous. The plumage remains downy through all stages of life, and both the males and females feed the chicks.

"Costa Rica?"

"Went with a birding tour, fell in love with the place."

"Well." Our mother holds the plate up once again. "We have birds, too. And you came here."

The cousin accepts a pale wafer, tooths a crispy layer off and licks the inside filling. "Birds are nice," she says, pursing her lips. "Is there a particular one? Cecil I remember was after the Resplendent Quetzal, originally." She comments that the lemon creme is tarter than she is used to. "Oh God," she says. "Can I just tell you real quick about my plans? I am on *such* a high. I have to see Masada, this I know, the Wailing Wall and David's Tower, Yad VaShem, Tiberias, the Dead Sea. All of those names! I can't believe they're going to come alive. You have to understand. Ever since I was a little girl in Sunday Hebrew school and Mrs. Milstein from the music period got me on this kick, all I could talk about was coming to see Eretz. Had to be her, sure wasn't my parents. She had just been, you see. She couldn't say enough. It was Eretz this and Eretz that and Eretz Eretz Eretz and, next thing that I know, here I am! Making it happen. Am I really? Someone pinch me."

Imma blocks a pincering hand. Our middlemost is prone to acting out on how we feel. We're tired and annoyed and we don't like her manner of speech. The Hebrew studded in the cousin's English is limpened by her accent and misuse of the possessive form. We've noticed this in other relatives, the scant unintegrated stash of

Hebrew tossed in like exotic peppercorns in a bland stew. A grammar lesson: Eretz Yisrael equals *The Land of Israel.* Lop off Yisrael, and your remainder? *The Land of.* The lack of resolution makes us jumpy. Six times in one breath makes us upset. To ease our minds, we rest our gazes on the glossy maroon suitcase, a large and handsome piece of luggage of a sturdiness recalling our door's. The outside looks to have been poured of liquid leather, hardened in a loaf-shaped mold, quite a thick loaf, abundant. An inside view would show every sweet pleasure in her world and, most important, a year's supply of Frosted Flakes, box after box festooned with guardian tigers, her personal effects serving as padding.

"If you will it, it's no dream," our eldest says.

"That's beautiful," our cousin says. "Isn't that beautiful? And so true. Look, here I am. But let me not forget my hosts!" She straightens up and snaps out the retracting handle of her case. The loaf follows, rumbling on its wheels. "There is something I would like to offer you," she says, as if we didn't know.

She rests her hand upon a silvery latch. She'll want to tip the suitcase over. We will want to help. We rise. She smiles and addresses us, more or less:

"Is this where I live now?" she says. We grant her the derisive look adults expect at purposefully idiotic quizzes. She puts on an equally broad aspect of bewilderment. "No?" she says. "Okay. You're saying that I'm not always hanging out on your couch?" We shake our heads in concert. "Really? Wow. Then what do I do? Where?" The youngest verbal sibling can take this one. "Great!" the cousin cries. "Okay. Let's get a little more specific. I live where in America?" Our eldest offers up what comes into her mind right after Disneyland. The Big Apple. "Great!" the cousin says. "Okay. Close. Actually Connecticut. South Meadowlark, proud home of Greater Hartford's first and largest Chuck E. Cheese." Most of this we don't get. The playful tone is meant for us, we know, the heightened animation, the little eyes rapidly widening and relaxing as she bobs her head, seeming to near us through the lower half of her bifocals, then to retreat above the seams. The esoteric wit is for our mother, who smiles drily as the visitor plays gentle puppeteer. Not that we mind. We're seasoned hosts. We recognize the prelude to a gift.

"So in conclusion," she says. "Your Cousin Tiffy lives in—" Can't hope to pronounce it, won't attempt. She fills in the blank herself. "And there," she says, "she spends her days camped out on people's couches. Yes?" Correct. "No! Silly Tiffy! Tiffy's ten years out of college. Tiffy holds down a job, a senior position, I might add, since not too long ago. The Lenzomat at Turnstone Mall, a pioneer in bringing one-stop, quarter-hour, exam-to-specs service to the Northeast. Not including frame selection time. I'm an optometrist!" she says. "Couldn't bring the mall, but I have my chief associate's kit." She looks at us. We glance at each other. They don't usually expect thanks at this stage. First we must have a taste. "In other words," she says, "consider yourselves my guests." Strange, but fine. Take it out.

Her finger stirs on the latch. We hold our breaths.

"Thank you," our Imma says. "No."

What! *Why?* No present? *Why* no present? Our youngest crawls over to sit on Tiffy's shoe. She strokes his head, her other hand remaining on the latch.

"There are a lot of you, I know," she says. "But I insist. My pleasure, honestly. The raise paid for my trip so what the heck. It's something I decided I would do. I get the glasses at materials cost. The fifteen-minute promise doesn't travel I should say. I'm going to ask for your indulgence while I wire the prescriptions to the grinders. Shipping will take seven to ten working days."

Our Imma's nostrils flare though she maintains the social smile. "Let's talk about sleeping arrangements."

"Homework time a challenge for the gang? Studies show fifty-three percent of cases, the reason's purely physical! A staggering forty of that's vision."

"In the area of the visual arts my children shine," our Imma says. "The annual school psychometric test proves preternaturally astute spatial perceptions, across the board. And no surprise. Their Great-Great-Grandpa Yokhanan of blessed memory cobbled the main street of our city. Samaritan limestone, cut by hand, transported by carriage. Laid them, too, not a gap. Never a set of lenses in the family then or since."

"Had to make do."

"Only thing wrong with his eyes, he sometimes had to close them. Killed in his sleep. Bedouin horse thieves. He had laid all but the last block."

"No kidding. You'll have to show me where he took that nap."

"Where he was felled there is now a modern quarry, massively mechanized, highly regulated and enormously explosive, closed to the public."

"Not a problem. I'll snap shots of his roadwork. Be great to send back to the crew. We'll take the kids out on location. What's your schedule looking like this week?"

"Asphalt proved better for the shocks, in time."

"Well, there you go!" Tiffy says. "Open your door to technological advancement is what I say."

"A well-established point of view," our Imma says, "holds that corrective lenses make for weakened eyes. The eye develops a dependency. The unassisted vision comes to be unbearable. Before you know, you always need them on." She claps her hands against her aproned lap and stands.

The cousin rises, too, our youngest sliding off her foot. We remain seated on the tiles, stunned, as mother, guest and suitcase move away. Why? Why? Hard wheels roll with an occasional shudder, which the tiles pass to us.

When we recover and catch up, they're in our bedroom, the suitcase gleaming in the shadow of our desk.

Our mother tucks the edges of a sheet under the corner of a

mattress. Cousin Tiffy dwarfs one of our chairs, exciting our space with her hands. When she sees us her arms extend in a full stretch, palms soft side up. We fall in her embrace. We press against her thighs and back. We drop our youngest on her yielding lap. Her sweet smell isn't of a soap we know.

"Delicious and delicious and delicious," she says, pinching every cheek. "Priceless. Whose chipped tooth?" Our next to eldest's. But the middlemost curls back his lips, as well, to show a compromised incisor. Him Tiffy proclaims a doll. She grins and her lip flips right up.

And thus we stand, half of our little group and all of her, flashing each other with the coverings of our hard roots. Even the frail connections to the inner-upper lip are shown. Our youngest joins right in, the pacifier falling out. Our eldest is a second mother to him, she melts, and united we grin.

Only our Imma keeps up her reserve. She twists a pillow through the opening of a case. "That's nothing to be proud of."

Tiffy's lenses sparkle with our wounded eyes.

"We broke our teeth because we fell," our Imma says. "We fell because we flouted better judgment. Who was in charge?" Our eldest bows her head. "And who rode who to the point of shared collapse?"

The guilty seal their teeth behind their lips, our eldest sputtering through them: "Who always works till late?"

"Kids!" Tiffy says, spreading her fingers in the air. "Kids will be kids."

Our mother drops the pillow in its place, her fists against her hips.

Tiffy looks down.

"Tiles!" she says. "Even in the bedroom? Wow, stark. Desertlike, barren in the elegant sense of the word. A little hard under the foot. Be hard on a kid's teeth. I was accident-prone as a child myself. My mother had the carpenter put extra cushion in. My choice was salmon plush. Forget it, though," she says. "I understand. If I were you I'd go for this exact look. I mean the specialness of life here is so apparent, even when you stay at home. Look at the stones. Look at the shells. That one's a fossil. Some have to be relics. What a concept. Every individual tile is basically an Eretz bar."

How can we but forgive this loving whimsy with our mother tongue? On the sofa she was happier than at the door and in the bedroom she is happier than there. We're off the topic of our broken teeth. Where this is going is clear. The future is bright. The sun shines through our shutters, tiger-striping Tiffy's mobile face.

If only Imma could be with us in our mirth. Her knitted brow betrays a mounting headache. "Take your cousin to the roof," she says.

Away we go.

And up, along the tiled stairs which rise from the kitchen porch. An ordinary wooden door opens into the high outdoors.

Ours is the tallest structure in the area, because the newest, but if a taller one were built here, it would see us like we see the rest: the bulges of utility rooms, prickly with antennae, the blinking solar panels angled at the sun, sending up postcards of the sky. The cousin is spellbound by the horizon.

The craggy hills resemble piles of scrap metal in the coppering light. A column of rich dust rises above the southeast range, nearly inactive in the breezeless evening, pale, whitish-yellow, lumpy, laden as a grandma's hose.

"Fantastic," Tiffy says. "Oh, perfect." She arranges us before this view, steps back and fumbles at her neck. She finds a strap. She draws a compact camera from inside her blouse. She aims, zooms in, out, in, and snaps.

The column slowly swells. The far-off blams of dynamite growl like a belly. Tiffy gasps. "Oh yes." The camera shaking in her hands.

Flash flashing, she goes oracular for a moment, not unusual in this kind of guest. The proclamation she recites comes from the third book of the Pentateuch. The scrolls of her flame-colored hair unfurl and stand on end.

"'. . . thou Lord are among this people . . . thou goest before them, by day time in a pillar of a cloud, and in a pillar of fire by night.'" We explain it's from the quarry. She explains it's the effect, and snaps another shot.

A bike with tasseled handles leans against a water vat, a tricycle stands by the generator, and a jump rope is slung on the antenna. She poses us in play. She poses us before our mother's potted cacti, as we holler, Cheese! in our tongue. Gveena! She laughs.

"Forget the word," she says. "Shows too much throat. Let's all just decide to be happy."

Again? All right. But as we organize the team, Tiffy's attention moves on. She is hunting for the source of a near sound.

"What's that?"

The scraping of a trowel.

"By whom?"

By Ibrahim, we tell her, not too loud.

She scrutinizes twilit pools of copper on the tiles, and soon her eye finds the man. He is kneeling, back turned to us. A softening beach ball has rolled down the slope and rests not far from him, beside the PVC lip of the rain pipe. His shirt is soiled, white-stained with plaster, suntanned where it clings, and pin-striped where the fabric remains unaffected. He is neither young nor elderly, about the age of our mother. In his hand he holds a trowel, which becomes visible each time he plunges it in a bucket.

"What's he doing?"

Working on our roof, as if it isn't plain. Repairs.

"What was the problem?"

Permeation, what else? Wasn't she just in our room? The results are there. A mottle, greenish-gray, above our beds. In the living room the evidence is older, yellow scaling. The symptoms are averted in one spot, then reappear on the next outfacing wall. Our contractor cut corners, our mother said she'd sue, the laborer became a fixture soon after we took up residence. He shows up every morning.

"Where from?"

The really curious fact is that he always comes in the same shirt. It's plausible he owns six garments of the same design, it's also possible the style is so related, that distinctions blur. Goes for a formal look, buttons and cuffs, slacks, never jeans, never a T-shirt no matter the heat. Always looks ready for a podium, before the dirt.

"He is a natty dresser," Tiffy says. "Let's have him step into our shot."

We let our heads slump to one side in consternation, east. The silly-grownup act again.

"I mean it," Tiffy says. "Why not?"

Just then our mother's voice carries up from the kitchen porch. It's time to eat, she cries, and we're glad to comply. Tiffy is slower, so her protests have a hard time catching up, though they keep coming. Once she's huffing at our side, downstairs, she gets her answers from our mother.

"He never has. He wouldn't expect or like it. His dinner is waiting at his home."

That night we stare at her round form under our sheets and listen to her adenoidal rattle. We can't sleep. How can we let ourselves, beside those eerie powers of mood infection, those strange ideas, and no gift. Still no gift! The next to youngest, and most impulsive, creeps up to the desk.

"Tomorrow," hisses our big sister. She's our conscience. She reminds us of our past: After the Frosted Flakes affair our mother made us swear to wait. How long? Until it's offered.

The suitcase is a black square in the dark. The cousin lugged the whole of it out of our room when she prepared for bed. She changed into a pair of baby-doll pajamas. Through the bathroom door, we heard each spring-latch pop and resonantly thrum in the acoustics of our blue enamel. Later we found this: the soap on the wrong side of the sink, her glasses soap-smeared in our dish, a sock hanging from the showerhead, the floor mat soaked. The toilet has been sanitized, and she's replaced our paper. The new roll doles out a double ply of staggeringly considerate fiber, fleecy, otherworldly, and— could it be?—infused with oils. Such a subservience to parts never so privately entertained. Is this the gift? Somehow it impresses only our eldest. Is this the thing our mother opposed? Could her sense of threat be this overblown?

Late in the night we hear the high emotion carrying into her daily summary, telephoned to our grandmother. "I know whose ass she's thinking of," she says. "I mean the nerve."

Our door is locked when we come home from school. It always is. We're latchkey children. But today, before we even fumble with the thick new key, the whole great apparatus shirks its job before our eyes. The bolts retract, the frame gives. The cumbrous door sighs and swings. Our surprise is something like discovering the staircase down has not yet leveled. Within this mind frame, it's a sort of comfort to find Tiffy on the inside, shouting:

"Guess who!"

The baby is wailing on the floor. The cousin sports our mother's apron, an old one we all remember well. Some stains are ancient but those red ones are brand-new.

Who let her use that?

"Mom's gonna be held up," our cousin says. "More work even than usual. And after she has errands, quite a few. She's a procrastinator, like I couldn't guess. Is she a Klein or what? I told her don't you worry, today you've got an extra pair of hands." These we eye, filing past: red-stained as well. She closes the door. "I'm making us all sloppy Joe!"

Which is what?

"You'll see. I could only find flat bread. A little more thickness would have been good. Whatever. Once the meat's in the pocket we'll have to eat quick. Listen, I could use a hand in here. I still don't have the hang of where Mom keeps all her supplies. Some of you could set the table. Some of you could run up to the roof and tell Ibrahim it'll be fifteen minutes at the most. He should just come down."

A sour smell wafts from the kitchen. Red flecks the edges of her lenses, red on the toes of her shoes, as they pivot, heading off.

"What do you mean?" our eldest asks.

Tiffy's bifocals sparkle as she turns again. "What do you mean what do I mean?"

Our eldest swallows and repeats our mother's words: "He never has."

"So? Until yesterday, me neither!"

"He wouldn't expect or like it."

"Talked to him. Seems like the first was true. The second, not so sure, there was a language barrier. What I *do* know, when I see it, is a mild but significant squint, what I would call strabismus. I offered him professional attention. Anyone could see the man was moved."

"His dinner is waiting at home."

"I guess today he dines from two cuisines! Look, why the hell not?"

"Our mother doesn't let."

"Your mother has left me in charge."

"To get us killed?"

"Holy crap." Our cousin scrutinizes us through every combination of her lenses. "You guys are genuinely upset!" She squats. She opens wide her arms. "Come here, you."

We hand our wailing youngest over, drop into a half-circle and look up. Our cousin holds the baby by the underarms. His diaper's wet. He whimpers, and she shakes him once.

"Hmm," she says. "Tiffy needs her hands to tell a story. A Klein or what?"

A story! Our eldest takes the child. He goes to sleep on her thin chest, while we three older ones forget our troubles once again in Tiffy's lively face.

"My Temple Nefesh music teacher," she says, ducking the head seriously, "as you know, Mrs. Milstein. The inspiration for the trip, not just in the past. Actively, now."

They're still in touch?

"I know, I know," she says. She makes her face absurdist now. She plumps her lower lip. "As if *her* teachers would still be alive! Old!" she yelps, then laughs and slumps. "But yes. She is alive. We are in touch. In fact she is now a dear friend, a friend who is slowly slipping away."

How awful. How terrible. Sick?

"The worst kind."

Oh no.

"Of the breasts."

Our eldest nearly drops the baby as she tries to plug our ears.

"What?" Tiffy asks. "Too harsh a topic for your age? The cancer?"

Of course not.

"Then the breasts?"

Shhh! Good G-d.

"Get outta here. I thought this was a largely permissive culture. I thought the majority is secular."

Yes to both. But not us.

"Then I guess I shouldn't tell you she's a dyke."

A what?

Tiffy explains in such a matter-of-fact way, that the idea simply strolls into our head and stays awhile, as ordinary as a sitter on a bench, whom we chase off, eventually, in a fit of giggles.

"What's so funny?" Tiffy says, in such a way that we're inspired to find our composure all at once. "Do you think it's wrong?"

Perhaps not. Truth is we simply never thought about the possibility. We knew about the boy and boy. Leviticus 18, verse 22. But girl and girl? We don't recall a mention. Maybe that's okay.

"The next part should be easier for you," she says. "Ultratraditional. Folks like you would have heard of the practice. Mrs. Milstein, Fiona, sent me here with her dying wish."

To be buried here? HaShem preserve us. She here now? In the case? That kind makes the very worst guest.

"She isn't dead yet," our cousin snaps

May He bring her full recovery.

"That is no longer an option," Tiffy says. She pushes a hand into an apron pocket, loose and shallow for easy reach, yet she fumbles. She takes a breath and works herself to equilibrium again. Finally she yanks out a small bag: "She sent me for this."

A sandwich bag, darkened, plump and prickly with crystallized instant coffee, about two hundred grams.

"No," Tiffy says. "Dirt."

But of course. A sprinkling of the holy soil of Eretz Yisrael. For the eyes in the coffin?

"That's right." She bites her lip and pushes the small parcel back in its storage place. "I got it from your building garden. Just a little. Didn't think you'd mind."

This is just dreadful. Where's our happy Tiffy? We must try to lighten things up.

So what else did she do today? Where else did she go?

"Oh, nowhere. Tour bus not leaving till tomorrow."

Not even a walk down the block? The local grocer offers a particularly fine fizzing sweet. There is the young mothers' clinic, Drop of Milk. The name itself is wonderful, and never has she seen so many infants and their mothers traveling up and down one flight of steps! There are apartment buildings older than ours in design. Different shrubs in different gardens, a deserted house.

"Believe me," Tiffy says. "Terrible sense of direction. I would find a way to get lost."

Did she at least go up to the roof?

"You know I did!" she cries. Because *we* asked.

Somehow, we brought the dreaded subject back upon ourselves. We, us.

"Oh come on!" she says. She punches a few shoulders, lightly, leaves the baby out. "Did I or did I not hear you say the man has worked up there for years?"

He stands for a continuous blight in our lives.

"But do you actually know *him*?"

Yes. He shows up every day in the same shirt. The shirt arrives here clean each morning, but, every night, it goes home stained.

"Not that again. Does he have kids?"

How should we know? And can *she* fault us? She, who did not know our demographics, names, or level of religious practice, her own blood and hosts.

Tiffy shakes her head. "Don't even know where he lives, I'll betcha. Bet you have no idea what kind of a home."

She, who won't set foot on our block. In and out of a taxi.

"He is your *neighbor*!" Tiffy says. "That's closer. You walk the same land. I'm only saying it's a shame, and to imagine what you might be missing, think of the cultural exchange. He probably plays something. I've heard that the musicianship is staggering. That artist sampled it, and I mean, yeah, a little goes a long way, but yeah! Amazing stuff, rides a completely different wave. I'm telling you. Just do it. Climb those stairs, extend that hand and flash that friendly smile. When you wish upon a star and so on. Thinking positive is half the game. Live your dream."

The woman is mad.

Her beliefs are inane, we tell her. Can we dream our walls back from their spreading problem? Can we think away the rot? And when we find ourselves wall-less, will a wish shorten the fall from a narrow apartment at the top?

"It's a moot point," she says. "I already invited him. He's coming. Try to remember we're just talking about a sandwich."

Oh.

How could we have known?

A skillet in the kitchen seethes, dispatching its aroma. Beef? Tomato sauce. In a sandwich? But that would be sloppy!

Oh.

We stand. We stare down at our mother's apron swaddling the bottom-heavy form. She is ripely shaped, maternally, you might say. We are young, our minds are flexible. We can imagine her part of the household. Tiffy leaps up to her feet, agile considering her girth. She has been spared the usual jet lag. She is full of energy.

"I am!" she says. "I can just feel the air re*storing* me. I also have this helpful little pill."

She gives us each a coated half. The smile returns.

The barriers have come down. No longer can we look at Tiffy as a guest. She is our *baby-sitter*, a whole different thing, an outsider who comes in as the boss. And entertainer! And brings prizes for good listeners, and have we not been that?

The cousin freezes. She regards us squarely through her specs, each eye divided by the seam. "That you should feel you have to ask!" She wipes her palms on the lined apron and leaves the pattern sloppied up. "My little angels. You had doubt?" Tears fill her eyes, then resolve. "Avanti!" And she leads us to our room.

One by one we plunk down on her bed, which crackles with a moisture-proof sheet Imma didn't think to take out. Tiffy approaches us, and then steps back, assesses, nears again, and shuffles us, arranges us by height, closes the gaps. She waits until we're absolutely still. She flips the shutters and submerges us in dark.

"Now close your eyes."

The first thing we all hear is the metallic clack and spring of clasps. We anticipate the whisper of cereal settling in its box, the crepitation of cellophane, perhaps the snick of Cousin's nails against the side of a glass jar. Instead we hear another, fainter clack and spring. We're stumped.

"Every head I tap opens wide," Tiffy says, and taps—each child in turn, oldest to youngest, one by one, and each one pops. The baby needs assistance, because of his age and as he is sleeping. One of us pushes up a lid, one steadies the head, taking care not to compress the pliant fontanel. The cousin bows over, pointing her narrow red ray. Slowly, the baby's irises uncloak of their own will.

We have already seen what he is seeing, and we see it still. The imagery endures past the removal of the tool:

The eyes are flooded with an edgeless flood of black, which seems to heave, although the heaving isn't seen. How one perceives the heaving one cannot define, and this throws off one's senses from a cliff. Not in a frightening way. The cliffs rise from the stars, it seems, as gravity pulls only faintly. Though the general direction of the fall is down, one floats, and presently the floating pupil fixes on a landscape hitherto unseen, but present all around, a glowing veiny network, like the intricate venation of a leaf, except not green but red, not flat but very deep, the circuitry like never-ending branches of a fragile blood-red tree.

We are suspended in a world of frailty, effulgent, tantalizing, begging to be touched. We keep floating down. While we are at it, we can swim, beneath and over luminescent intersections, our only burden to avoid collision, not to interfere, to leave the glowing system unimpaired. The craft is painstaking, but in this slowness, we can learn. We exercise—we *become*—delicacy, heedfulness, astuteness, fine, fine care.

Until we hear our cousin's happy sigh. The darkness suddenly is ordinary, the daylight sifting, dim, through the thick plastic shutters.

"Wasn't that neat?" Tiffy asks.

The middlemost skips to the window, forces it ajar. Upon our particleboard desk the suitcase lies agape, blooming with clothes. On these a smaller case perches, open as well, the inside lined with velvet cavities, harboring metal tools. One of the cavities is empty. The cousin holds her implement. The handle is black, the head a one-eyed, silver cone, which still emits its concentrated ray, until she clicks it off.

"So?" she says. "Wasn't that mind-blowing?"

We're sure our mind remains largely the same. We've tasted no new flavor, smelled no new smell, masticated no new texture. That was it? Nothing else?

"Sure there's something else!" Tiffy says. "Did I or did I not give you the pitch already yesterday? I saw you sitting there. I saw you listening, or so I thought."

Again she reaches in our mother's apron, this time producing a catalog. Our eldest receives it. The publication is thin, notebook-sized, but densely paged, the pages slick but also powdery, sharp-scented, freshly inked. The language we can't read. The photographs, in rows and rows, page after page, show eyeglasses, framed or not, in metal or plastic. Glass glints over the infinite eyes of numberless stiff-headed models.

"Little girls often like page six," Tiffy says. "The pearly hues. The pink looks amazing on a redhead."

Our eldest casts the catalog aside. She rises as it hits the floor. Gently, she lays the baby on the bed, and smoothes the khaki skirt over her adolescent hips. She steps up to our cousin till her forehead nearly brushes the plump chin, then spins around to face our way. A stain darkens the area where the baby sat.

"She think she's going to make us four-eyed," our big sister says. "Like her."

We know a call to action when we hear one. That's the present? We arise as one.

We swarm the guest, immobilize her, search her suitcase: skirts and skorts and peasant blouses, baby dolls, bras, panties, fifty rolls of toilet paper. Nothing! What is left to do, except tear our mother's apron off this fraud? The cotton sashes remain tied in a bow while the stitches break on one end.

Our next-to-youngest reaches in the pocket, and removes the parcel of dirt. Then the little monkey jumps up on the windowsill. Perfectly safe; our mother has furnished the window with convex bars. Hanging out, he rips the parcel and shakes it out. He watches as our soil rains down brown and disappears below our myrtles, back in place.

Tiffy never resists. She waits until we loosen our grip and, sneering at her, back away. Our eldest hurries to the baby, whose wild motions have impelled him near the edge. He has been howling with delight at the melee.

Tiffy exacts no vengeance. She does not explode in a burst of temper. She never says a word, after these four: "Seven to ten days." She only leaves.

She tramps, heavy-footed, to her nesting cases, closes the small one and the large over that. Head hanging, she hoists the suitcase off the desk, lowers it, and stands it on its wheels.

A shudder passes through the tiles as she leads the case away. We hear the heavy key turn with the smoothness of ball bearings. Our Pladelet slowly swishes open, yet more slowly swishes closed, and is received.

We gallop through the flat to end the sequence. Our eldest turns the key.

Our kitchen is filled with smoke. We switch the gas off. Baby on slim hip, our eldest slips her free hand in the oven mitt. Our mission she describes as twofold. We must drive the fumes out of our house and change the dinner plans, both before our mother's return.

Taking the skillet to the roof does it all. Ibrahim can see. Whatever ocular deficiency our cousin found in him is indiscernible by us, if one exists. His eyes are very like ours. He watches the smoke rising in between us with a beetled brow, much like our mother would, flickering his lashes much in the same way, over eyes similarly lit, sleek as two oil-soaked black olives.

Our mother was once beautiful, and so was he. Although he is stooped and thickened and begins to wrinkle, his hair retains the pigment of his youth, a Nordic blond, some new or ancient history of influx dyed into his locks. The black smoke billows in the wind, tilting aside, unveiling the pillar of the quarry dust, far-off, white, stolid. Black waves in, and again rises.

We have talked to him before, but only as messengers from Imma. These are our first words to him which we ourselves compose:

We would like to go air out the house. Would he mind the skillet?

"I could douse it if you like," he says.

He could do what? We don't know the word.

"Such clever children?" he says. "Your own language?"

They probably teach it in the seventh grade, our eldest says, setting the skillet on the tar.

"Tar burns," Ibrahim says. He reaches through the smoke, his plaster-whitened fingers graying, ungloves our sister of our mother's mitt, and slips it on his own hand. He bends and takes the skillet by the handle.

The column of smoke scatters and regroups as Ibrahim straightens again, then slowly travels west, towards a water tap that curves out of a segment of our building's silver pipes, though every shine in twilight appears copper. As in the same time, yesterday, the solar panels duplicate the sunset. Copper spokes our bikes. A copper droplet quivers from the tap's ridged copper nose. We rise and follow as the column from the skillet, unreflective black, inclines east as though resisting, as Ibrahim walks on.

Though the roof is not so sprawling, the journey is long. The sun sinks lower in the sky. On any other day we would be gaining in abandon as we lost the light. Perhaps the mention of the middle-school grade has made us tired, all the hard work still ahead. The eyelids wish to close as if the worker is our teacher.

Is this not one too many radical shifts for children so young as we, in so short a time? We should turn and leave. See the stains on his shirt, see that rigidity in the attire.

But again we hear our mother's words. He might not expect or like it.

He is our partner in mid-conversation. We would not like to leave him wounded. The door connecting our home to where he works is nothing special. He is as locked in here as we by our Pladelet.

So what to say? And where to go from here?

Our next to youngest comes up with a subject. "Do you play an instrument?"

"Why yes," Ibrahim says.

His gloveless hand appears behind him and undoes the button in his slacks' back pocket. He comes up with a pen, and tosses this over his shoulder. In the shadow of the trailing smoke the pen sails in an arc. It is a common pen, a ballpoint cartridge cased in bright blue plastic, which we catch. We hand it to the baby. He puts the barrel in his mouth. Ibrahim throws another, and another. Some we seize out of the air, some we collect from the soft tar. He throws one still enclosed within a pouch of cellophane. His fingers seem to feel this too late.

"No!" he calls out as the thing bumbles towards us. "That one don't take," he says. "I shouldn't have thrown it. The ink has never moistened the tip. A virgin pen knows only to gash the page."

The Roberto Touch

✤

INWARD THE STONE was pale and scrolled with grooves, like soft Galilee cheese, grated and gouged. The tunnel turned, the outside light began to flinch. Another turn, darker. A lengthy explanation for this subterranean network had been given by the guide, but Shulee wasn't academically inclined, although the details of a lesson were welcome to grab her attention if they could. From the guide's launching speech these words had made it in: *Ancient Rome, Bar Kokhva, Akiva,* and *escapeway.* They rattled in her mind as she crawled through the tunnel on all fours. The atmosphere in here was close, thick with a scent as off-putting as it was fascinating. What was it? Many things at once. Gravel, ground up with some living exudation—sweat, and something faintly dungy, footnoted with ammonia.

How would it be to use the escapeway for its intended design? How could you stand it? Bar Kokhva had managed. *This* very rock floor would have pressed *these* jagged dimples into *his* knees and palms. This selfsame darkness would have slowly commanded his eyes, this moisture weighted his garments. But this terror in the heart would have stood for a threat far worse than claustrophobia, the Ancient Roman methods of authority. They who raked the flesh off poor Rabbi Akiva's prayerful old bones, the tissue off the sage

114

who was remembered for having said: And you shall love your fellow as yourself. In this very stink the rebel would remember the seer's dying cry: Hear, Israel, Adonai our God, Adonai is one! And the sorrow in this call would mingle with the tragedy of this fetor constituting his last air. But perhaps a rebel leader wouldn't have odors on the brain. He would have more reason to be desperate, more cause to quash his fear. He would be armed.

"Mmm, how Roberto loves you!"

A hand cupped her buttock while the girlish voice moaned; on the last syllable the hand squeezed and let go. This time the touch had truly caught her unawares.

"Koos amak!" she said, with the hiss and snarl fitting the slur. The potency steadied her even as the Dress Patterns teacher whined faintly in protest, far in the dark ahead. The provocateur behind added a rude fingering. The narrow tunnel didn't allow turning around to crack her a good one on the chin, so once again Shulee passed the squeeze on to a buttock of the pair ahead and, once again, there the practice died. Every time it ended with Yona Rodelheim's tight ass. No fighting spirit, no healthy spite, no sense of duty to the joke, only a choked, bleated lament.

"Enough."

The eleventh-grade girls of Keeshor Vocational Religious had started off stooped and gradually come to this crawl. The Roberto touch had been set into motion soon after the guide had led them into the hole, advising the students to imagine the Romans at their backs. The practice would have been the brainchild of a girl from Clerical, who was known even outside her division for her love of AS Roma's top goal scorer. At first the touch was passed on with enthusiasm, cascading forward in bouts of giggles and snorts. As the light lessened and the walls contracted, the sounds of provocation were becoming isolated, the responses progressively tense, the Dress Patterns teacher's voice in their aftermath increasingly spiritless in her declaration: "This simply will not repeat itself!"

One wished the time required to cross the mountain through its heart would have been defined in advance of the crawl. But what difference? When anyway you weren't able to read your watch. The one Shulee had taken on the trip was of the cheaper models from Uncle Chelomo's case, a band like stretched pink bubble gum, and hands that gave only a feeble phosphorescence, short-lived, gone by now. Had she covered far less distance than she thought, with far more ahead than she would allow herself to conceive of? No, the exit lay just beyond the next turn. This was quite possible. But if the tunnel would soon be over then the teachers would again stand. Why in the world then had she cut loose with words of such power as to guarantee a girl's suspension from school? The curse was simply the strongest that came to mind in a moment calling for strength. Not only Arabic but invoking the private parts of an opponent's mother. Would such a milksop as that Dress Patterns teacher even know the meaning? Maybe not, but she would know the type.

The ceiling grazed the crown of Shulee's head. She ducked her head and continued. Would she take the tunnel over a teacher? A teacher over the tunnel? Her ear was grazed. She groped, found the turn, and followed it. The ceiling dipped lower. She tried to manage the new conditions by crawling much as she had done until now, only the torso lowered in the manner of a lizard. In the first try she understood this way of life required a sustained, sinking push-up. Her arms collapsed. She dropped to her belly and lugged her body by her forearms like no animal she could think of except for a paratrooper. The surfaces continued to close in, dank on every side. She trained her thoughts away from the smell.

Bar Kokhva. Release the language from the old-fangled mold and it made all the sense of words now: Ben Kokhav, Son of Star. Hadn't she sung the great name countless times? In rousing minor key on the annual festival of the Lag BaOmer bonfire, before the orange shape licking a black spring's night, every year of her life until, when? Until never and at no time. Who ever sang the hero songs at the fire? The bonfire and the singing children circling in a hora maybe went together in picture books. In life, any songs that night came out of the radio your uncle planted on a rock. The melodies were much more interesting to the hips. If you danced, it was never in a circle, but alone in a merry shuffle, or in a pair.

Bar Kokhva in that case stood for a good time, his yearly bonfire an occasion for all ages in the city to stay outdoors after dark and do their favorite things in the sight of high fires. Greet, talk, eat, play, sip a soda and court, connect and go off on a search, the air moon-cooled and aromatic with the smoke of kindling and grilling meats. Radio sounds and conversations roaming from the neighbors' fires, and those in nearby lots. Before you reached the age of courting your high point was the effigy. On the eve of the holiday, you would draw the final touches on the dummy's face in marker, and at the fire's peak toss into the flames whoever you had sculpted in his full bad looks, Nasser, in her childhood days, with limp arms of cloth, or the evergreen perennials you still saw now: Eichmann, Arafat, Hitler, Hafiz al-Assad, the ink features quickly eaten and the rag stuffing next.

So there was the message, and plenty good it was. The Nation of Israel lives, destroys its enemies, and loves a party. Did anyone think to sing of Bar Kokhva while they were at it? Not in her neighborhood. Then why the hero song thrumming in the mind? Because in school you learned it in the early grades, and she had always liked music. She still remembered the lyrics word for word.

> *"Oh, come," the tall man thundered. "He who'd sooner sever*
> *his own finger*
> *Than suffer idols in God's Place."*
>
> *Hailed by Akiva, followed by the brave,*
> *Bar Kokhva, freedom's arrowhead!*

"A star!" gentle Akiva cried. "Shot forth of our father Yaakov
And alighted in our midst, a man of our times, our guide
    hereafter."

Hailed by Akiva, followed by the brave,
Soaring eternal, freedom's arrowhead!

"Fie!" quoth the cynic. "Grass will shoot up from your cheeks,
    Rabbi Akiva,
Ere the star of true redemption shine!"

But green the palm fronds flourished in the arms of rebel
    Israel,
And though Edom reddened our valleys yet the arc of valor
    flares today.

Hailed by the man of peace, joined by the brave,
Ablaze eternal, freedom's arrowhead!

Too bad that period was discontinued with her enrollment at
Keeshor, although the kind of music she liked now they wouldn't
teach.

The passageway narrowed again. The floor became more pitted
and the pits more full of moisture. All talk had ended, replaced by
perfect lightlessness and quavering breaths. She shoved her belted
canteen from hip to rump and pushed through. Another turn in the
tunnel was approaching. She knew this before any part of her was
chafed. She reached through the dark and there it was. She slipped
around the protrusion. Some extra guiding sense was kicking in.
Anything could become known. On her next move forward she
began to plummet, no, sink, hand first, into cold water. She was
becoming submerged, or just her forearm. Her palm hit rock, slid-

ing on slime. In a heartbeat she pulled herself out, shaking drops off her fingers.

"I could have broken my jaw, you ugly," she said to the classmate ahead, that Yona again, a vexing presence even unseen and silent. "You couldn't warn me?"

She heard the toes of Yona's sneakers, scraping onward in the dark, farther up than she had expected. She dragged herself forward with fresh haste, ignoring the sharpened impact of the stone's grain, glad for the little scare having awakened her. She advanced rapidly, yet sensed no gain, until ridged heels of rubber suddenly grazed her chin. There, she had caught up, but now would have to slow down. Why should she? The crawl had flown by in the catch-up moments. Her palms no longer felt battered, merely informative, succinct in their rapid reports. A rebel leader's thoughts move fast. He must execute many decisions in no time. He must never allow an obstruction.

In the full dark Shulee lifted a hand and reached out. She found what seemed like the back of a knee, both tender and taut, and over this she closed her fingers, flutteringly, then hard.

"Mmmm," she said, with high emotion. "Who but Roberto could love you so much?"

Yona stopped and would not move on.

Knuckles crashed into the swelling of Shulee's calf. A chin lodged in her backside. She felt another, muffled impact as the girl behind was also collided into. Shulee pushed against the shoes ahead. She couldn't see them, but she knew them, orange Pumas. They wouldn't budge.

Then Yona Rodelheim whispered something.

"Move," Shulee said.

"I can't," Yona said.

Voices began to tumble forward, each query occluded by the next.

The sharp weight lifted itself from Shulee's calf. "Come on," the girl behind her said, as if the trouble were her fault. The impression was corrected at once by Yona, whimpering again.

"I can't. I can't anymore." She called out for her mother and then simply stayed where she was.

Within seconds the tunnel was clogged with despair. Shulee screamed. The sour air left the lungs hungry. She tried to punch Yona's legs, but was not able to establish good momentum. Her own ankles were grasped. She kicked. The hands receded. Yona's crying became higher and thinner until it was no longer like a voice, more like an instrument of warning, a police whistle. The pressure built in Shulee's throat again but now, like Yona, she remained silent, the suppressed cry turned back on itself, flooding the thoughts with an appalling insight, black as the dark.

They would never see the bus. This was no passage but a fall into Gehenna. They had been swallowed, eaten, the pick of the plate. And for what crime? For wanting nothing but to stand again. This was all she wanted.

"I want to stand," she cried out. She had never said anything truer. She wanted to say it again. "I want to stand."

Many behind concurred. Many wanted this with her. They joined the shout. She shouted with many, while others began to greet their Maker: *Hear, Israel. Adonai, our God, Adonai is One. Blessed is the name of His honored kingdom, forever.* Apparently even the girls ahead of Yona were paralyzed by what carried towards them. They joined both shouts, and the ordeal dragged out.

Later it would be revealed that the Dress Patterns teacher had had to coax the foremost crawlers, each by each, out to the target chamber, that when the way to Yona finally had been cleared, she could not be talked out of her surrender. The hired escort, an old but sinewy Civil Guard man, reentered and bodily dragged her out.

In reconstructing the event, some wondered how he could build up the proper leverage, confined. The elbows couldn't bend enough. Yona's pants knees were eroded, but so were everyone's. Perhaps he'd simply been persuasive. It was proposed that he had trained his weapon at her forehead. An exchange indicating so had been picked up through the cacophony by several sources, unallied. Yona Rodelheim couldn't be made to weigh in.

Once she had been dislodged, each newly mollified girl passed the message of delivery to a recipient behind. Gradually the tunnel was unclogged.

A chalky palm beckoned to Shulee. She crawled towards it, reached, was hoisted out and to her feet, and pushed aside as a new head emerged.

She stood in a stone cell. A ventilation notch let in a dim sandcolored light. All of the faces here acquired stony tints. The girls confederated into little bands, some still crying, some passing furious opinions nose to nose, some cramming close like mute litters of cubs. Yona was sitting by a wall, not one but two teachers standing over her, demonstratively calm.

Alone, Shulee kicked out a foot, then stomped. Her breathing slowed but wouldn't ease. She scraped the other foot forward and stomped again, and the same again, shoes punishing the grit, grit punishing the shoes. Lucky her, lucky all of them, to have been delivered to the inside, with one of them a proven cork. Predisposed to becoming stuck. Little had they known, as they had filed one by one into the tunnel, a saffron-yellow efflorescence striping the velvety green meadow around, which in the heat of noon had seemed to swell and fall like the rib cage of a sleeping cat, curled around them.

Would it be the same on the other side? Of course not. Rather, even lovelier after this punishment. And more achingly tantalizing, more profoundly out of reach right now, as she stood trapped in a miserable notion of responsibility for the whole disastrous episode.

Why was she responsible? Because she had awaited her turn at the tunnel's entrance beside Yona Rodelheim, and entered behind her. She shouldn't have chosen a place so near a girl who played on her nerves. Why had she chosen that place? It was only natural. They were meal partners for the length of the trip. They had pooled their money. They had shopped together for provisions to last the whole three days. Well, *why* had she partnered with a classmate she disliked? Because she had had no choice, that was why! If her most recent hordeolum infection hadn't kept her home from school for a week with her eyes under warm compresses and her lonely ears bathing in radio hits, she would have been present in class the day the alliances were forged.

Why hadn't anyone signed her up with their name? That was the real question. Did her own classmates really expect her to believe they had thought Yona and she were friends, so had said nothing when the teacher made the match in Shulee's absence? Shulee Bouzaglo a friend of Yona Rodelheim? The mute? Practically, tongue-tied to the point of strangulation. Oddball! An oddball! Sure, Shulee herself was regarded as a bit of an independent. A maverick! A life force. She was a godsend when the lesson dragged especially low. How they all laughed! Whereas, Yona Rodelheim? A scarecrow, if humans were crows.

How could her own division, the Graphics girls, have done this to her, one of their own? Maybe not the strongest in execution, but she had great ideas. Low on patience, high on creativity. Shulee Bouzaglo! Or, as they would hear it in roll call each morning, surname first: Bouzaglo Shulee. Their only one. Had they forgotten all their affection for her as her sick week had stretched on? Was it her fault she suffered from a chronic condition? Could she have been expected to leave the house with the eyelids still so inflamed even past the infectious phase? Several young men in her neighborhood, and many more older, considered her deeply attractive. You respected your admirers at least so much as to not willfully tarnish what it was they saw. Because of this she suffered now. Because of this, for the length of the trip, she would continue to be associated with the disgrace.

But she was letting herself off too easily. Not just for the trip's length would the stigma cleave but for all time, for all school time, she the friend of Yona, in a league with a weak mind, suggestible to fear. Yona had earned them both the grade. For an Annual Trip posed tests unlike those back in school. A blister on the foot translated every step into pain. The sun wouldn't relent. A gully at the end of the long rope approached too slowly while the curious wish to spread the hands came right away. Sloshing through standing water lively with mosquito babies your imagination reduced to a transparent, writhing worm. Or a stench got to you. The torment might rise higher than the resolve, the horror stick like a nasty case of hiccups. If you stopped you would not continue. Later the failure of a girl to see herself making it through would be her lasting disgrace. The Trip would become known for this one test, and she for having flunked it. This was the big risk, and how much more so if your position among the girls wasn't pivotal in the first place. An individualist was too easily recast a pariah. The only way to try and work around the terms was to remain on the bus, but who did this? Never anyone of stature or the hope of it.

And who wanted to stay on the bus? The annual trip was the one school activity she looked forward to. Here, finally, your labors were rewarded richly, with novel sights and the distances crossed, and scents like strange jars being continually opened. Dropped figs fermenting in the sun, goat-crushed hyssop. So maybe also carrion, in full sight and shocking detail, but you saw purpose as clearly. Baked paths beneath a scalding sun eventually took you to shade, a loosely anchored plank spared you the fall into fast water, a hill slope lobbing rocks under the feet presently led you to the rare view. All of them saved you from hours pinned under a desk. How she despised a desk. Because she despised a desk she had drawn out her stay at home. She had brought the whole calamity on herself.

In the powdery chamber she spotted a crumb of grit almost so large as to pass for a pebble. She kicked it, or rather tried, but her forearm was grabbed so that the endeavor had to be abandoned—forcefully grabbed by the strong fingers of the Civil Guard man. He sucked noisily on his tongue looking down at her. His neck was very short or perhaps settled deeply with the weight of his thick-skinned head. He said that she should gape a little less at him and mind the floor. She looked to where he pointed. The chamber floor was scooped out neatly, like a massive gameboard, with row beside row of craters.

"Each one of those depressions at one time contained a jar of precious fluid," he said. "The heart of a way of life. I ask that all of us here keep in mind that this is not a sandbox but a national treasure."

She hardly craved a lesson but she liked the personal touch. She checked around to see how his attention to her was being taken by the others. The girls nearby all feigned indifference and on the other hand she was indifferent to their pretense. Everyone was antsy but with his brassy voice he had singled out only one, and who? And why? Because of her looks? Her pluck? Her mystery? All three. A man, a man, the one man accompanying them, hers for the length of the trip, with all the others looking on.

When he unhanded her she stuck beside him. The girls all looked at him. From his armed side she looked at them.

"This way," he said, and she did not follow but rather walked along.

He was old but just like a young soldier smelled of cigarettes and gun oil, though also something more interior, similar to the cave. She wasn't afraid of the cave. She was afraid of nothing. The Trip's defeat had already taken place and it had not taken place in her, thank God. It had chosen Yona.

He led them to an adjoining room and asked that they observe the cisterns. Shulee observed the others as they complied. He said to notice the stone wells, notice the crushing wheels. She noticed the top cartilage of his ear, smeared with the gray secretion of the cave. She could imagine following him around in here for days, leading the others. She pictured how her face would be affected by the transformation in her state of mind: smoothed, hardened, no time for expression. He would teach her to convert her fear into intelligence. That was bravery, one acceleration of the senses made into another, the judgment rising to every split-second occasion. She would take up smoking. Smoking helped the nerves, didn't her mother always say.

"Insidious," he said. "To put it plainly, insupportable taxation would devitalize—"

A girl from Textiles handed a classmate her canteen and watched her drink. After a spell, she reached a hand out, seized the canteen. With the other hand, gently, she pushed her friend's forehead up, separating her mouth from the mouth of the vessel. She screwed the cap back on.

"So industry goes underground," the guard said. "Now, step this way."

In the next chamber he tapped another chipped and pitted cistern. A girl sank to one knee, untied a shoe and retied it.

"Of course oil for the Holy Temple," he said, "but also ointments, cosmetics and shampoo, soap."

Shulee heard a whispered demand for spearmint gum, followed by thanks.

"Flax seed," the guard said. "But without question, and having everything to do with the most popular fodder recipe of the time—"

Someone was snuffling drily, in an increasingly obsessive way, the nose more and more self-interested. A girl from Textiles was scratching a friend's back. She stopped and picked a chip of stone off the grayed shirt, then went back to scratching, up and down, gradually moving sideways. The man had lost the crowd. He should be relying more on his personality and less on the knowledge. The lecture was too long. He took a breath and moved on. He paused beside a dark, lopsided cleft in the chalky wall.

"All because of an obscure feud of the Second Temple era," he said. The shoelace-tier bent to deal with the other shoe.

"Doesn't that hole in the wall look a lot like an ear?" Shulee said.

The guide swung his heavy head as if annoyed by a gnat. The girls murmured. The scratcher had stopped scratching. The snuffling had ceased. The shoelacer's fingers were frozen mid-task.

"At the heart of which," the guide went on, raising his voice. "Stood one stray ram of a prized lineage. Now naturally our interest turns to lanolin."

"For the history of hand cream we had to crawl through the sewer?" Shulee said.

He took a slowly swiveling step to face her. Those from Shulee's division looked at each other. Perhaps now they would remember her as they should. This was her excellence. Once in a while she rose up like no one else.

She slurped her upper lip into the lower, then released it. "I'm sorry," she said. "It came out."

"Came out," he said. "Maybe you still need diapers."

"You should watch out what makes you curious," she said. "I'm a minor," whereupon a woman's voice cried out from an adjoining chamber, reedy, echoing, sepulchral:

"That is really quite enough!"

Even the armed guard's cheeks seemed to blanch, before he recognized the whine of the Dress Patterns teacher.

"Join her," he said.

Shulee opened her mouth to continue the conversation, but thought better of it. She swung a hip around and skipped over the nearest threshold.

The space in which she found herself was exactly like the one she had just left: gray concavities in the floor, black holes in the walls, a few incomplete cisterns. Beside one of them sat Yona Rodelheim, her legs crossed oriental-style, the toes of her Pumas orange as dusty persimmons, her eyes closed. The Dress Patterns teacher sat a little higher, on a stone shelf that protruded from the wall. She glanced at Shulee and pointed at the floor next to Yona. Shulee found a place across the room.

In the next chamber, a shuffle and mutter reorganized into the continued lecture. A dark face poked through the portal, regarding her briefly in the punishment room, then retreating.

Several times Shulee thought to advance a point of view or hum a song, but in every such instance she recalled the teacher in the room and refrained.

Had the woman recognized her voice as the one uttering the foul language in the tunnel? If so, she didn't let on. Perhaps there was no recognition. Shulee was not a Textiles teacher's charge. Would the teacher remember a voice without the context of a student? Maybe not, hence the hopelessness in her own voice at the time, knowing she would never confront whomever she had put on notice.

But everything about this woman came across hopeless, a wan member of the Reverent sector. You wanted to tuck this kind of person back into one of their crowded neighborhoods. The mere sight of them, so much more fabric than skin, made you drip sweat. Knowing the crippling frequency of the Holy Law's interference in their day made you recoil in fear. It was better to know less. The less you knew, the less bound you. For the Trip the woman had put together a particularly cumbersome outfit. The Trip was the only occasion on which the school relaxed the traditional ban on trousers worn by their female students and staff, in school or out, and indeed today, in concession to the inevitable thistles and biting things, the teacher was wearing unfashionable track pants. Over these she wore a long denim skirt to keep secret the fact that her legs split at a higher point than the ankles. To this woman every girl in the school would look like a whore even in a skirt, whereas to Shulee the thought of a body so thoroughly concealed all its life nearly brought tears. She herself braved expulsion from the school on a daily basis, squirming on the hindmost seat of her bus every afternoon, as she pulled tight jeans on under the skirt, then peeled off the skirt and unbuttoned the uniform blouse to reveal a tank top, a halter top, a bustier, to feel the sun, feel the breeze, to signal to the modern nation that she was a part and feel the eyes of her men pleased.

She drew a heart in the grit of the floor. She sifted out the larger particles and formed a small mound. She looked over the shapes cut in the walls. She observed the dust-dulled strands of her meal partner's hair. The hair was dull to begin with, an ugly blond, like terrier fur.

If only the lecture were audible here, no matter how stultifying. When she applied herself to listening, she found she could, with some effort, discern the words through the wall.

"The perdurability of human hair!" he said, as if he had been following her eye around the punishment room. "Provisionally, of course. Conditions allowing, climate permitting, stability, exceptional dryness. Naturally our thoughts turn to Masada."

Masada? They were nowhere near Masada. Masada was last year. She put her finger to the floor again, then raised it to her mouth, discreetly, tasted not much of anything, or rather much of nothing, coatingly, chalk. At Masada the lecture had been as needlessly abstruse, as unending, but at least it had contained the grain of a better story. The men killed the women and the young, the men killed themselves. The Roman slavers found dead bodies. For the generations after there remained a girl's braid, in a glass display case, caked with a gray paste of desert dust. She saw it herself. Very dry hair. Time tore the braid from the head and time conserved it. That most definitely had been a better Trip. On Masada there had been other groups. She remembered seeking shelter with a Japanese tour. Their guide she hadn't understood at all, but the propulsive intonation tilted her, and tilted her, till she was angled in among them, equally, and they had made room, respectful. Of her kinship to the braid. They had seen it: where her curls ended, hair unlike theirs. They could imagine her two thousand years needing shampoo.

She knew of their regard for suicide. She had followed every episode of *Shogun* on TV. In class of course they'd all been mad for Richard Chamberlain but Shulee liked the samurai. Squat though he was, but what ferocity compressed! And how she had triumphed in bending the eye to see the facial strangenesses as ornament. No one in class had believed that she could. On a woman, all right, they'd said, on the women it was like makeup, like adornment, for example take Chamberlain's love interest, a doll, a stunner, but the men? The men were not like men, too strange, fierce as beasts and fussy as girls with their silks and hairdos. Impossible that her feelings for the samurai were real. They said she was just trying to stand out. Untrue. His single-minded hatred for the leading man had won her heart. Then the hara-kiri episode had come and after that nobody scoffed, she was given space. The act had shaken foe and friend alike. What would the show be without the samurai? At break she had chalked an elegy to him upon the blackboard, just his name, over and over, Omi Omi Omi, with the proper honor suffixes: *san* and *of blessed memory.*

But that was last year, a somewhat childish episode—sincere, but after all a character on television. This year she was committed to Marcus Bentov, the drummer from the rock group Neft, the bald one, a real personality. Everyone went for the pretty singer boy, but there was always so much more life behind the frontman.

When at last the time had come to leave the manufactory, Yona Rodelheim was roused and made to crawl out first, practically, the Dress Patterns teacher before her, the armed escort behind. All the way out, a murmured comforting, or goading, could be heard ahead.

A grate was slammed, the emptied crawlway swallowing the echo. From her seat Shulee could hear the Dress Patterns teacher urging a more efficient drift towards the vehicles. Through the broad windshield just ahead she saw green all around, swept by silvered ripples in the breeze. The driver peered at her through the rearview mirror, spitting a lump of gum into a coffee can electric-taped onto his dashboard. She saw the guide adjusting the strap of his gun and climbing onto the Clerical bus.

Finally every girl had boarded the two buses. The drivers started the engines, but did not yet pull out. Two teachers stood facing Shulee, who was sitting on their assigned front seat.

"Bouzaglo, Shulee." This was the Art History teacher, her head turned so her left eye honed more sharply on her student.

"Present!"

The teacher closed her eyes, then opened them. The Dress Patterns teacher stood beside her, gazing off along the center aisle.

"What is wrong with your assigned place?" the Art History teacher said. "I see your partner is doing a fine job of saving it."

"I want to sit with you," Shulee said.

The teacher anchored her fists at her waist. Under the caked dirt, her jeans, a good fit and in vogue, confirmed the rumor sparked in school by something in this woman's bearing, in the composition of her clothes, in her unsaddened spinsterhood at very possibly already twenty-five, that outside teaching hours she wasn't observant. These jeans were well worn and an investment. They had a life outside of school, as did this woman, admirably lean, with flat, wide hip bones propped on widely spaced thighs. To school she always wore silver filaments in her earlobes and sleeveless dresses of Indian cotton with sleeved shirts underneath to comply with the code. Now her mouth was curving in a sealed, downturned smile, succumbing.

Shulee smiled back. Normally their relationship was troubled, the teacher too often distracted from the substance of Shulee's in-class observations, too hung up on their loudness and sweep. But on the Trip there was a hope. Here academics were irrelevant except for having forged a preexisting, intradepartmental fealty, familial warmth. Shulee knew this woman and the woman knew her. This teacher would have heard her swearing in the tunnel, would have recognized the voice, and didn't care.

"The jeans on you are something, Teacher," she said. "Where did you get them? You're a bomb. You look good normally but these show off your figure like we can't see as a matter of routine. That I should look so good when I'm your age, Amen."

The Dress Patterns teacher took a deep breath, and blew it slowly out, mastering her envy. She would have to. Her colleague was everything she was not, lovely and dark, with black hair cropped close to a delicate skull, a Yemeni with deep brown skin, today splotched with gray. Clean her up, and she belonged on the chair of a sidewalk café in an artist's neighborhood in Tel Aviv, where she would sit engrossed in conversation, uninterested in people-watching, since she was the people to watch.

"All of our clothes on all of us right now are something," she said. "We're all coated with deposits."

Shulee enjoyed the sound of this. The teacher's throaty accent beautified a burnished university Hebrew. "Are they from Dizengoff Center?" Shulee said. "Billy Jean Modelle, right?"

"We're all tired," the teacher said. "Not one of us had an easy time in there. I'm sure we'd all appreciate a measure of release right now but, Shulee, you must try to find yours via channels more constructive than this incessant unruliness."

"Authentic," Shulee said. "Not the knockoff. I can tell the knockoffs."

She locked her eyes on those of her teacher's. Now the teacher knew. Shulee, also, was a contemporary woman in her private life, regularly shopping for pants, knowing the popular labels.

The teacher sought the pale face beside her, then attended back to her student. She squatted down. Her thighs even squashed in this position remained thin and Shulee admired this like everything else. A near bus honked. She found the teacher's eyes peering at her level.

"I'll go sit with your friend," the woman said. She rose and left Shulee's field of vision.

The bus gathered its strength, strained, growled and pulled away as the Dress Patterns teacher sank into the window seat. Shulee sat stiffly, looking forward. The teacher twisted in her place, probably reaching in a pocket, then put something in her mouth, probably a pill. She gulped water from a canteen, and swallowed.

The cord of a microphone whipped back and forth below the dashboard, Shulee following its movements. She had gotten what she wanted, a seat away from Yona. Why was she still unhappy? Your friend, the teacher had said. Two wounds dealt as one. Shulee was not Yona's friend! Yet her favorite person on this Trip thought so, and had seen in her the betrayer of a friend. Once again Shulee was stuck in the Reverent woman's grim company, and once again she had brought the punishment on herself. The sins were only building up with every hour. She meant so well.

By now she was nearly positive this teacher did not recognize her voice. As a final test, she cleared her throat with resonance. The woman did not snap her head, accusatory. She didn't recognize the voice. God above had chosen to deal with Shulee in addressing that especially bad case of swearing. If she had only sat with Yona, as a friend, she would have been entirely redeemed by now.

The microphone cord swayed back and forth with the leanings of the bus. The wire-covered head sparkled. Very soon the girls would be bidding again for turns to sing. She turned towards the window seat. The Dress Patterns teacher returned the scrutiny, then attended to the task she had been busy with, arranging a bundled shirt against the shuddering pane. She leaned her cheek against the shirt and closed her eyes. She emptied her lungs with a sigh. Her white neck was glossy with sweat, her hair visible only at the nape, where it protruded in a tangle of dark wisps from under a traditional wife's kerchief. Soon her shoulders mellowed, slumping like butter in the sun. She reverted to a curious breathing pattern. The lips locked just prior to each exhalation, so each breath emerged with a soft pop.

Slowly, Shulee rose. She questioned the driver's eyes with hers. He shrugged. She extracted his microphone from its clamp.

She spun slowly to keep her balance, and blew into the mike. The Dress Patterns teacher stirred but didn't awaken. The steel mesh of the mike was cool and rough against the lips, and smelled like batteries dipped in mint. The instrument was narrow but weighty. She pursed her lips and sang:

"She loves the pain in him the pain of him she left me for his pain, ooh wahh! If she could see mine now."

Two Textile girls in the neighboring front seat watched, scowling, incredulous. Of course they wouldn't know this song. This was like nothing witnessed on the bus so far. Not a ululating love song from a market stall cassette, not the latest winner from the Eurovision fest. Not sung-poems of high purpose, love of land and sacrificed youth. No, this was the nation's first homegrown hard rock, a new sound for the nineteen eighties. And on the drums! Her beloved. Her baldie Marcus Bentov at the drums!

He didn't sing, she had to simulate him as the verse repeated. She turned her gaze skyward, enraptured by a mounting strain. She saw the roof hatch cracked, showing a crescent of blue, but screwed her eyes shut at the view as Marcus always did, sticking the tongue out as far as it would go. She turned her face towards her fanship, nostrils flexing, but did not engage their eye. Hers opened only to the drums.

They were everywhere. They were diverse. Her Marcus was a traveler as he told the interviewer sent by Maariv for Teens. He didn't use the ethnic instruments as much as he would like but when he could he liked to augment the sound, when the hide could be heard he liked to use it. She couldn't remember any of the names in his collection. She could only see them. Mosty, like her Marcus, she stuck to the modern ones, with a pounding of sticks. The solo grew more and more complex, the grimaces more wrenching. She wiped her brow.

She was almost at the point to give the crowd their first real glimpse of naked fury when her vision was interrupted. In the aisle before her stood the Art History teacher, looking on all this with high esteem. She was tapping her foot. She ran a palm over her elegant scalp but stopped the motion early to correct her balance. She watched the performer and nodded, and of course she would. She would appreciate a Marcus Bentov, an overlooked beauty, stumpy and cold-eyed, bulky and snarling, shorn so that the private details of his skull were common knowledge, young but imaginable as old and still as furious—a woman of sprawling aesthetic horizons would see why him. This was after all a teacher who could project onto a screen nothing but smears and dribbles and say, Now here we see before us an artistic milestone, very controversial in its time.

Light beamed through the cracked roof hatch, illuminating the aisle—not an aisle, the middle longitude of an enormous concert hall.

The teacher held out a slender brown hand and removed the microphone from Shulee's grip.

"You have gone over the acceptable time," she said. She turned and called for a showing of interested hands. As she awaited the next singer, she shifted her feet in constant adjustment to the vehicle.

Shulee ducked deeper and deeper into the woods, glancing over her shoulder. When the time had come to sit to lunch there was no avoiding the girl any longer. And now Yona Rodelheim was at large, tramping over the loose red soil with their food, under the pines. Twice Shulee had heard the quiet voice call for her.

That was a long time ago. Now she was safe. Black pearls of goat droppings gleamed on the ground. No one but she would venture this far from the group. Only Shulee. When she returned she would be in spectacular trouble, a star, and she would also have eaten. For, looking out from the bus, over the teacher's sleeping head, she had seen a food stand on the side of the road. She stepped onto a gravelly shoulder and gazed across. An old Arab woman sat on a bucket, selling treats on a rough table of plywood propped on cinder blocks. No traffic was coming, and it seemed none would come for a long time.

There were pines on the other side, too, the same kind. Needle leaves hissed mildly all around. Needles had fallen on the woman's table. Some rested on the silver tops of unfamiliar soda cans. The branches behind the woman let through shards of man-made color, far-off Arab laundry hanging, and doors and shutter slats painted in Arab blue. The cans were brighter than any of this. The type *was* familiar, after all, though also unfamiliar. This was Pepsi, which you could not get in the country because it was not distributed in the markets, due to the Arab Nations Boycott, as her cousin Tomer would have explained whenever he explained it.

How was it, then, that she beheld the beverage in its canned form, only four bus hours' distance from home? Of course. The Arab Nations had asked Pepsi to boycott the state of the Jews, this woman wasn't a Jew, so Pepsi decided, why should she suffer? She was a private distribution channel. Many more like her no doubt existed. Who knew? Uncle Chelomo went to the Arabs for his sausages and skewer meat; this was why Grandpa Daoud would not eat meat in Aunt Yvette's kitchen. Perhaps next time Shulee would go along with Uncle.

The plywood was laden with dented metal trays, as well. One was crammed with triangles of baklava speckled with radiant green pistachio dust. Another was laden with date-stuffed domes of maamul, and another with cubes of rahat, glowing dark amber through a frost of sugar powder. All this put off the same smells as the same treats sold at Central Station. But Pepsi! Who would have guessed it? Pepsi-Cola.

She examined the cans again, a dozen of them. She reached for one and took it, the warm metal dimpling in her grip. The only other time she had held this, the can had been empty and the occasion upsetting. Tomer had brought it from a tour of duty in Lebanon. He had brought also Lebanese cherries, and a macabre aside, which he told those who gathered to enjoy the fruit on his parents' porch. She herself had still been fascinated with the smell of the can, planning to lift it to her nostrils again at the time when he said what he said. The scent had recalled that of the Sabbath wine cup, the silver sticky after the blessing and the meal.

So Shiko finds a Hezbollah jaw in a shoe. The shoe he leaves. I tell him, What's wrong with you, take it in the shoe. He says, Shoes we find all of the time. I say, Not with a jaw in them. He says, The jaw I got. I tell him, A jaw you'll find again, too. He says, Not in a shoe.

No response had come from the family and no commentary, even though to say this he had cut Grandpa off. Tomer had been strange in his demeanor and abrupt. And worse, when no one responded he looked to her. They were close in age, they had played together. That very stare had often goaded her towards feats of nerve, public accomplishment, once even to ring the doorbell of crazy Kokkinos down the street in the course of a game Tomer and she had refined to one rule, that the designated player inquire of an ominous third party whether he had lost a given object that couldn't possibly be his. The winner was the one to start an angry chase, then come back and tell all.

On that Shabbat afternoon, in the presence of their elders, she had found Tomer daring her again, but with much more vehemence than ever before, and much less persistence. For soon with a nauseous expression he had turned away and walked off, smacking the base of a new pack of cigarettes. She recalled the muscles jerking in his back. He had brought back from Lebanon also the habit of smoking nearly constantly, one cigarette lighting the next.

The youngest of the adults could not bear responsibility for the group! It was not for her to have orchestrated a turning point as the tension hung, and Tomer shouldn't have expected it. He couldn't have. He wouldn't have required her to issue the response. Was there one? *The terrorists should all be crushed, Amen. Good going.* But it had seemed to her you should not keep the bones. Was she to have gasped at the manners of the battlefront from the safe center, a schoolgirl turn her nose up at a foot soldier? Maybe that was his point in the first place. What was the point? She couldn't even follow the plot in the dialogue. Did Shiko end up taking the jaw? Maybe not. Maybe the whole thing was soldier banter. Was Tomer's goal humor? Perhaps the only contestable issue was that he had brought up the matter with her little nieces playing Five Rocks in the corner with five brass cubes. Someone should have told him to watch his mouth. Could you tell a man defending you with his life to watch his mouth? They were right to have said nothing at all to him, but couldn't someone have explained it to her, later? Very soon no one had seemed bothered anymore.

About the Pepsi, Tomer had said it tasted different from any other cola, but it was difficult to say how.

The old Arab said something. Shulee nodded to indicate she was still making her decision. Did it cost the woman money to let her make her decision? It didn't appear that she was in a hurry to rise from her bucket.

"Just a minute," Shulee said, but when she caught the vendor's eye she almost regretted sneaking off. In all her sixteen years and nine months she had never stood face-to-face with an Arab in order to interact. The woman peered with the gaze of steel rivets in a square-jawed handbag, more glint than character. Shulee set the can back in its place.

The old Arab spoke again, shrilly, and Shulee found she no

longer wanted the drink. If she was to skip lunch successfully she needed solid candy. A breeze lifted a mist of sugar powder off the rahat and carried the scent of rosewater to her nose. The old Arab tapped the tray and lifted three fingers. Just out of curiosity, Shulee pointed to the soda, as well.

The old woman raised all of the fingers of one hand, then folded them, and raised two. Outrageous! Pepsi was the finest soda in the world, or else the Arab was doing her part to impose the ban. Shulee pointed back to the candy and raised the finger to point up. One. The woman raised two. Shulee nodded. The old Arab reached down and tore a section from a stack of newspapers on the ground. A child emerged from behind her, stretched on the tips of her toes, picked out two cubes of rahat, took the paper and wrapped them. She turned the small packet over to the old woman, who looked at Shulee and waited. Shulee prodded at her jeans pocket, but found herself distracted and inept, staring at the child with all the fascination she didn't dare impose on the elder. The little one was beautiful! Like a kitten, miniaturized. Wearing a too-short tricot shirt, a small tan stomach exposed, tiny hip bones and a dainty knot of navel. On the fabric above, an image of the television muscleman, Mr. T, bulged shirtless.

"Mister T!" Shulee said. "Mister T, right? Good. I like, too!"

The child said nothing, but could it be that Shulee's efforts with her were softening the old face, or did the leathery jaw simply jut less than she had first perceived? And why not a softening? If a woman put up a table she wanted to sell, that was all. And here was a buyer. There was no malice. It was only natural that Shulee should have distrusted her at first, travel was dangerous. But had an old candy seller and her helper girl ever knifed a hiker in a waadi? Hijacked a bus and burned the passengers alive? Floated landward on inflatable rafts to massacre a hotel lobby full of tourists? Or taken high schoolers hostage on their Annual Trip, and shot twenty-one of them dead on their sleeping bags? Those had been eleventh-graders.

No. Buying candy was not what got them killed. They had been asleep. It wasn't a sought encounter. In a daytime engagement, entered willingly, it was up to you. You could pay attention, you could use your eyes. You could see what kind of Arab you were dealing with, a murderer or not a murderer. This Arab wanted only to sell. Shulee would buy. One very successful interaction for the record. Once she returned to her group, she will have done something here. If someone in the woman's village should say, The Jews are a dark spawn which must be liquidated, the old woman would answer, I met one and she was perfectly delightful. In turn, when Shulee boarded her bus with rosewater breath, she would say, Bought it at an Arab village, sure; my Uncle Chelomo purchases certain items from them, too, and afterwards sits there and drinks coffee.

True, how much more impressed the girls would be if she managed, in all this, also to thwart the boycott and show up with a cola they had never tasted. Not this time. It wasn't meant to be.

She twisted her canteen on its belt to better work her hand into the pocket. The old Arab observed, uttering her harsh sounds. Wind mussed the pines and exposed more of the village beyond. Shulee found her coins, yanked her hand out again, dropped everything she had into the Arab's waiting hand, disregarded the packet of sweets being held out in exchange, grabbed a can of Pepsi, and ran like the devil.

Goat droppings stuck to her soles and pine needles stuck to that. Through the leaning trunks she saw the roadside clearing where the group had stopped to eat. She saw no girls, but there was the hindmost bus, the exhaust pipe smoking.

The exhaust pipe moving, the bus rolling away. She could hear its companion, rumbling ahead. She came to a jolting stop and watched as the vehicles revved up around a bend and vanished. Running footfalls came from the direction of the trees behind her.

She whirled and collapsed on her haunches, fear draining the power from her limbs, the soda can dropping.

She closed her eyes to spare herself what she knew was coming: By the supernatural powers of hate the old woman had hauled up the sheet of plywood from her table, and with it dashed across the road, and through the trees, and back to the road in an arcing path, to crush the skull of her enemy's youth. Or the child had fetched the mob she had been sent for. Murderers! Bandits. She had given them everything in her pocket, even if it was short of the price they had named. The price was exorbitant.

"Can they do this?" someone said in Hebrew. Shulee opened her eyes. Yona Rodelheim gazed at the clearing, wonder-struck, her orange Pumas set widely apart on the bed of needles. She approached Shulee and squatted beside her. The weight of the backpack she was lugging nearly upended the girl. Her eyes acquired a sudden shine. "Can they leave us?"

"Don't you cry." Shulee retrieved her soda from the dirt and stood up. "Crying we don't need."

"I would think there are regulations. I would think by law—"

"Stop that," Shulee said. "Slow yourself down." She couldn't stand the girl's voice. When a sentence finally started coming, the words streamed out in too much of a rush, with too little variety in the inflection, the harried disclosure of a robot with a gun at his back. At her forehead, hadn't the girls said. "Why didn't they wait?" Shulee asked.

"How would I know?" Yona said. "I was with you."

"You spied on me?"

"I thought that you were going to the toilet. I thought you'd want a lookout."

"Did I ask for a lookout?" Yona seemed to consider this. "Did I go to the toilet?"

"No."

"But you kept sneaking after me."

"I was trying to catch up. If I shouted the teachers would hear."

"Do you even know how to shout?" Yona had nothing to say to this. "Maybe today we'll find out, now you've got us stranded here. We'll have to see what happens to us now because of you." Shulee reached for the girl's hand, pulled her to her feet, spun her away from the road, and herded her back towards the trees. There Shulee took the lead, walking among the trunks.

"Where are we going?" Yona said.

Shulee continued the retreat from the road. A songbird alighted on a low branch before them, but fluttered up in a frenzy just as suddenly. A crow shouted nearby. Yona's panting quickened. Shulee passed the soda can again from hand to hand.

"The Art History teacher has it in for me," she said. "She can't stand my level of self-confidence. It bothers her, she has to be boss. She's trying to get back at me for having a mind of my own. She'll be showing up again, any minute now." Her wrist was tired. "They drive a ways more, she's satisfied, she comes back to get me, here's what I tell her: The Bureau of Education is going to hear about this."

Yona pulled a breath sharply through her nose.

"No crying."

"I don't understand why we're running from the road," Yona said. "If they come back they'll come by the road. We don't know our way here. I'm hungry."

"And that guard," Shulee said. "What's his problem? Oh, you have a gun, big man. You get to bore us senseless at gunpoint."

"You're acting like we can't stop," Yona said. If indeed the guard had held his gun to her she was doing a good job of hiding the trauma even at the mention of him. Her voice continued to stream over in the low, controlled rush. "Is there a reason we can't stop?"

"One human being has the balls to stand up to him, look what happens to her. I cannot tolerate that man. Can you tolerate him? That one also wants to teach me a lesson. They'll be the ones who learn. The school's going to be closed down, it deserves to be closed down. The teachers are substandard. The principal is a rat face. You think this won't be on the evening news, you're crazy. There's going to be a scandal like there never was, a stain on the whole system. They're going to ask me and I'm going to tell."

"We should stop," Yona said. "You should stop. I think you should get ahold of yourself. You're very upset. You acted strange on the bus."

"That was air drumming!" Shulee said. "It's only strange to know-nothings like you, idiots out of contact with the modern world."

"But you should have seen your expressions."

"How can you talk to me about *my* behavior?"

"Why was the Arab upset?" Yona asked.

"What Arab? What upset?"

"She was shouting at you. You ran from her."

"I ran because I heard the buses. Goat shit again. Be careful."

"But I saw—"

"I was counting on you to make sure the group wouldn't leave without me," Shulee said. She kicked a pinecone out of her way. "If you'd have been able to stop yourself from spying on me, they wouldn't have taken off. Why couldn't you leave me alone?"

"For meals we're partners."

"Maybe if you respected that. Maybe if you didn't act like that meant we had to walk together the whole Trip."

The food pack was rustling, items inside knocking together. Shulee was hungry. She would feel better once she drank.

"You were trying to get away from me?" Yona said.

"Did I say that? Did I say that? Koos amak! Will you please shut up? Please?"

"I don't think it's good that you should curse in their language here," Yona said. "That's a very bad one. They might hear."

"I'm afraid of *them*?" Shulee said, more quietly. There were no teachers around now, but she did wish she hadn't uttered the damned words again.

"You shouldn't have said it back there, either," Yona said.

"Tell me," Shulee said, kicking more and more pinecones out of her way. The scattered layer suddenly had become a crowd. "Do you really want us to talk about what happened in there? Do you really want to put yourself through that again?"

"*You* put me through it in there. You put us all through that. You should admit your part." Even now the girl sounded composed, or subdued, or both, as if everything were rehearsed and then recited through a blanket. Hard to believe her hysteria, so recently.

"I don't remember *me* refusing to go on," Shulee said.

"You should see your role," the girl said.

"I see it fine. It's to be stuck with you. Stuck in there and stuck out here."

"I didn't like the touch," Yona said.

"Can't you take a joke?"

"I didn't like the touch in the tunnel. I was concentrating very hard in there. I was getting faster. I was keeping my thoughts away from the smell. I was working hard at it."

A rusty pine tassel fell on Shulee's shoulder. She brushed it off, striding on. The trees all looked the same, except that from time to time a yellow stripe would appear on a trunk. The crow shouted out of sight. She tried to fit the can into her back pocket, and couldn't. She kicked a rock over. An agitated millipede skated over her shoe and disappeared. The sky was visible in spokes of blue among the highest clumps of needle leaves. Spindled light was thrown on the red soil, crossing out the very pebbles and twigs it brightened.

Again she passed the can from one hand to the other. She thought of cracking it open, but she would wait. Somewhere safe, she could savor and sip, slowly as if this were a bowl of well-known stew in a strange house, the tongue deciphering, little by little, the decisions of the unfamiliar cook.

"Tell me the location of Margoah," Yona said.

"What is this, geography class?"

"You don't know," Yona said. "All your life in this country and you don't know."

"And you're not from here?"

"I was born abroad."

"That's right," Shulee said. "Before the National Matriculation test in English all the girls were milking you like a cow."

"You say unpleasant things," Yona said. "You should think before you speak because you will have to think about it after."

"Listen to her," Shulee said. "Good girl. How many Adages of the Fathers do you have memorized? Your parents must be terribly proud."

The spindled light withdrew, leaving the details of the turf blandly discernible. Shulee slowed to a march, looking up. A cloud was trailing across the sun. Yona fell in beside her. Shulee looked down, kept walking, the orange Pumas keeping equal pace.

"That wasn't an adage and you don't know where Margoah is. I can tell you. Forty-two kilometers north of Jerusalem, in Samaria. From the highest point you can look down to Shiloh." She swallowed, took a breath. "If you live in the settlement, you look out your window in the morning, your eyes might hit on the exact spot where Hannah prayed for a son. Hang your laundry, the wind on your clean sheets is also stroking the same ground where Eli the Priest lay his head at night. From another angle you can see the precise location of the decisive Hasmonean victory over the Greeks. Take a Shabbat stroll and walk where Judah HaMakabbi marched. Go to Beit Knesset, you may be praying where Eliezer prayed a day before he gave his life under the belly of the pagans' elephant, three days before, a week. He would have passed here."

"What are you talking about?" Shulee said. "You live in Petakh Tikva by the zoo. Maybe from there you got the elephant."

"My brother lives in Margoah," Yona said. "I practically live there. All of the kids there know me like I live there. I'm going to live there. This is my plan. I'll get married and live with my brother for a neighbor, and his wife and their children as a part of my family. I love his wife and I love their children. I love life in Margoah. I have two nephews and a niece," she said. "We'll build a house next to them and our children will grow up together."

"What about your parents?" Shulee said. "An old man and woman alone in the city?"

"They have friends. They'll come to visit like they do now, with me. They gave us the ideals to want to live there," Yona said. "They taught us to love the land, and that's where the land is. You see it all around you wherever you walk, hills and hills and hills and hills. The first time I set foot there I thought I was on the moon. I said so. But the point is, no, exactly the opposite. The point is you're exactly where you belong. Physically you feel very small, so why is that? Perspective. Sure, you're small, but you're a comma, you're a period, you're a necessary part. The hills are the chapters, all around you, past and present, future and the end days, so you see. You see exactly where you are, and what you are, what you've come from and what you're bringing about. Like Avraham in his time, the same comprehension. In the city you go to a park to sit under a tree and stare at a fence. Everything's hacked, chopped up and coated. You can't see the land for the concrete. You could be living in Los Angeles. That's what we're here for, to forget that we're here? That's how *you* prefer it. Have you ever even been in Judah and Samaria not as a tourist? More than just passing through on a school trip? Even just as a guest in someone's home? Just for a Shabbat. A holiday. Should I invite you? There are risks. Maybe you're afraid."

The girl had never spoken at such length and at this level of passion. "If you're hungry you could eat while we walk," Shulee said. She stopped and faced Yona. "Need help with your zipper?"

The toes of Yona's orange shoes were pointing slightly inward where she stood. "I watch my brother's children when they play outside," she said. "I come up with new games for them and all the time I'm watching them like a hawk. My sister-in-law says I'm a natural mother. I see everything all at once and I remember it all. And I *am* like the children's second mother, except they like that I have energy to throw a ball. On the east there are olive groves and from the other side of them have come hostilities." She slipped off the straps of her backpack and let it drop to the ground. She crouched beside it, laid her hands on top, looked up. "My sister-in-law, driving home from her mother in the city one night, was shot at, but they missed. Her neighbor from two houses down, similar story. Only she wakes up in the hospital with one eye gone and no more sense of smell. In that case it was rocks. I help her, too. With her kids, but especially with her cooking for Shabbat. She can taste salt and bitter and sweet, but that's it. She won't eat what she didn't used to like. The empty eye is always crying. She's always with a tissue. Could you stand that? I can look her in the face even when she comes out of the bath without the patch. I'll tell you exactly what I see. I see everything the Jewish soul endures, and still survives. You would look away. You would talk about something unrelated."

Shulee squeezed her soda. "I'm for Peace Now," she said.

"So now more lying," Yona said.

"Lands for peace. Peace for lands."

"You will say whatever comes into your head to stand apart."

"I would marry an Arab," Shulee said.

Yona unzipped her pack and reached in.

They heard the spray of gravel under tires and the rumble of an engine. Yona sprang to her feet, abandoning the pack. They ran towards the road, but when it came within view, saw only a brown Peugeot with an Arab license plate, blue. It had already passed them but now it seemed to be slowing. It *was* slowing, coming to a stop. The handbrake rasped and the driver's door opened. A white sneaker tested the ground, above it a blue jeans hem. A heavy-thighed young woman in a floral head-kerchief stepped out, turning to look their way. Shulee punched Yona's waist. Yona looked at her, wincing.

"I think it's okay," she whispered. "It's a woman alone. Maybe she can drive us somewhere? Maybe she can make a call."

Shulee made her eyes ferocious, and undertook her earlier job of shoving the girl back into the woods. This time she kept pushing. Yona's legs seemed persuaded, hurrying along, but the mouth kept arguing.

"At worst she maybe won't help. Think a minute. You're not used to talking to Arabs. You never see them where they live. If you lived in Margoah you would see Arabs all the time where they live. My brother talks to some of them. With some of them you can tell it would be all right if it wasn't for everyone around them."

Shulee guided her roughly to avoid a tree. "My uncle purchases some items from an Arab that he knows," she said. "Don't think you've got some special experience."

"We'll send her for help and hide," Yona said. "When they come for us, if we don't hear Hebrew we'll keep hiding. It's starting to get dark. This is the first car that passed through all this time."

They reached Yona's pack, and the girl leaned down and grabbed it. A can of pineapple rolled out, a bag of Ringo peanut puffs. She bent to gather these but Shulee wrenched her up by the collar, spurring her on.

"Why won't you talk to this one?" Yona said, hurrying. "You had no problem before."

"Now there's no bus in case of emergency," Shulee said.

Yona hugged the pack. "What happened? What was going to happen? You're always lying."

"She wanted to cheat me."

"Who runs from a cheater?"

"I didn't let her cheat. I paid her a fair price. I left her all my change."

"You stole from her?" The girl was shouting, crying, too, the suddenly powerful voice warped.

"Keep it down," Shulee said. "I gave her plenty. Everything I had. I still paid more than it was worth." She vaulted over a fallen nestling. The dead bird's details differentiated themselves sharply from the blurry ground: a naked pallor, a deflation, and a supervision by flies. She heard Yona jump, too, then the girl was beside her, gasping, water pooling in her eyes, her mouth contorting.

"You stole from her."

"Stop that," Shulee said. "Don't you dare." She stumbled on a pile of fallen needles. No, a mound of hard earth capped with red-brown needles under which a colony of scaled gray land crustaceans had been resting. She skipped and hopped to remain upright, clutching at Yona's quaking shoulder. She could feel herself coming to tears, as well. "Don't you dare slow us down." She grimaced and let go of the girl. Crying was like nausea. You could overcome it.

"You didn't like the price, you didn't have to buy," Yona keened.

"Quiet, quiet!" Shulee could hear the distortion in her own voice now, the sorrow and plea. She tried to keep running close by the trunks, so Yona would have to fall behind, but the girl merely kept switching sides, plaguing her with a horrified face.

"A stupid soda, when you had a full canteen," she cried. "You stole from an Arab. From an Arab you had to steal. HaShem have pity on us. You're insane. Isn't there enough trouble already?"

"What do you know?" Shulee wailed. "What do you even know, at all. Don't even think to ask me for a sip!"

A momentary silence canceled the trees' susurration. Then the woods resumed, and the girls tore through. Behind a rock the size of a hunkering bovine, they collapsed hip to hip. The crow shouted. A faraway rooster answered more ornately. They waited for a long while. They drew apart and crouched, listening. Songbirds grew raucous in the trees.

They looked each at the other's face, seeing the jaw slack, the whites of the eyes inflamed.

"And even so," Yona said, dully. "I think that it was as big a mistake to run away."

Shulee ground her teeth together and got up. She tossed her can from one hand and caught it with the other. She licked her lips.

"I shouldn't have listened to you," Yona said. "I should have assumed that you'd be wrong. What did the first have to do with the next? The young one in the car and the old one you insulted? If you catch any connection at all you catch it wrong. At least we have food."

Shulee climbed onto the rock. At the top she teetered, then raised herself to full height, planting her feet and raising the soda can, then her empty fist. She brought them down, one after the other, as if beating drums with unsteady wrists. Yona reached in her pack again. She produced a roll of dried salami and a transparent disposable knife. She sawed beneath the metal tourniquet cinching the purple casing.

"Two slices bread or open-faced?"

Shulee stopped drumming to test the seal of the can with her thumbnail.

"Mustard or dry?"

She pulled at the tab. A geyser of pale brown froth drenched her shirt. She held the can away from her as this continued. Soda streamed down the rock and was swallowed by the dirt.

"I'll put the mustard on the side."

The brightness through the trees had lessened, remained less, and was thinning.

"There's also lima beans in sauce."

The birds were at their loudest before sleep. High on the rock an evening chill frisked the wet skin of Shulee's breasts. Soda trickled between her knuckles. She tipped the can, slowly, over her mouth, with care, preparing, to shake the light remainder onto her waiting tongue.

"I'll give you some of everything," Yona said. "You'll do what you want."

Part 2

veYordim
(and Descending)

Anatevka Tender

FINALLY THE KITCHEN drawer came open, slamming into her stomach and spewing the obstruction towards her face: rubber bands. Snarls exploded and spilled over the sides, red, blue, and amber. Bunches crumbled in the hand, while others glued themselves to the skin, the younger units, still sweating out their resilience. The clingers she shook off and the strays she kneeled to collect. All of them she stuffed into a Hefty bag.

"Yitz," she called out. "Please!"

No answer. When at long last he would appear, he would insist he hadn't heard her any of the other times. If she could hear his sandals crunching on the Astroturf of the porch, couldn't he hear her shout? He would say it was a matter of focus. She believed this was true. The boy had an excellent mind—the young man, rather, the sergeant who made the rank despite the early trouble with compliance, just as in the years of double schooldays at Yeshiva he had excelled while garnering a reputation for disruption, as accomplished in the morning sciences as in the sacred texts of the late afternoon. What did he know from housework? The dullness he seemed to have a good sense of but he had no idea of the scope.

More wormy clots clung to the bottom of the drawer, coming

away with offensive sounds. She grabbed a scouring pad and a viscous detergent. All but the faintest tracks of rubber melted off the white surface. What remained was like the ghost of crayon vandalism, red, blue, and amber, washed off a wall. She rolled the drawer shut and moved on to another, also stubborn but surrendering sooner. Prone stacks of Styrofoam cups squealed in emerging, soft shards breaking off, concavities tinted with drink.

The bags of garbage were beginning to dominate the kitchenette floor and the job wasn't even half-done. The lessor was in too miserable a shape to be held accountable. The old man, the dying condominium owner whose name she could not seem to recollect although the nephew would have printed it on the lease, had hoarded also plastic bottle caps, salt packets, red coffee stirrers, cocktail swords, cruise ship napkins. She thought of the phone, mounted on the wall by a dry erase board, which still bore the words *pilot light* in a wavering hand. The mouthpiece had smelled spitty when she had spoken to Harvey the night before, and she had noticed rust-colored stuff caked around the pushbuttons. She didn't want to see that again when he called tonight. Cleaning supplies were piled on the counter. She soaked a paper towel with rubbing alcohol, strode to the phone, and rubbed. She had neglected to ask Harvey was he using what she froze in tinfoil. She'd left heating instructions on pieces of tape, but he should peel those off.

She erased the board while she was at it. The alcohol dissolved the words.

"*Now* you're talking," Yitz said.

She pitched the paper towel, the solvent drying icy on her fingertips. Yitz hadn't shouted, but she had heard him as if he were just outside the doorway, and he was, across the dining area, still on the porch. She had to remember the facts of this apartment.

"Now *who's* talking?" Once she was done with the big cleanout, she would have a radically easier time housekeeping than she had had in years. There was so much less space now. Mopping, only in here and in the bathroom, maybe sixty square feet of linoleum, everywhere else carpeted. "Your little brother's with you? Eytan, I thought you were getting ready for bed."

But she heard only Yitz, clearing his throat in a farcical manner. He and his brother must have struck up a clownish mood and were preparing some sort of presentation. Yitz would direct and Eytan would perform, the little introvert briefly turned out by his big brother's theatricality. No food matter stuck in an ear, she hoped, or nostril. The desired audience would be one taken unawares, so she walked over without clearing the fatigue from her face.

But Yitz alone stood on the porch once she had skirted the glossy oval of the dining table and pushed through the heavy folds of the floor-length curtains, the shock of changed location hitting her once again in the outdoor smell, Maryland at summer's peak. The humidity had brought out the curl in her son's black hair. Where was his kippa? His head was bare.

She couldn't see what he was looking at, just the evening sky, still fully lit and yet amazingly permissive of examination, the glare hung with a filter of thick clouds, lush with the details of a slowed or building storm. Another slice of this phenomenon was visible at foot level, framed by the iron stilts on which the wall was raised. The Astroturf disguised the unforgiving cement only by prickling at her feet through her hosiery. Each step forward reawakened the long miles of the passenger-plane flight stored in the vessels of her calves. She wondered if the pull of gravity at this height was worsening the congestion. The complaint dated to her first pregnancy, this boy, this discharged soldier, who at the start of their travels had been a nine-year-old charged for a historic climax, a permanent return, they had all thought, from Hoboken to the land of their Fathers. Through that journey, too, her legs had been such a bother that she still remembered. Coming or going the blood did the same, striving towards the ground the whole airborne way, but how much longer now it took the legs to return to normal.

She stopped just short of her son's side. When she saw his view she forgot her legs. Across the freeway lay the suburb, but sub-arboreal would have described it better from these heights, as it was entirely sunk beneath the trees, all evidence of human development shielded by a blanket of green, though not truly a blanket. In the layer, shaggy shapes swayed this way and that, pressed together, like a woolly-shouldered nation hunkering in prayer, or rather pending decision, given that the movement seemed to flow like a debate, circulating, splitting and returning. The chirr of some abundant local bug surged suddenly out of the dark divisions, and she would not have been surprised to see a ponderous neck drawn up from bowing, here and there a face turning up, in a time when the coming evening was announced by a great peal of silver hammers, ascending and descending, against aluminum it sounded like. The damp air bore sweet rot and verdure far above the fertile soil.

"Look at that," Yitz said. "Boom. Green green green. That's trees for you," he said, with nervous admiration as if he hoped to be one someday, at which ambition she could only raise her eyebrows. With the *boom* she had snapped out of the spell.

Why boom? Like a cry in a magic trick, to announce an immense change? And of course, yes, three days ago they would have regarded from their old home the rails of another porch set in stucco across a street where boys would pause from playing soccer when a car passed, their shouts rising in Hebrew when the conditions for play returned, whereas here today—boom! Nothing but green, green, green beyond the graphite streak of the far-down thruway. But unlike a magician he had extended both arms joined, right fist squeezed against left forearm, and jerked them like the mechanism of a rocket launcher. Boom.

"I need a chair," he said. "I'm going to sit here."

"The nephew could have taken that monster of a television and left us deck chairs," she said. "Look at the grooves in the Astroturf. There were deck chairs."

"I dig that TV."

"With all the woodwork?" she said. "Horrible. Dig?"

"It *should* be ornate. It's a shrine. It's a God."

"Please with the nonsense. You don't say this kind of thing for your brother to hear, correct?"

"I'll buy it off the old dude. That thing's an antique, circa, what? Nineteen-something-or-other Americana, electronic Americana, electronicana. Dig it. First thing I'll set up when I get my own pad. Could use a new antenna, could use a better antenna." He had started speaking at a normal pace but now he was racing. "Caught cartoons on it at three A.M., three in the morning, man."

"I'm your mother and not a man, please."

"Any time of day you can watch anything," he said. "There's never nothing on, which I find very cool, my learned gentlemen and fellow prodigies. Let us say grace."

"Cool I don't think you even say anymore. That's from the sixties." Did he need the indiscriminate greed for local idiom to mark him even more a stranger? The nonsense talk would be enough of an impedance when he began to make his way here, and with a faint Israeli accent now to boot.

"Cool's cool," he said. "I heard it about five times from the bagger at Safeway."

"That's from who you'll learn?" she said, but she allowed herself an ironic smile. She had been touched by the experience herself. "Did you hear all the Have a Nice Days from the cashiers?" she said. "And two How You Doin's on the way, from perfect strangers."

"Have a nice day, now!" Yitz said.

"It's a pleasant practice," she said. "Really agreeable."

"Let's get kitchen chairs."

"Okh, all those bags collecting on the floor. They won't fit in the chute. You saw where the garbage room was downstairs?"

"Five minutes let's enjoy the panorama."

"View," she said. "A panorama's only from a pinnacle with visibility all around." From within the apartment came a childish voice: *Imma!* "What is it?" *To use it?* "Use what?" But even as she shouted her voice declined towards the pitch of conversation, because who knew what he had found, and she would have to go and check. "I have to go check," she told Yitz, turning to go back in. "Come soon. There's so much to do still inside."

"That family is finished by now," he said.

She turned back towards him. "I don't understand this," she said. She didn't. Why he must continue to invite the war in Lebanon into their daily routine she could guess. What determined his timing, she couldn't. "Now, Yitz?"

He gazed past her cheekbone, as if expecting other company, more important. As always he proceeded to look down, annoyed, having been stood up.

"The Hezbollah by now would have come in and finished them off," he said. "Collaborators they finish off." He kicked the Astroturf, studying the action. "Did the poor schleps ask us to set up camp on their roof? Does the Hezbollah make fine distinctions? Wonderful questions, thank you, Yitzhak Hirschhorn. Discuss."

"Please," she said. "You can sit with me later. You and I, later we'll sit." Again Eytan called out. "Wait!" she shouted.

"Just you and I?" Yitz said. "Bring him out with you, so he can hear what he won't have to see. They had three girls, one his age. She liked to bring the soldiers lemonade. Finished," he said. "Boom."

So there, the chilling sound again. And there, the momentary nausea that she had barely let herself acknowledge when, in the kitchen, she had thought Eytan was out here with his big brother, alone on the porch. What was that fiction she had told herself, a skit they were preparing for her? The boys hadn't done that in over three years.

"You should think," she said slowly. "Before you speak about your little brother in this way, please think, a child who only knows to idolize you, a boy entering the second grade as a foreigner, your baby brother. He would have been perfectly happy staying in the one place he knows."

"When he's eighteen I'm sure he'll hold the sacrifice against you," Yitz said. He used an expletive from the army, which struck her only with the ring of deep spite, but no meaning since it was in Arabic. The gallop of the furious words vanished into one of his farcical throat clearings, at the end of which the raging Arab reemerged as her surly son. "They had a dog," he said. "I liked that dog, I always wanted a dog, yeah, dig it. I'm going to get myself a mastiff."

"Not according to my lease," she said.

Again she approached the curtains and pushed through. Again she stood in the old man's apartment, and an old man's apartment it still was, a much too fully furnished rental, choked with the choices of an uninspiring lifetime and the odors of canned soup. In her rush she nearly knocked a heaping bowl of furred wax peaches to the ground. She found Eytan sitting on the toilet, pants down, smooth thighs squashed against the seat. The seat was transparent and contained the shells of mollusks. He was looking at the ceiling.

"What's that?" he said.

"A heat lamp."

"To use it?"

"Not to use it." She flicked off the switch. Eytan watched the glare behind the glass shrink to a dot. "Don't look," she said. "Harmful to the eyes. Remember to hold the flusher till the water starts."

Through the hallway and the living room, the mustard carpet spared her legs and assaulted her eyes, likewise the oat-mash curtains and wallpaper, and doilies everywhere like fallen moths. What was this passion for draping, cloaking, coating every firm surface with something soft? She felt as if she were negotiating the folds of a great, slumped sack. A giant hand could gather up the edges and lift her up, out and away. She would find herself floating over the treetops, Yitz watching her from the porch, his face blurring until altogether swallowed by the tower. The toe of her hose caught on a steel carpet border as she crossed the threshold of the kitchenette again. She yanked free and heard a run begin.

Among his other puzzling comforts, the old man had hoarded a colony of sealed sandwich bags stuffed with a mysterious substance, dark and dry. She could live with the mystery. She threw the bags out by the handful, but soon she had poked one open, rubbed a pinch between her fingers and sniffed, what? Tea leaves, but weak-smelling and silty, not the cut of leaf sold loose. He had salvaged the contents of used teabags.

She was washing her hands for the umpteenth time that day when the phone rang. The best rates had set in there hours ago.

"How You Doin's on the street from perfect strangers," she told Harvey. "Have a Nice Day in every shop. You having a nice day?"

His time it was the dead of night, he said. The voice came across corrupted, not altogether him and the retort uncalled for. She knew what time it was for all of them.

"I should say reaccustomed for myself," she said. "I find I'm touched. I find I appreciate the civility, and not to mention Yitz. This morning at Safeway I thought he was going to propose to the cashier. I told him, Yitz, I'm positive the sentiment is genuine. It also happens to be in her job description. Eytan dropped a blue-berry yogurt in the parking lot, and the cart collector offered a replacement. It wasn't even cracked, only caved in."

He said there were still some loose ends at the department, some last-minute demands.

He had his ticket, though?

Yitz muttered on the porch and shuffled his sandals. Harvey must have heard the shift in her attention. He was waiting.

"Monday you said you would book it at lunch," she said.

Soon as the pace let up, he said, a lot of administrative loose ends. Considering his appointment as department chair he owed his colleagues a thorough wrap-up.

"Your chairmanship ended a year and four months ago," she said. "And the buyers?"

The closing had to be rescheduled.

"Why?"

"A few remaining questions."

"But we had cake and coffee twice. They were looking to renovate. They didn't mind the parking spot, they met the tenants' council. They got along with Abukasis!"

"Only a few remaining questions," he said. "Leave it to me. You have enough on your hands right now. Trust me. Are you having a nice day?"

"Thank you," she said. "I am indeed." She let him know she had set all the important concerns in motion. Yitz's application at the college was missing only his discharge papers, Eytan and she were to meet the principal at Jewish Day tomorrow.

Harvey asked where the principal had gone to college. She didn't know. Had the boys made it to morning prayers at the local shul? he asked. Not yet.

The line was lousy. At times there was a delay in reception. She would hear nothing and then he would come in with just a fraction of the first syllable shaved off, so that there was the unpleasant but really unfounded sense of omission. Other times it seemed her voice was being transmitted to him more swiftly than it could travel to her own ears. He would interrupt.

She already had one job lead, she said, from a member of the community who— Yes, very homey. Only a little tidying up. She wondered if she shouldn't be the one to call him tomorrow, so the—

"Leave it to me."

"That phrase again," she said.

"That what?"

"Leave it to me," she said. "Twice now. It sounds glib. You never say that."

"Bonny."

"Are you punishing me?" she said.

"What is this all of a sudden?"

"You won't answer the question."

"Can I be punishing you when it seems I'm the one being prosecuted?"

"So this is debate club and not a conversation."

"I'd rather not go looking for extra grief," he said. "I called to see how you're all doing."

"We would do better with you here."

"Is this a choice that I'm making?" he said.

"So it's *my* choice. Terrific. He is punishing me."

"Is this a choice that I'm making, having to wrap up our affairs here. What are you trying to stir up, Bonny?"

"Get your ticket," she said.

"Don't speak to me in this manner, Bonny!" She moved the phone farther from her ear, heart quickened with the disconcerting thrill she always felt when she had managed finally to provoke open resistance. "Don't treat me like some self-indulgent balker, a child, a foot dragger. Don't trivialize my task here. Don't—"

"What else?" she said. "God knows I could use the help right now and this is enormously helpful, Harvey. I shouldn't do what else?"

He said nothing and in fact she had been primed to carry on, but someone was addressing her from outside.

"You can give me one more job?"

And if only this had been Yitz expressing interest in a useful outlet. However the voice was the voice of a second-grader and the syntax that of a native Hebrew speaker. Eytan stood in the doorway with bright red shoulders, in Israeli pajamas consisting of a thin tank top and shorts, hair dripping wet beneath his kippa, crocheted of white thread bordered with green.

"You ran the shower too hot!" she said.

"I did what now?" Harvey said.

"So I fixed it," Eytan said.

She told her husband she had to go. She would call him tomorrow. He told her to have it her way.

She herded Eytan back into the bathroom, where she removed his kippa and wrapped his head in a towel. The container of ointment was lined up on the rim of the sink along with all the other new pharmaceuticals awaiting a clean shelf.

"I can do some more with the blue spray on where there's glass?"

"No, enough of that," she said. She smoothed the cream onto his shoulders. "Next time before you shower you call me. Does it hurt?"

"No," he said. "So another job. What one are you doing now? I can help?"

"I'm in between. Listen, you have to learn the settings before you run it alone."

"One more job," he said.

She returned the ointment to its place, unwrapped the boy's head, and secured the tightly knit kippa back at his crown, with a metal clip that clicked as it shut.

"One and no more," she said. "Then we call it a day."

A White House snow dome, a Miss Liberty snow dome, Mount Rushmore in a snow dome, Abe Lincoln cleaving pewter logs, cork-backed coasters, two sets intermixed, one celebrating aspects of Virginia, the other stamped with simplified Chagalls.

Two glass bluebirds, two ruby cardinals, a Disney-type woolly mammoth, ferocity replaced with dimples and a lolling tongue cast in a rubbery polymer. She transferred everything to Eytan, where he squatted by the tasseled sofa, ripping the *Times* for padding. For each new artifact he paused and with a ceremonious gesture extended his hands, received it but did not yet wrap, instead arranging everything in rows on the sofa. She piled doilies on the armrest. Her eyes began to itch. Once in a while Eytan sneezed.

The oak-entombed television served as the site of a ceramic shtetl. In the shadow of the bent antenna, in valleys of wrinkled lace, enameled huts and figurines staged a nonsensical production of the stock Old World tableaux. The band of wedding musicians swept bows across strings and blew wind into instruments, as the dairyman slogged by with morning buckets, chickens pecking underfoot. On his path a man and woman whirled together, dancing, gripping edges of one handkerchief, free arms stretched out; the woman's grazed the ear of a Melamed, who in turn wagged a glazed finger at a benchful of schoolboys, behind whom four men in black caftans and white stockings held up the four poles of a canopy, which sheltered a rabbi and a bride and groom. This last piece, like all the ones before, she handed to her son, followed by doilies. She fetched a canister of Lemon Pledge and sprayed down the fuzzed areas.

Olive-wood camels, olive-wood mules, olive trees painted on olive-wood slabs. Isaac's binding pounded into the soft foil of a single bookend, a midget Rachel's Tomb in clay, slotted on top for alms. Impossible the old man wouldn't own a brass King David's Tower on a chain. She looked behind a bureau and there it was, on ropes of dust.

Perhaps the carpeting should be professionally shampooed and suctioned, perhaps torn up. How, otherwise, even once the residues in the whole place had been eliminated, would she overcome this stubborn case of crawling skin, knowing that the main surface of the place was a sponge? True, she disliked mopping but she loved a floor just mopped. She hated to have given up her tiles, hard but ever cooling to the feet, back home. And what was it, only three days away, if not still her home? Harvey was in right now. Standing on her spotless tiles and cursing her for making them leave, yes, though he wouldn't admit it, hard at the task of chronicling the move as a concession to her and not to circumstances. She had been coming to see it in his behavior, like the sickened way he had looked at her the night before the flight, standing with his back against the kitchen tiles they had chosen twelve years ago, a harvest theme, persimmons and blue grapes. He had reached to hold her hands and she wouldn't make her hands available. She'd been koshering beef liver! Chopped liver freezes very well. She told him, You don't want to touch my hands, and he could see that—had seen it well before his gesture, and still chose the impossible time. Bacteria, juices, blood, she had said. He walked away as if she'd meant these as personal slurs. The slightest motion between them nowadays connoted disappointment on a massive scale. How could it but? When their last domestic project had been to dismantle their existence.

Mezuzahs wrenched off their door frames, closets emptied, the white walls bared from batik tapestry, a woodcut print, a copper platter, an oil painting, original calligraphy on simulated parchment.

Not much, at the end of the day. Few and commanding foci, that had been the goal twelve years ago, for the home that had been not only their first owned, but also the first with a concept of design. They had stuck to local craftwork, the minimal touch or the marvel of intricacy, religious themes as well as secular, befitting the vision: the grandest old hopes alive in contemporary garb, Modern Zionist Orthodoxy. Here the days would move by the map of Law while the heart beat for Zion, and all the time the mind would remain immersed in the developing world, which again was Zion, rising around them in fresh asphalt, new cement foundations and young trees, close by the sands of the Mediterranean. Inside their apartment they invoked the outside, sand-colored tiles set off with a blue wool kilim, not too broad, not to obscure the stone reflecting the pure walls, clean, fixed planes in an apartment just finished within a building similar to scores rising in sprawling blocks of bright white multistories, contractors' signs blazing all over Herzlia, squares of color silk-screened on tin. The ficus saplings in their wire enclosures fended off the heat with quavering fig leafs. This was their place, an M.A. and a Ph.D. in scientific disciplines, chemistry teacher and metallurgist, the daughter of a beadle from Trenton with her Harvey, the would-be heir of a Bronx grocery, who had engaged her to him in Hoboken with the wall of Jerusalem in sterling silver around her finger.

The furniture they sold. Any notion of attachment fizzled once they had looked into shipping costs. This time there would be no subsidy. No establishment supported the descent, which was instituted on what principles? One, mercy on her sons. And the practice? A very big move. And after that?

Yitz's throat-clearing kept announcing his presence on the porch, but the farcical delivery negated the insistence. Eytan remained busy at the sofa. He had sorted the old man's collectibles into groups, according to what categories, it wasn't clear. She had specified only two: storage or keeps. He took a step back to appraise the inventory. He was taking profound satisfaction in the work. There stood Harvey, but very small. There he had been, too, in the altitudes between Ben Gurion and JFK, in the little boy's fantastic self-sufficiency. Eytan had kept himself diverted the entire time with only five slim storybooks, a box of crayons, and paper. No, paper she had forgotten, so he had drawn a family of puppets onto travel-sickness bags. The use of these had kept him busy the rest of the way, the only fuss coming after the long nap, when he awakened thirsty. He wouldn't push the call button. *No, you, you,* he whispers through tight lips, scandalized.

Footfalls crunched on the Astroturf outside. At the sofa Eytan raised a hand behind his head, twisted a tuft of hair near his kippa, stepped forward and made a selection, picking up the mammoth and looking closely at the tusks.

The curtains billowed, writhed, then separated into panels, Yitz bursting through, droplets rolling down his sideburns onto stubble. "Summer shower!" he said. "I remember the smell!"

Eytan gaped big-eyed at his brother, then at her. "Here in the summer it rains?"

"I saw lightning," Yitz said. "Dig it. We're going to get a show. We need some chairs out there. Let's get some kitchen chairs." Thunder broke and he jumped, but wove the motion into a decision-making gesture, smacking a fist against a palm. His little brother hopped to, beginning to walk in his direction, still holding the mammoth, scratching his neck with the trunk.

"Eytan!" she said. "No."

He hid the mammoth behind his back, as if the toy were at issue, and as if it must be hidden from Yitz.

"You cannot go out," she said.

"Let the kid have some fun," Yitz said.

"Sixteen stories up, Yitz? Exposed in an electric storm, on metal chairs?"

"Ahh," Yitz said. "Guess the fun's only for me."

"No," she said.

He took a step around the sliced oval sheen of the expandable table, towards the kitchenette.

"Those chairs stay where they are," she said.

"Who are you talking to like that?" he said. "I'm twenty-one."

"Who are *you* talking to, Yitz?" she said. "You are in your mother's home. I allow no willful self-endangerment at any age."

"Oh," he said, taking another step. "Interesting news. I wonder how you plan to enforce this."

As usual these days his gaze was shifty but he knew when he was being looked at. He hesitated very briefly before breaking into a rush. Three paces and he was in the kitchen. Garbage bags rustled. Chair legs scraped. Chair legs knocked against the table. The bags rustled some more.

"Fuck it," he said behind the wall. "Shit-pile blockade." He emerged chairless, walking with the same haste as before, but towards the bathroom.

"I could use your help," she said.

He seized the doorknob, by which he heaved the whole door

upward in its frame, this was the method, and then in. He walked inside and closed the door, unnecessarily hard. Eytan returned to the sofa and put the mammoth down. He reached for a scrap of newspaper and wrapped the standing bass player.

"Do double layers on all the porcelain," she said.

"Them that's like this kind?"

"Yes."

They heard the toilet being flushed, once incompletely, then success. The medicine cabinet latch released. A bathroom object clacked, tumbling into the sink. The sky thundered again.

"What's the blessing for thunder after lightning?" she said.

"'Whose power and might,'" Eytan said.

"Very good," she said. "So let's go."

Blessed are you, Adonai our God, King of the universe, with whose power and might the universe is full. He recited the Hebrew fluently.

"Amen," she said.

The bathroom door opened. Yitz, in just his briefs, strolled out, one hand slowly massaging salve onto his belly, the other gripping an unfamiliar pink tube, any print or logo worn off. He settled on a damask ottoman, legs splayed. Eytan looked up a moment, and turned back to wrapping. He lifted another newspaper strip, but let it drop again, instead selecting a full sheet with which he wrapped a bookend.

They each attended to their task. Between clashes of thunder newspaper crackled, cleanser fizzed, and scar tissue softened with moist, private sounds.

If Yitz insisted on treating them to a freak show this evening, on the other hand spirits were remaining calm now, and he was making no more moves to step outside. She believed he had never meant to, had come in to get out of the storm but sought to import one indoors. The current attempt was as unpalatable, but quiet. To comment on it would only fix the little one's attention on this weird public tenderness and its object. The scar was dark red, raw as a scrap of organ meat, and self-inflicted. The boy's body would have come out undamaged by combat, had he not burned it by his own hand on sentry duty, with the embers from bowls of hashish.

To explain the practice he would say only that it had helped him focus, all at once on every tree in the surrounding grove of cherries. And in the green sickroom where this practice landed him, could he have been diagnosed as focused? Trapped in the full length of hours throughout which a young man could sob without resting, isolated high upon the terrifying pinnacle of his young experience, the vision of boys just like him exploding all around.

But what right had she to decide that hers, of all the boys of Israel, should be exempted from this vision? No, what right had she twelve years ago, to decide that Yitz would be a boy of Israel. This was what the sacrificial ram was asking now, having jumped out of the fire into her living room, eyelids burnt off, very angry.

Crisped around the glaring ovine eyeballs, very nice, a very pleasant thought. Perhaps Harvey was right and she did like to amplify misery. Yitz had gone nowhere near his eyes with the embers. And he could be meaning nothing by this conduct, now. He could be doing simply what you would do in the army, taking care of your private business in the group's full view.

She set the canister of Pledge down with an inadvertent knock. "Yitz?"

He looked up.

"Yitz," she said.

"Yeah," Yitz said. He kept going with the salve. "What?"

Eytan turned around, holding a papered clump, his hands inky.

"We're doing housekeeping in here," she said.

"Yup," Yitz agreed. "I can see that."

"Yitzy." For once he looked directly at her. "Right now this room is for housekeeping."

"Do I offend you?"

"Housekeeping," she said.

"It's not so bad," he said. "Take a good look. Hey, little bro, want to look?"

"You take your personal hygiene to the proper room, now!" she screamed. "Eytan is busy with a job!"

Yitz shot to full near-naked height, upsetting the ottoman. He marched to the bathroom and again disappeared inside, again slamming the door, but even harder, a nerve-racking number of times. Boom. She set her face in a slim smile. Boom.

"Housekeeping," she said. She strolled towards the ottoman and righted it. Boom. Skipped away on her aching feet. Boom. Something metallic fell and skittered on the bathroom floor. "House-skipping," she sang, dancing on to inspect the box, the half-cleared sofa.

She told Eytan he was a champ. He snickered, wiped a hand across his nose, let the hand cover his mouth a moment, then rubbed an eye. Boom. His hand traveled to the back of his head, and tugged at a tuft of hair.

She had started removing pictures from their nails, Eytan had returned to mind his stock on the sofa, and Yitz apparently had run out of steam when she heard the warped beginning of a familiar tune, four notes and no more.

"Show how," Eytan said. He was struggling with the stiff key of a music box.

She walked to the sofa. The box, belonging to the shtetl set, was modeled after a poor cottage with, what else, a fiddler on the roof. For whatever reason he had grouped it with Abe Lincoln. Thunder broke again. She wound the key.

She stood the contrivance on an end table and Eytan watched it spin slowly around, tinkling a number from the musical, maudlin and hesitant and ending with the inconclusion typical of these cheap novelties. In the bathroom Yitz turned on the ventilator and turned it off.

"Again," Eytan said, and she recognized that he was crying. Why would he not cry? Still she was shocked, not having seen tears from him in so long.

He cried differently now. No longer the crumpling of the face, not shoulders shaking, no more sound, only the eyes welling with water. When he saw her looking, he smiled, chin tipped bashfully towards the chest, his gaze flitting to the carpet.

"Here," she said. Her arms still recalled his baby weight, the small spasmodic heft.

He pushed her away with surprising force. "Again," he said.

She wound the key. He wiped his eyes and left gray newsprint streaks. He wept some more. His seventh year's smile, perhaps his one for life, chided the indulgence, but for the moment he demanded it, again and again, and she provided.

Barbary Apes

✥

A PIGEON PACES THE external sill, ruffled, red-eyed, fat and in a stupid panic. Beside the radiator Dassa pretends to lose her traction on the desk connected to her chair, deprives her head of a supporting arm and swings an elbow at the glass. It's a lost cause. The pigeon knows the girl in lecture room 500 to be of zero consequence, all show. The panes are sealed, the panic undisturbed.

Intro to the Sephardic Diaspora, a social science credit class. Rabbi Haziza has been standing and lecturing for forty-seven minutes from the same spot and in the same posture: one fist, cupped in the other palm, pressed to his chest, primed to administer his own CPR when ultimately the strain overcomes him. Why should he strain at all? The dullness in the eyes of mandatory credit students drains a teacher's soul. Well, sustenance is near. In the region where the radiator valve dispatches a perpetual hiss, there sits the Rabbi's most committed freshman, alternately broiled and chilled. The outside cold may puff in through the spongy caulk, bearing from the streets below the smell of motor-oil mingled with Manhattan rain, or it may not. The girl is oblivious, captivated by the Rabbi's teachings. See her shining eyes.

She checks the inner corners for dried sleep. The left is clean. The right smoothes with a rub.

"And that topography seems to have borne a direct influence upon the vocal stylization of—"

A natty, oldish man, clean-shaven and small, the Rabbi is a Jew of Gibraltar. She loves that about him. Yes, with the monkeys, he replied in the first session. Everyone knew about the monkeys, or at least pretended. Only Dassa brought them up, hand flagging even as the teacher introduced himself.

Please. The student in back.

Gibraltar with the monkeys?

Yes! he answered. With the monkeys! he said, struck. The Rock Apes go hand in hand with the mention, he said, to those who know.

Thus nearly four months ago, but the impact remains fresh. He will set eyes on her today. He will remember Dassa with the monkeys.

There is a value to these monkeys, far and above the starting worth of any monkey, already high. A monkey of any kind is at the very least likable, but a Gibraltar monkey has a reputation. The Monkeys of Gibraltar: It rang a bell for everyone, or at least the pressure was on to feign the knowledge. What the reputation is, she doesn't know. This kind of reputation is much stronger than the kind you have the details on. You must create them.

Monkeys. At the zoo aren't theirs the most popular cages? You not only glimpse them in passing but stand and study. From the best enclosures, one will study you back. Gorillas break your heart because of their sad pace. A mother's black fingers go on grooming her baby while her gaze slowly sweeps the crowd beyond the moat. The male might contemplate a tire, then lay it down and settle as on a raft from which to stare up at the sky. Consider living side by side with these wordless family units, but a variety with smaller individuals, minding their business right along with you and yours. You come and they go, casual as park-goers and birds, except that on occasion pairs of eyes would recognize each other briefly, from across.

"Codified," the Rabbi says, "in the least lavish thread in the embroidery."

A series of far sirens cries. A second pigeon joins the other on the sill, on landing frightening its predecessor, whose fright alarms the new arrival. Both birds race to opposite ends and keep these posts, the small heads pulsing around and around, the beaks the second hands.

"The gold of course," the Rabbi says. "In preexpulsion tapestries you know it would be actual—"

The first bird's plumage is pink-brown. The new one is the same. Occasionally the breeze reveals the underlayer, pale wisps overresponsive to the air.

"As I, as I, as I—"

She turns towards the blackboard and finds the Rabbi looking out, through her window.

"I pointed out to you," he says, back from the momentary absence, though continuing to gaze afar. "Also in the case of the Toledanos, so here, again, we see force of necessity converting heirlooms into tender—"

Dassa trains her gaze to follow his: Gibraltar, rocky, gray. Blue ocean waves whip wet crags upon which famous monkeys rush, ecstatic. Various aquatic fowl circle the pure sky. Beneath them, a youth, a young Rabbi Haziza, bids good-bye to his favorite monkey, who, alone among his peers, crouches inert, grave and attentive.

I will miss you, says the Rabbi. I will miss you, my good friend.

And in a blink the noble Rabbi is a man, displaced, stranded high in a cold city, in a lecture room, where torpid figures meld into the shapes of desk-chair combinations. Steam spits. Beyond the windowpanes, bumbling pigeons roost in the eye of skyscrapers gray as cliffs. It is to them the Rabbi lectures. Round and small in his lovely old-fashioned suits, he hawks his line of goods to the Manhattan towers: the golden history of oriental Jewry, Sepharad. Samples include clarifications of the Laws for living penned in Egypt, rabbis counseling to Spanish kings, poets of Yemen penning glorious unrequited hymns to distant Zion. Habits of celebration among Syrian Jews of modern Brooklyn. The Rabbi labors on, regaling the skyline.

But towers are content in rising up, blind to interiors. When she checks back, the Rabbi has returned to the room, still wistful—bitter, never—sweetly tolerant of life's indignities. An easy A. He is forever gentle with the girls and would extol even the most insipid commentary. Anything. Today not even drivel issues forth.

The radiator chokes down a wet sneeze. The Rabbi starts, looks over.

There she sits. In attendance all along, everything a teacher wishes for, an audience to whom his story is alive. He widens his eyes: How have I been coming across? She stares back: good, poignant. The Rabbi smiles with a mild rise of the brows: Now don't go overboard. He isn't here for sympathy but for the purpose of providing texture to the thoughts.

And indeed there he is, again back in boyhood, the same roly-poliness of his adulthood, but scaled down and in a sailor suit, navy and white. He sits in the shade of a stunted Mediterranean tree, in a circle made of many more small boys, all sailor-suited, partaking of the Torah which flows from their schoolmaster's lips. It is a Friday afternoon. A procession of mothers marches by, over a dusty footpath, conveying cauldrons of raw stew to a communal hearth. Their sons may sense them but they don't look up, rapt at their master's feet, enthralled, naïve. Little do they know. The beatitude will soon be shattered when the War compels them all to sail for asylum in New York, where they'll be charged with roomfuls of dull-witted college girls. The last of the Gibraltan mothers marches past the children, the flicker of a long, dark hem. Then she is gone, with her cauldron of stew. The blue ocean thrashes against wet crags upon which monkeys, vehement, alarmed, guffaw and rant as if they might be heard above the waves. A frantic pantomime display. The waves overwhelm every sound.

"Please. If you would, please, Miss Lvovy. Your thoughts regarding Kurdi bridal rites. Hello there."

Rabbi Haziza breaks away from the Gibraltan scene, standing full grown in a Manhattan lecture room, forehead wrinkled, hair thinning, suit brown. For the first time since the beginning of class he disunites his hands, awaiting.

"This week's assignment, chapter nine."

"I don't remember?" Dassa says.

"Not the end of the world," the Rabbi says. "Happens to all of us from time to time. We'll leave the subject open, then. Something you found evocative. An aspect of Jewish life on the slopes of Mount Ararat. Or the life cycle of Iraqi Jews, or Parsi, should you have skipped ahead for extra credit."

She is months behind.

"Anything at all you'd like to comment on?"

No. The attention drifts to more pressing concerns. In her bunk bed every night Dassa experiences with stark immediacy the life of her dorm-roommate's feet. Margaliss, a tiny girl, steps every night out of her Dr. Scholl's, climbs up the wooden ladder to the upper berth, below which Dassa lies. And it begins. The feet dangle over the border of the mattress. Hands reach down and anoint with Vaseline Intensive Care: heels, arches, toe by toe, each digit attended to with loving, squelching deliberation. The slickened feet are aired out briefly, then secured in white cotton socks, before retiring. The roommate's hips are slight, her legs tender, without muscle. When she disrobes completely there is the shock of a soft paunch and cumbrous breasts with huge, dark areolas.

"Evocative or curious," the Rabbi says. "A question is at least as good as exposition."

"To me I personally!" She would enjoy some privacy right about now. She stops, slows herself down. "It's just. I mean for someone like myself, they, those, like, I'm from Rhode Island?"

And Rabbi Haziza merely gazes at her, seeming smaller even than before, abandoned. His only ally in the class deserts him, fuses with the heartless New York skyline and becomes a flinty speck. He is alone again. And she feels sickened. He is lost to her. But it's his fault.

A muffled argument of car horns rises from the street. One of the pigeons on the windowsill is dozing. The other pulls up a loose feather, burrowing for pests. The feather coasts towards the street. The radiator gurgles and is still.

She walks back to the dorm through the exhaust of pretzel carts, vapors of toasted dough corrupted by burnt salt. It's November, cold and clammy after a night of rain, but the clouds overhead seem unportentous, otherwise engaged. A vendor whisks out a white sheet of tissue paper, snaps it in the air, and with his other hand poises a pair of tongs. A flock of Perl Memorial girls approaches him. They take no notice. It isn't kosher. Dassa walks behind them.

—*top of the Empire State Building. The drops are blowing up instead of down, I'm freezing cold. But do I kvetch? He—got the notes for Rabbi Semp's—*

She passes the pretzel vendor and again he tries to lure, but Dassa, also, shuns him. She doesn't eat. The head is buoyant, full of holy noise. The rift between her and Rabbi Haziza has only upped the giddy static.

—*maybe this is news but you are not the only one who lives in— cold? He says, You should put on—the Kree'ah laws.*

She watches the girls' striding ankles. Perl Memorial enforces a modesty code but no uniform, and yet as if by decree the girls all wear the same clothes. Modern tailoring conformed to the pre-scribed lengths, the permissible clingage, has produced the same results across the land. The skirt in vogue is mid-calf length and narrow. The fabric could be said to be a stretching of the law, fre-netic rayon, at rest indeed smooth, disconnected from the limbs, but each step sets in motion a flurry of ripples, fluttering connotations of the body beneath. Three razor-sharp pleats at the back fan out, fall back in line, fan out, revealing opaque cotton tights and hints of variation. The forms beneath the cloth assert their differences in generalized terms. Dassa anatomizes the defects, as always finding a bad case of nerves relieved in private furies against girls. They yammer on.

Out comes this pair of gloves, not really me, but cute— Body stood up to her. She's— Somewhere private— Pink, angora. At this point I'm a little— Punch your stomach right under your navel, just enough to— But for a parent you rend by hand, though you can start it— Fuse your nervous sys— One on. He says, Maybe the other hand isn't as cold. I say, It is, it is! But he keeps noodging me, So put it on! So put it on! What are you waiting for? And all I do is cry, because, the ring finger? Is drooping. Drooping.

Before Dassa can adjust her pace, the group comes to a stand-still, and she plunges unprepared into the fluid interaction of the Perl Memorialites.

"Oh. My. Gosh. Ohmygosh! It's gorgeous!"

"Mazel Tov!"

"Hey!" It's Margaliss, with naked joy detecting Dassa in the crowd. The little roommate yields a stream of dialogue just as Dassa's powers of perception are sucked into the maw of an invisible revolv-ing door. Now she must push the grinding cage back to the starting point, only to be ejected back onto the street. What's the idea of a revolving door? She thinks about this. Draft prevention.

"I'm sorry?" she says. "What?"

"Yirmy Meltzer and His Vilde Khayes," Margaliss says. "They're back from their European tour and they're coming to Queens. We're all gonna go Wednesday to celebrate with Shayna. You?"

"Oh, you should come, you should come!" someone else cries, maybe Shayna. "They're hysterical. And they always put up a screen so we can dance."

They pelt each other with their favorite tunes. *"The Tshulent Tzha-Tzha." "My Mammeh Tzippoyreh." "A Shindig for Shabbos!"* "Ahh!" They exclaim, as if bested but glad of it, until *"The Valtz for the Vedding"* gets a bigger response. But *"A Kopf Full of Torah"* merits a screech.

"No-nonono*no!*" Margaliss adjudicates. From the neck up, she's adorable, with a toddler's suckle lips and wine-red ringlets, and they listen. But she doesn't speak. She dances, right there, in front of a Korean deli. As quickly as the Perl Memorialites can gasp in unison, they form a living wall around the girl, locking Dassa into the construction. Margaliss shows how it's done.

The movements called for are precise, swift, governed, not involving the hips. One claps in a certain way, shuffles sideways in a certain manner, hoofs and scrapes in a particular sequence of steps. The face is almost solemn, tranquil with know-how. Red curls fly out as barrel-shaped Margaliss spins and then halts.

"That's *The Posken,*" she says. "It's a cinch. I can teach you."

Dassa's empty stomach snarls and bubbles. "Me?" she says. For this phase of the day she likes to be alone. The hunger will mount, and then plateau, and then she'll be rewarded with a special shake with all its festive scents, sights, sounds: vanilla dust clamoring in her blender, four ounces of skim milk to four of water, six cubes ice. Finally, the filling of the glass. The level will rise thickly, dense with vegetable gums and bright with Yellow Number Five, rich with a generous percentage of endorsed Daily Allowances, richly deserved. The warmth of sweatered shoulders pushing into her is not part of the plan.

Margaliss waits. The other faces are arrested in anticipation, in a pitiful dare. There is no temptation. Dassa is the staunch descendant in a line of women who hate to dance. And no mean feat, this remove, pitted against a calendar full of occasions for cooperative steps. A Jew must dance. Again and yet again the circles form, the summoning recurs, hands on the women's side of the division reaching out to draw a girl in. Dance for the giving of the Torah, for the victory of Ester and the hanging of Haman, a newborn brought into the Covenant, a bride joining a groom. There's no avoiding it, but at the very least a girl can pick the hand with which to link. Her mother's, say. Within the pandemonium a daughter can seek out the strawberry blond wig for special days, the guarded smile for such occasions, the warmth and roughness of the dishpan hand. For several revolutions, then, the strange grip on the other side can be endured. And soon, abetted by the circle's many shrinkings and expansions, a mother and her daughter neatly trim themselves away, and head for the buffet.

"We're going to Slice of Zion before," Margaliss says.

The others turn on her.

"We said we'd vote!"

"Kosher Delight."

"Nah, Lou G. Siegel!"

"Avshalom Shawarma."

"Ooh, I could kill for his Lemonchick Kebob," Margaliss says, and in this moment, seeing the girl's vast, vastly satiable love of broiled meat, Dassa feels something so like rage that she must break away immediately.

"Wednesday I got plans," she says, and glances both ways crossing the one-way street.

By a subway shaft a patter of leather soles catches up with her, and she prepares to find out whether she goes mute in times of peril as her dreams have claimed. She won't find out today. It's only the Rabbi, who'll soon hurry past on the way to his train. They both must go their separate routes, move on, pick up the pieces.

He falls in step with her. "Miss Lvovy, good afternoon." He is slightly winded. "Are you in a hurry, Miss Lvovy? Do you have an evening class?" His pronunciation is so crisp, it is the clean lack of an accent, a neutral, supremely logical implementation of the English alphabet. He wonders could she spare a moment, gestures towards a green street bench. In class it is apparent that he isn't tall. But that she towers over him, this is uncomfortable news.

She sits. Like pressure on a dented soda can, the sitting frees her stomach of a pesky crimp. The Rabbi lowers himself, too, but perches only at the very edge, so that his feet won't hang short of the ground. As always, he seems absent something. Absent Gibraltar, yes, but moreover. Absent a walking stick. The old-fashioned kind, not hooked, having an ornamental bulge on top, an intricate brass knob to fill the fist. A graceful prop would really pull his look together, plus afford him more security on the high bench. His shoes are russet, pointy, buffed. He wears a three-piece mahogany suit, a creamy shirt and a blond satin tie. His yarmulke is of blond satin. A faintly lustrous hankie, blond, protrudes from his breast pocket. He is not so swarthy as she had pictured oriental Jews before enrolling in his class. There is in fact an illusion of fairness, not because he is light, but because the tans of his skin and his thinned hair, his brows, his irises, are so complementary, he seems monochromatic, made of gold. This must be how Jews of Gibraltar look.

"You're close to failure," the Rabbi says, and this is more fantastical than anything she could have dreamed up alone. The monkeys, in a sudden hush, observe a life raft sailing, through the air and out, over the waves. "There's time for you to make a comeback," he says, "only just. I should have caught it earlier perhaps, but that's the nature of a college, the sheer numbers. A student can slip by. When I consider now that at the start of the semester you were among the strongest girls—"

The raft crashes far from its mark. She doesn't like the stamina of *strongest*, the sputter of consonants. Hardiness is an adversary, constantly setting her back. The more she checks the scale, the more the progress of the indicator seems to slow. One can still tweak the skin over one's ribs. One shouldn't be able to do that. There is an ample pinch of buttock, cushions of pudge about the kneecaps. The upper arms still register a tremor when one sternly wrings the flesh and then lets go. Her hips she likes, she will allow this. Sharp, pleasing to the touch, framing a quiet hollow, inner functions simplified of late, the bloody clockwork stopped. She can and does give herself credit where it's due.

He strums the space where the tip of his cane should be. "Of course, you're not surprised," he says. "This doesn't come as a surprise."

More of a discombobulation. Hers is such a visible medium, there is inherently display, petitioning, but closemouthed. Anything offered in response must be spat out.

"I propose," Rabbi Haziza says. A beggar in pigeon-gray garments comes and begs. The Rabbi reaches in a pocket, drops two quarters and a nickel in the man's hand. Almost immediately another man moves in. Him the Rabbi turns down, shaking the emptied pocket. The beggar looks at Dassa. He stinks of drink but seems frightfully sober, rapidly assessing and inferring. "I suggest independent work," the Rabbi says. Behind the bench, doors open, letting out a smell of forced-air heating and a flood of people, into which the beggars are absorbed. "I strongly recommend you take advantage," the Rabbi says. "I've never failed a student," he says. "I don't wish to now." Down the street, a bus backfires, repeated shrieks alert of a reversing truck. "A presentation is one option that occurred to me," he says. "You could, of course, take on an extra paper, but since the last two posed some hardship, I thought—"

"What's my subject?" she says.

"Yes!" he says. "Yes, good. Well. I would like to give you the full range of possibilities. We've covered a fair number of communities so far, their rites of passage, holiday observances, attire, history. Any of these you'd like to zero in on would be fine. Or you might want to branch out in a new direction."

"I can do it on the monkeys," Dassa says.

His hands fly up and fasten on his yarmulke as if a stiff breeze threatens. The fancy walking stick would have gone banging to the sidewalk. In the time he would have taken to avail himself of his hands again, scramble down, try to retrieve, she would have reached out and secured the rolling cane. He'd take his seat again, beholden, compromised. Flipping her palm up, she inclines the cane towards him, but he doesn't take it, only grasps the brink of the green bench with his small hands. She sees their aging iridescent skin.

"The monkeys," he says.

"Of Gibraltar. Where you're from."

"The monkeys," he says, reaching for his breast. He pulls out the handkerchief and dabs his nose. "They aren't Jews, you understand."

"Everybody knew about the monkeys," she says. "Nobody knows what. You never covered that."

"I see."

"So that could be my subject."

"Miss Lvovy."

"None of us knows what it is. The reputation that they have. The Monkeys of Gibraltar, okay. What about them?"

"Apes," he says. "Barbary macaques." He folds his handkerchief. "I don't know why you test me."

"If you made something up I wouldn't know the difference. How can I test you? I'm asking."

"Asking what, Miss Lvovy?"

"Why the reputation?"

"Noise," he says. "The Spanish tried for a surprise attack. The apes were startled first, raised an alarum, the British took it as a personal favor and bestowed the status, as they will." He checks his watch.

She sees the face, white, with no numerals. He pulls a cuff over the platinum dots. She snatches at her bag, tears at the zipper and pulls out a notebook, then a pen. "What kind of noise?"

"Ape sounds."

"Made by the monkeys?"

"By the apes."

"Which look like what?"

"Like apes. Furry, humanoid, stocky, tailless. Apelike, Miss Lvovy."

She frowns as she masters the buckling notebook, digs in a full stop. She squints at him. "They do expressions?"

"Very active faces. Grins. Pouts. That's the cue to make your getaway, the pout. They're threatened, you'll be harmed. After a quarrel they reconcile by chattering their teeth. Now, Miss Lvovy."

"Describe your favorite one." she says.

The Rabbi presses his hands against the seat and stands. "My study partner will be waiting," he says. "Once you find a subject for your presentation, come and see me during office hours."

"I got a subject."

"The Barbary macaques won't do."

She turns the barrel of the pen between her fingers. "I should just drop out."

"At this point in the term it would go on your permanent record," he says. "I don't recommend it. I don't think that's the right choice."

She caps her pen. He checks his watch again. A batch of subway travelers surfaces. The beggars reemerge.

"The freshman year is a demanding one, I'm well aware," the Rabbi says. "I can be flexible. I don't insist on the conventional approach."

"So I can do it on the monkeys?"

"Miss Lvovy," the Rabbi says. "Please listen closely. I am touched by your enchantment with the island. I ask that you recall our subject." Again he checks his watch. "Have you ever tasted haminados?" he says.

She strokes one sneaker with the other. He takes a sideways step. A pigeon makes it presence known with flapping wings.

"Eggs in their shell," he says. "Slow-cooked inside the Sabbath bean stew. Show me a lineage of Jews without a Sabbath legume stew. In ours you will find eggs. The color they acquire is rather beautiful, the richest caramel-brown. The flavor is like nothing else." He doesn't sit again, but he stays put, his shoes moored on the shores of a silver puddle. "Show me on the other hand a student so indisposed towards study that even food won't engage her. This has worked before," he says. "A former student of mine could not write in essay form, simply could not write down her thoughts in a meaningful sequence, though no problem orally. She, as a case in point, made up the needed credit by becoming a Moroccan chef. The presentation was a smash! The whole class feasted. We took business from the cafeteria that day, teachers and students stole in from adjoining rooms. It did a lot for the young lady's popularity. Now, granted, she lived in Flatbush. She had access to a kitchen. You're from New England, I recall. The dorm facilities won't be conducive. Our kitchen is at your disposal," Rabbi Haziza says.

She can only stare at first. She tries but is unable to conceive of his present home. All she can say is, "You live close?"

"On the Upper West Side. My wife is always thrilled to meet a student. You'll find her quite an asset in research. She's a superb Moroccan cook."

"I might not like the food," she says.

"Very well. Find some cookery books. Consider Turkey, Tangier, Bukhara."

"Why not Gibraltar?" she says. "Can't I do Gibraltar?"

Rabbi Haziza pulls out his handkerchief once more and passes it over his brow. Strange, on a day so chilly. The cold is recorded in the seized muscles of her back. Her teeth chatter.

"Miss Lvovy," he says. "I am not asking you to entertain appalling truths, only the barest understanding of our path in the diaspora. You must progress beyond the spell. Our community did not spring fully formed out of the Rock. I am Moroccan by derivation. My wife is Moroccan by derivation. Gibraltarian cookery is Moroccan by source. Remember your notes. Even your apes, as their name testifies, are travelers, North African exiles."

"The Monkeys of Gibraltar?"

"Barbary, Barbary, Barbary," he says.

"I'll leave it in your hands," he says. "We're listed. Telephone my wife." The Rabbi jogs away, and down, into the sooty subway shaft.

The beggars draw near. Dassa turns and walks in the same direction. A white-robed perfume seller lauds his vials: Nile Essence, Congo Musk, Cypriot Potion. She holds his hawking eye in an unwitting promise, so in passing him reneges. He curses. She opens her notebook and walks on through the moving crowd. "Watch yourself, child!" A woman's angry voice.

But Dassa never bumps into a soul. She dodges fellow walkers by continuing to register their basic pace and post, compared to hers. She riffles through the pages of her notebook, searching for the arbitrary spot she chose for writing.

First the notes of the beginning of the term parade, columnar, bulleted and underlined, highlighted in three colors. Then the ranks break up. They scrabble into small unruly mobs of words, huddling, more and more tight-knit, until they curdle into odd unlettered shapes. Finally: blank. But only till she finds the monkeys.

She overshoots initially, but leafs back and locates the notes. Holding her place, she finds a wall out of the way, leans her back on dry graffiti, smoothes the page, and reads her work.

Some sentences are incomplete. The penmanship was hampered by conditions and an enigmatic shorthand dominates from time to time. *Gib eggs.* She tries to picture the interior of the Rabbi's home. His door, she is convinced, will be ornate. She thinks the wife will be the one to answer when she knocks.

A female version of the Rabbi, those Gibraltan looks, the self-same gilt of foreignness, the classy dress sense. She'll welcome Dassa in. There will be a hallway.

Patterned wallpaper and three brass hooks. A winter hat, keys, a light coat. Above the hooks, a photograph in a brass frame.

The yellow metalwork competes with the exposure, an image compromised by some mechanical incompetence, a loss of light's gradations, maybe age. The sky is the same silver of the water, the rock as black a shadow as its creatures. The largest of the figures is rotund, his silhouette describing skullcap, suit, a walking stick. The manner of the company he keeps is one of greeting, reaching, long of arm, long-fingered, naked, bony and succinct.

The Worker Rests
Under the Hero Trees

※

A SLACKENING IN THE pit of Adi's stomach warned her just as she approached the curb outside Fern Orthopedic. An individual she hadn't noticed on the empty street was suddenly closing in, too vividly purposeful, targeting her.

Turn back into the store, she advised herself in the calm, compelling voice of a public service ad from childhood. The voice, male, spoke in formal Hebrew, a trained narrator's delivery of a televised manual for the avoidance of common dangers in the house and out. This sort of ad was used to fill the commercial-free gaps between the broadcast hours of Televizia Leumit, the national channel. The short productions were often highly dramatized and diverting.

Here, out in the world at present, the message was this: On the event of torturers advancing in an unpopulated area, seek out the nearest venue of commerce. In this half-wild strip of Cape Cod, that would be Fern Orthopedic, and she had already spent far more time in there than she liked. The shopkeeper tried to lighten the message of impairment on the groaning shelves with unsuccessful humor. A male mannequin posed center-floor, jointless limbs forever crooked in sitting, face blank as a lima bean, body a gross

188

parody of pain. No part of him remained unslung, unbraced, ungir-
dled, unsupported or unsoothed. He held a cane and was fenced in
by a walker. His wheelchair was padded with a blue cervical pillow
and his feet bathed in an electrical basin. He wore a rosary around
his neck. Humor had to be the object. And today along with him
there had been also a live patron who had arrived before her and
stayed beyond both their transactions, no doubt still stoking the
discussion of his ganglion cysts.

What to do, then? Where to go? The safety ad narrator's voice
had shut down with the first argument as always. On her own she
came to the decision to think her most hostile thoughts. Glaring
curbside, she found the threat gazing back. A tired pane of Plexiglas,
scratched, weather-beaten, sunk in the frame of a newspaper dispenser of the yellow plastic variety hawking the *Midgmouth Town
Crier*. Because a change of routine was always good for the nerves,
which had just now made today's big statement, she responded with
a quarter-dollar coin. She pulled out a thin copy, the edges scalloped
from the past weekend's rain. She rolled the paper and held it like a
bludgeon at its base.

At Fern's she had deposited the polymer leg orthosis of her
employers' son, which was cracked and required duplication. He
would use a metal brace for a couple of weeks and she must remain
alert to the skin of his leg. His leaning would have changed since
the last time, the metal would dig in new places. Any reddening
spot was to be cultivated into a callous using a pad of gauze and
rubbing alcohol. She hoped not to tire of the heightened scrutiny,
of what she would keep seeing so close, a body encroached on by
nature and devices, brutally and long, the damaged brain in those
eyes, the brittle seams of her pity.

No tourist cars tore past as with the paper in her hand she wandered across Massasoit, a street not paved on a known footprint of
America's New English start, not housing the hand-churned ice-
cream shop or the short row of antique vacation manors, and not

leading to a beach of the Atlantic or the cranberry production plant with visitors' center.

The next morning at breakfast she found the *Crier* on her table in the caretaker's quarters adjoining Clarence's rooms. She had dropped it in Clarence's kitchen, she was sure, and didn't remember ever picking it back up. The mother must have come quietly in the night.

She filled a coffee filter with grounds, eyes on the front page. The lead story was of course a cranberry plant feature. The lower article displayed a color photograph, a man in his late twenties, square built, a touch fleshy, black curls balmed and beard groomed calligraphic, fine and very dark along his jaw. She switched on the coffeemaker and returned to him. Portuguese, she thought first, then Cuban, remembering the community by the shore. He stood smiling in proud leisure as if he had always known the cameras would come, fist to hip before a turquoise wall that glittered like an overpierced face with all manner of fishing tackle, pretty and sharp. She got as far as the headline: LOCAL COLLECTORS EMBRACE ONLINE AUCTIONS, FIND HISTORY. Then she went off to wash for the day. By the evening the paper joined the *Boston Globe*s delivered daily from the distant seeming city, heaped in new and near-new condition in the milk crate where she kept them between recycling dates. She considered keeping her eye open for a covered container to replace the milk crate, maybe something more attractive that might go with other small furnishings that she might add to what Clarence's mother provided.

When the night came to fix the papers for disposal, she read through the days in a sitting. The plague in China was continuing its drift forward while the carnage back home had receded to the inner pages. In Lowell a Cambodian dry cleaner was celebrating a second generation's dirty clothes. Thirteen Hindus had been massacred in Kashmir, elders to children in one predawn. The missing dictator of South Boston had been twice spotted in Belfast. Burlesque was on the rise in the western suburbs. The war was coming next Monday. The boys of Brit pop phenom Ladzilla enjoyed a witty rapport and in Holyoke a grandmother had died in the sight of neighbors, stabbed by her old lover who knifed himself too after a chase. One neighbor described him as having done like the Japanese, though the man had arrived from Cape Verde. The war would come in the first week of the next month. Creperies were back. Girls' schools were unprepared for the economic decline with no women alumni donating. In the south a child kidnapped six years ago had been found alive but very different. Sour plums would add spark to a cold meat sandwich.

Just past five that morning, the spool of twine having rolled off along a crooked floorboard, she unfolded the *Crier* and snapped it flat. In the photo feature the man with the nice beard and impressive tackle, a Felix Esquivel, was quoted saying this: "I just puzzle over how they used to make them. They're terrible. Either they had a whole lot more time then or there was a lot more fish." She turned the page. On the reverse side came into view two words alone.

Neer Shabazi.

The name appeared in unexceptional print within a single small article continued from the first page, but the letters pulsed like a gaudy zone. She did not see letters at all. She saw a narrow teenager with black, wing-shaped brows on a young forehead complected medium brown. She saw a row of white apartment buildings, rust trailed down them in long stains as if from ducts at the lower corners of repeated porch rails, in the city where they had both lived. She recalled the upper-story view, the rocky hills west of Jerusalem blurred through a haze of distance and factory mists.

She had gone through so much before happening on this, disaster and achievement, violence and attempts to change the law, caricatures, thumbnail portraits, telling and less telling shots, recipes worth studying or not, mystifying rows of numbers, the outside layer of Sports, readership letters, and her own reactions by turn curious, afraid, sorrowful, hostile, tickled, proud, hopeful, distracted, despairing, prurient, and exhausted, dreading the workday when she saw the time. At last she felt peace. Neer Shabazi, here where she lived now. A morning breeze blew through the kinked venetian blinds, scented of seaweed. Birds had wakened in the walnut and were agitating for activity. At the gate the bottle gleaner sorted through the recyclables with a methodic chiming. Neer, here where she was now, this peaceful place, this cape of cod.

Spell the name, the phone voice at the cranberry plant requested when the workday kicked in at nine, and recited the letters back in a convincing show of ignorance. For nearly two weeks Adi was made to go along with this. No matter how she pressed, the voice promised only that he would receive the message if he was there. One morning she picked up a call to hear a man verifying her name in the proper accent. She said in Hebrew that it was she speaking. He identified himself, unnecessarily. She asked did her name mean something, and he said, Of course. The younger Poresch girl from the top-floor flat.

Seven years old. She had been making her way home late after school one day, having attended her extra music lesson in the Conservatorion by the city hall. The streets would have been wakeful in the dimming afternoon but emptied of contemporaries in her school uniform. In her backpack would have been the bone-colored plastic recorder which she had considered a great thing.

What she had learned at the Conservatorion that afternoon who remembered, but the first full tune the teacher taught to them stayed. Slow-paced fingering within one octave, to these words: *The worker rests under the hero trees*—pause, and the same again—*The worker rests under*—the last notes altered to resolve—*the hero trees*—and climbing higher so the phrase closed like a call before response—*The river wind through eucalypti leaves caresses the bent neck.* A melancholy song but accessible to beginners, written before the time of radio for the men and the imported trees who had dried up the malarial swamps and built this city, the neck referring to the lives the disease had claimed.

It would have been something to walk home and consider certain trees great, but on that mid-year day this wouldn't have been the song. With the recorder on her back she had reached Alfasi Street, or Captain Wingate, or was it Alterman? On a street within a radius of more or less three blocks from Mendeleh Shapira, where she lived, a man in a white shirt had taken her hand. Together they had turned to bring her home by a new way. The man knew to predict that this new way would pass a garden. In the garden stood a dwarf poured of cement. On the dwarf's feet would be seen genuine Dutch clogs.

But before they had reached the Dutch dwarf, an Israeli boy had approached, medium-brown skinned, a son of Yemeni Jews, teenaged, with a familiar thinness and floating gait. At some distance he had stopped his floating, and had looked, and kept looking, and finally had said, She's my neighbor from my building. This was true. The man in the white shirt had walked away with calm dispatch.

The Silhouette was empty when she arrived to meet him, closer to the happy hour than lunch. Behind the bar watching Comedy Central was a serious young woman with a punk pompadour, hair bleached to a frazzle, teased and fastened with conspicuous clips. The television was fairly loud but the near absence of the bartender's voice seemed unrelated to the blare. Adi read her lips, guessed at their message and responded a little too loudly. The woman poured a liberal shot, then added mixer and pushed over a napkin.

At the end booth Adi sat facing the entrance. In this way she faced also the television. She gazed up at the skittering light, sucking a thin streak of cocktail through the stirrer. For a while she kept noticing also the bartender with her aura of damaged hair.

Soon Adi was sinking into her seat. She pushed a broad strap off her shoulder and let the weight of her backpack shift entirely off.

On the screen a figure popular in cinema was collaborating with the regular crew of a TV skit show. Normally he was cast grimly but now he was eager for a laugh, his eyelids popped wide. His pleading smile mesmerized her, his premature timing. Her skin crawled. Worse was to know that since his poor performance the guest had died, and died violently, at the hands of the mad wife for whom he had been caring many years unbeknownst to the public. A passing van blocked the afternoon shining through the bar door. She felt her face frozen in an anxious gawk. This would be the sight of her to anyone walking in. She rose and moved to the seat across, facing the area of the toilets and games.

To touch a major influence. To reconnect with the past. To press the hand that eighteen years ago had blocked a push to turn her life badly against her. A girl who had left the country that had raised her risked surrendering this kind of opportunity. Yet here it was.

The television continued to broadcast the skit, involving a catchphrase that drew increasingly uproarious laughter on being repeated. The phrase was "Honeychild, don't you even *go* there," and each new character would arrive at this same exclamation after a setup with the guest. During one tense interlude between catchphrase and uproar, Adi heard footsteps. She splayed the fingers of both her hands and clamped them over the vinyl edge of her seat. A man in a blue uniform strolled past. Not Neer Shabazi, but a thickset repairman, hair nutmeg-colored striped with white. He stopped by the pool table and set upon it a heavy canvas tote. He smoothed away the strap and undid a zipper.

He stood not far from her booth. She could see the marbled rose of his hands, the thickness of his fingers, but she couldn't identify the implements that he went on to produce from his bag and arrange side by side on the green felt. Several objects were box-shaped, flat and rectangular and appearing to be covered with narrow drawstring sacks. He set down a tool with a coral grip. Beyond the pool table an electronic lottery screen flashed the minutes remaining to the next drawing in gold on blue. A wall-mounted jukebox was colored to appear flaming, a transparent window in the middle displaying greenish stacked disks.

He took out a fistful of something and then in his other fist the same, brought both fists together and joined the two items into one with twisting motions. What resulted he placed on the felt, no more than a thick, nutted bolt to judge by its appearance. Whatever it was, it disappeared when becoming obscured by a pair of tan slacks worn over narrow male hips, which had come between her and the repairman at work.

"So I found it," Neer Shabazi said.

"My directions were all right?" she said.

"I have a map," he said. He slipped between the opposite seat and the table. She pushed upwards.

He leaned in. She extended her arm.

He kept leaning in. His forehead, finely lined above the brows, neared and neared until it could be only that his habit of greeting was to kiss the face. If this wasn't the custom around here still there was no reason she couldn't cooperate except for blind panic, which she wrested down just as he canceled his motion, attempting to disguise it. He was tall and made a long descent to sitting. When the seat stopped him, his bowed trunk straightened slowly in its collared shirt of gray tricot. She watched the phases as he settled on the other side. He smelled good, if somewhat too powerfully, of lemon cologne. She guessed he was someone for whom to feel fresh and clean was a festive high point. More exciting to her, more promising of an enduring chapter, would have been a man careful to walk around with rips in his pants and enjoying a tipple. Could there still be hope? Neer was holding a brown bottle of beer, a Budweiser. He lowered the bottle to the table and spun it slowly on its base, one half of a full rotation, so the insignia faced him while she remained in view of the ingredients and warning. Nevertheless she went on to picture his legs, hoping them not entirely smooth. The more thought she gave the legs the more hair she added, aspiring ever closer to the density of bear pelt. Such man fur would have shocked her in the past but with every year now she was finding she wanted more hair. He arranged his legs under the table and prepared to plant an elbow on top. Next he would cup his chin in his hand.

He stiffened and glanced impatiently away, as if she and not gravity had brought him down. She snapped alert, mortified. These after all were Neer Shabazi's legs she had been furring in her mind, legs of a savior, not some guy in his clothes. He looked back. He cupped his chin in his hand. His brows were not wing-shaped but rather straight.

"It was hard to get the cranberry people to admit you were even here," she said.

"Admit?" he said. "I'm no secret."

"You're telling me you're not," she said. "You're in the paper."

"I was in mid-interaction when we spoke on the phone," he said. "I thought, but then I dismissed. Really? *The New York Times? The Wall Street Journal?*" Even in this heightened state of interest it seemed he was distractible. He peered up at the TV and back. *"The Globe."*

"The local *Crier*. This was my point to the receptionist. They release a statement, I call, and they deny it."

"They denied our award?"

"We never got that far. I asked for you."

"You expected the person at the telephone to know my name?" he said.

"I expected? I assumed. You were in the paper."

"Have you been to the plant?"

"Big?"

"Not every level is equally engaged by my visit."

"I misunderstood then," she said.

"You never know."

"How do you mean?"

But he only flipped his palm up to dismiss his last remark. He raised his beer to his mouth. He drank in a manner that suggested he wouldn't drink many more than one. He appeared to be listening to what he drank, the sound neither pleasant nor unpleasant. Having made the observation, she found she resented him, as if this right now were an insult in a series. Distant neighbors before, close-mouthed strangers here. She was surprised at how quickly her mission had switched to sour corroboration.

He was not handsome. He was very narrow-headed. She imagined the trait had made it easier on his mother in birthing but she couldn't go any farther to picture him as a child without altering his features too improbably. Big eyes, big wise dark eyes, she had remembered beneath the gracefully shaped brows, which indeed were here today, if unwinglike, but his eyes were small and sunken and tending to flit. Perhaps she had been recalling his older brother, Yiftah, or his little sister, Kineret. She remembered Kineret, her own age, on a bike looping among the stucco pillars in the building's parking lot. She remembered pretending not to see her, although she herself would have been playing alone by the tough oleander where the cats hid. Why hadn't they hit it off, two girls in one lot? Above them four floors, eight porches, and not to mention the posterior flats: sixteen families to a building. Bonds couldn't be established among everyone. Her family was religious, the Shabazis not. The children wouldn't attend the same schools. They would never meet in synagogue. Their conventions of greeting would differ. If you were short an egg you would knock on a nearer door.

Everything could have been different had his family kept a strictly kosher kitchen and scaled the stairs to ring the Poresch bell.

Hers would have climbed down for a meal every so often on Shabbat and would have reciprocated. But yes, first genialities on the Shabazis' part would have been required, the outreach, because in that country her family had been checked, mannered too mildly, correct by the norms of another place, correct or conserved, newcomers and their kids waiting for a handle on the scene. The Shabazis on the other hand, parents and children, would have been two native-born generations since the grandparents had newly come, though to think back on their demeanor, perhaps newcoming wasn't bound to lift away on schedule.

So, a balance if not a relationship. The Poresch family the guarded Americans on the top floor, the Shabazis the guarded Yemenis downstairs.

Flat Four, southwest. Flat One, southwest. Draftswoman and pharmacist. Nursery school assistant, courthouse guard. Eldest a daughter, middle child a son, the younger daughter by the oleander looking for cats. Eldest and middle both sons, and the youngest riding solitary through the pillars on her bike.

She raised her glass and tipped it. Oily threads of vodka twirled through the cranberry juice. "Congratulations on your accomplishment."

"Mine?" Neer Shabazi said. "Not mine. It's a whole team." But anyway he slanted the neck of his bottle without touching her rim, shrugged and drank.

What else to say? Eighteen years had elapsed since that day when she had barely known him and after which nothing had changed. She would have passed him on the block with even more haste than her disposition prescribed, a sneaking horror now, though by some tacit covenant of children she had never told her parents, and he had never reported, her lapse of judgment, his presence of mind.

"Do you still find yourself on twenty Mendeleh Shapira Street?" she asked.

"Nu sure," he said. "Sabbaths and holidays. Supper sometimes."

She supposed this meant his parents were still alive. She smiled. "Are the Livyatans still there?"

"No."

"Handsome kids, the girls more than the boys, boys on the portly side. I liked their hair."

"They moved," he said. "A few years after you."

"Lovely hair," she said. "Each one of them, thick like honey. But that endless piano practice, all of the time the same mistakes, each sibling exactly as bad as the other. And that dog of theirs," she said. "Oy."

"A tan chow chow."

"You remember!" she said. "That dog."

"She made a lot of noise."

"Nu sure," she said. "With them leaving her so often on her own, the howling, but besides."

"I don't know what else I would remember her for."

"The tensions," she said.

"Someone protested the howling?"

"No," she said. "The waste. Mr. Tzadka."

Behind Neer the repairman had stepped away from the pool table and affixed the implement with the coral handle to the underside of the jukebox where it projected like a lobster claw. The door of the jukebox cabinet was open now, the man concealed behind it. A nutmeg-colored sideburn remained visible through the window, a ruddy cheek and the sun-bleached fringe of a mustache, framed by the printed flames.

"The air traffic controller," Neer said. "Seamstress wife, two girls, a boy my age, Oded. Iraqis."

"That's right!" she said. "That's what he was. At Ben Gurion Airport. I had forgotten that. His ears were shot from the jets."

"The howling wouldn't have bothered him then."

"On the contrary!" she said. "His hearing came in and out and he hated noise I guess for both reasons. The wavering effect drove him mad. I had forgotten that. When the Livyatans practiced the piano he would go berserk. He would shout down the dog. To me he was never anything but polite. I was very quiet. How could I have forgotten that? He lived on our floor. My mother did business with the wife. Their porch was next to ours. The dog was in the porch beneath, Three southwest."

"We heard her very well on One. But the tensions you say concerned waste?"

"That's what I said. Now I don't know. How could the ears have fallen out? I remember knowing about them. His wife would have filled my mother in. My mother would have told our father and we'd have heard."

"But the matter was the Livyatan dog waste and not her noise, this was your impression?"

"One day he smeared her shit on their flat door."

Again Neer Shabazi rotated his bottle on the table. The repairman continued to fuss with the interior of the jukebox, his booted feet shifting as if he too were embarrassed. Why the bad language? Of all the anecdotes she could have chosen for a sentimental journey. A neighbor boy to whom she owes a debt of gratitude turns up for the first time in her adulthood and she talks shit, literal shit. Television may have influenced her. Another skit was wrapping up, the cast members endeavoring to sound much older than they were as well as drunk. The dialogue was thin and they had lost it for hysterics.

"Where had he collected the shit in order to smear it?" Neer said.

"How do you mean, where?"

"Dog shit in the hallways I would have thought would get around. I'd expect even downstairs occupants would have been aware of the infraction."

"Outside. He collected it outside."

"The dog was soiling the exterior common areas?"

"Dog shit on the street is enough of a problem. The path and garden I remember clean."

"How then could he have attributed the waste with any certainty to the chow chow?"

"I don't know," she said. She was growing sad. "Watching from the porch?"

"One way or another his behavior seems extreme."

"Yes," she said. "That's I suppose what I was getting at, extremely humorous, I must have thought."

"Rather I'm puzzled that this story in particular should have come to mind."

"I was puzzled before you," she said.

She considered coming clean about her state of being. Shorter shifts would help, a few more chances to clear the head. Could she raise this with her employers? A live-in position meant accessibility. And how to put across to them that, nearing his fourth decade, their son's mind no longer was infantile but rather that of a very old infant tired of pain and wanting a quiet corner, where he found lust continually new, with any source of friction? The ottoman today, yesterday the carpet, the giant exercise ball, and more and more household items as every day she generated less and less chatter, since he couldn't talk. They had trained her in a slew of rehabilitative drills but the man had been this way from birth. Joy came pouring out of him at the slightest prompt. His teeth were shortened from constant grinding.

Neer raised his bottle and drank.

"Not puzzled!" she said. "No, to think of it. In my line of work I deal on and off with anything that comes out of a living body. The friend I see most often does the same thing, my weekend relief. The worst cleanups are a natural part of the conversation. You could say we compete."

"You're a nurse?"

"A live-in caretaker," she said. "But you're not. I apologize."

"No need," he said. "I've considered secretions myself. You do lose sight of other sensibilities." He drank thoughtfully. "But returning to our conversation I remain most puzzled that I don't remember the bad smell. It would have bothered me." He set his bottle down, not rotating it this time. He seemed to expect them to return to the previous topic. It appeared he might stick to it as long as they had here, less than an hour left before each of them must resume his and her work.

"Good beer?" she said.

"It's fine."

"I can recommend a local brew if it's just fine," she said. "Let me buy you a drink." She prepared to rise, turning one shoulder a little more towards him than away.

"Thank you," he said. "This is fine."

"Or one of these," she said, brandishing her glass. "In honor of your accomplishment. What's your vodka?" She smiled again, thinking back to herself at seven years of age, when he had saved her. Instead of more demonstrative she grew violently shy, the smile stretching like a surgical mask. She looked to her drink, watery pink around the liquefying ice, ruby red elsewhere.

"Thank you," he said. "I don't enjoy the juice other than medically."

She returned her shoulders to where they had been. "The stuff has to be sweetened and they sweeten it too much."

"On its own it's terrifically tart," he said.

"You're the authority." She tapped her drink to indicate again that she had chosen it in his honor. He would confirm this and she would confess.

"The tartness is not my finding," he said. He shifted his elbow on the table by the lottery cards and clamped his narrow jaw between his thumb and pointer. "Unless you mean beyond the sensation, the underlying nature."

"Exactly," she said.

"The anti-adhesion properties in this particular astringency."

"Yes."

"Or rather what we found to be a very certain compound in the berry which inhibits the adhesions present on the pili of the surface of pathogens, effectively disabling their cling."

"Yes!" she said.

"To one another as well as the teeth."

"What they put in the new red toothpaste!"

He took a swig of beer, sitting nearly languorous, but the eyes prowling. "No paste yet," he said. "So far just a dentist-administered glaze. The color soon fades."

"I for one look forward to your product very much," she said. "Red teeth or not."

He held the bottleneck by his lips without drinking, head still propped as on a tripod, his small eyes darting to the chattering TV again and again. He loosened his lips and released the bottle. "The name on the final product you can be sure will not be mine."

The old-seeming displeasure surfaced again, curling her nostrils. Did he take her for such a nitwit as to think his name would be the brand? *Shabazident!* on polka-dotted squeazy tubes, authorized by the ADA. The TV ad depicts knee-padded cyclists in a ruby-toothed stream, grinning, invigorated by the voices of a gospel chorus, thundering hope: *Bring out the Shabazi in your smile.*

The man was simply unable to cull theories of personal intention from the length of sentences, not even as short as, I look forward to your product. *She says this to encourage me?* No, not even, *An interested consumer!* At the jukebox the repairman cranked the coral handle once, twice. Something clicked.

"My mistake," she said. The repairman moved slowly back and emerged from behind the open jukebox, drawing out with him a wide cartridge, painted white but of metal, judging by the heavy scrape and slide of many coins against it from inside. She checked the time flashing, gold on blue on the Keno screen.

"Not on the pending patent," Neer said. "Not even the latest grant proposal." He squeezed his small eyes shut. He opened them. "I'm astonished I made it even to the local sheet."

"Team Honored," she said. "You're on the team." She stared at the seat beside her. She was losing interest in this personality across, this Neer Shabazi of the cranberry dissection squad, zealously dry, maniacally factual and now revealing himself also a disgruntled employee. Altogether a joy. What had possessed her to arrange this? Perhaps this was the time to say, I owe you my life, and wrap things up. Neer remained silent, seemed not to mind that the conversation had died. She examined the black vinyl of her seat, then the chipboard wainscot, the different ways in which the chips had aged, the remnants of a bumper sticker, and in a rush returned to the vinyl. "My bag!"

Neer checked his own seat, hoisted her backpack by the hanging loop and passed it high over the table. The canvas bulged strangely where it stretched over the new orthosis, showing the one-of-a-kind outline of Clarence's calf and heel. She set the backpack by her hip and knocked through the canvas. The polymer responded with a hollow sound. The dread retreated. This wasn't the time to fail in the eyes of the mother. The mother was alert to a worker's fading investment. She was familiar with it, she could tell, therefore the mounting tests, antiseptics misplaced, the surgical gloves missing, ointments and powders gone, the electric toothbrush, the super calorific shakes. If Adi didn't ask for a replacement right away the mother would magically find what had been lost, and wonder how the aide could have done without.

"I don't need a little plaque for my office!" Neer said suddenly. "Only proper credit and accurate placement in the group. This is important much less to my pride and pocket than my lasting impact in the field!"

She watched the currents of emotion in his forehead.

"Along the way you must reflect on your engagement I suppose in every human dealing," he said. "I understand. I know. A scientist today must be not only a politician, but also a salesman and a lawyer as well. You are your handler. Any other setup is fantasy." His gaze examined hers over a sharpening second, sought the television and returned, his small eyes large in their effect. Each time they came back solemn, solemnized, gems in skin settings. "I don't have the natural flair," he said, his irises glistening, black as coal. Not black as coal. Converged on her, each bounced blue doorway shapes notched with dark cutouts of her skull. When his eyes flashed up, each mirrored the TV. "I also have no choice," he said, "but to develop in this area. The research cannot lose my perspective because of a nature I can learn to flex."

He looked at her again. A bus rolled by outside, judging by the action of the engine and the duration over which the doubled light of the door left Neer's eyes. He glanced up, eyes again mirroring the TV, down to her again. In the time before the light returned it dawned on her he could go on like this forever.

"I hated to sacrifice the focus of my research," he said. "Of course it's just this maximizing notion which incites the peripheral unseens. I relied on my representation by others. I woke up to find I had been underrepresented. The fault is mine, I don't deny it. The self-promotion was my labor to carry out like any other assigned to my post."

"You've had a regular place in my thoughts," she said.

Neer recoiled in his seat. His knees knocked the underside of the table.

She said, "Thank you."

"There is no need."

"I have the need," she said. "I won't make a big show, I'll say it once and with restraint but this is what I came here to say. The man in the white shirt took my hand, you took the other and he let go. If you hadn't passed by who knows what I'd be today. Because of this I will always think of you. You will always be in my thoughts."

Neer took a long drink, swallowing three times. He returned the bottle to its place on the table, on a water ring. "I didn't take your hand," he said. "I stood at a distance so I could run if I had to. I made it apparent that I was memorizing his face."

"I don't remember his face," she said.

"Nor I. Not back then, either. Seemed I'd retreated while maintaining the aspect of inspection. I had never been so frightened."

"Do you remember walking me home?"

"No."

"Stands to reason," she said. "Me neither. We wouldn't have exchanged a word."

The repairman was back at the pool table, though plainly he was not that but rather the earnings collector. He had propped the great repository of jukebox coins on the green felt and now, one after the other, drew the box-shaped objects, each from its fitted sack. Each sack revealed a repository like the big one, of metal painted white, but smaller. Each of these in turn he fitted with the gizmo like a nutted bolt and what protruded of this he inserted in the larger case. Each full connection caused a rush and clank of change that rang each time in a faintly new way. When each bout of streaming stopped he detached the receptive unit, rewrapped it, and cinched the string.

"Why did your family descend?" Neer said.

"That word," she said. Meaning *emigrate* but applicable only when the launching point was Israel. Immigration was ascent, and emigration, the fall. The lingo wasn't new. *There was a famine in the land, and Abram descended into Egypt to sojourn there.* Under similar circumstances, Jacob and his sons went down, but never again came up.

"I apologize," he said. "Charm is not my strong suit as I said. Why did you emigrate from the land?"

"The land."

"Now you're quibbling."

"We thought we were ascenders for life but were only for a time," she said. "Am I supposed to be able to explain it? In that case all right. We were never sufficiently absorbed. We left, and now we're here and not there." She flipped her palm to let the subject go like a balloon.

For in the period leading to her family's descent she had been happier than ever before, but why would she tell him? Did he require recollections of her late-coming and short-lived period of acclimation to assure him of his native country's worth? Would he find this in the details of three ordinary girls from her middle high school?

He might have saved her life, but Natalie, Pazit, and Colette invested in it, welcomed her onto a trail hidden to her until then, into the ways of less observant Orthodox schoolgirls, or rather girls observant of other things. They'd known how to negotiate the markets, striving through leaning stalls to treasures of stretch cotton and fake gold. They had brought her to dance halls, urged greater attention to the hips. On double, triple, and quadruple dates they had planted her on the rear seats of motorbikes on which the cutting wind had taught her with what tightness one must hug the waists of boys in army uniforms. Colette threw up her meals to stay lean. Pazit's brothers slapped her when she disobeyed. In the tenth grade Natalie wrote Death to Arabs on a sole of her running shoes.

The good old times. In hindsight, yes, times that had been drawing a new itinerary for her in the land, by a way different from the old heroic songs. On foot, on bus, and on motorcycle, the girls had stayed on the move, the girls had got around. The girls had loved the street, heaving with crowds of coexistent human wills, malicious and neighborly, all desirous in their way. When she had left none of the girls had wept. The Poresch family after all had only been taking a sabbatical leave. No one had anticipated that same year would furnish the Israeli street with so many more trapdoors than before. Who would have let themselves predict so many sounds of walkers falling? Or the Poresch family remaining in the stiller landscape.

"Can you recommend points of interest?" Neer said.

"Sure," she said. "Boston."

"Locally, I mean. They send us only on the tourist route. The beaches are too quiet. The pocket watch museum is thoroughly covered in two days. I don't like ice cream. One mansion was enough. Where do I find the human scene?" He reached behind him and took out his map. He spread this over the area of their table above which two other patrons might speak.

"We have a watch museum?" she said. His finger traveled three or so miles over a shore route and stopped. She stared at the point.

"Do you find you like it here?" he said.

"Something in the local character speaks to me."

"You must have to live here awhile to pick up the sound."

"No denying," she said. "I miss the people on the streets. Wait a few weeks. It gets thicker. Or hire a captain, go fishing."

He folded his map. She pinched the tip of her stirrer and turned it, blending the liquid ice into the darker stuff surrounding.

"How's your drink?" he said.

"Once the ice melts it's not so syrupy."

"Is there a vodka you prefer?"

She looked at him. He didn't know he was recycling her earlier small talk. "No."

Music began to play through the jabber of television comedy. The earnings collector was at the jukebox again, thumb on the coin slot.

"Christ, not again." This was the bartender, fully audible now. An Irish accent aerated her final *t*'s to a soft whoosh.

"Don't like it?" the collector said. "I'll let you choose the next one."

The first selection continued playing, voices of women harmonizing, a song ubiquitous as of the winter just passed, streaming from mall and film house speakers, radio, music TV on which the video revealed three fiddler ladies, ordinary-looking but lovingly groomed, figures shown off, instruments trained at shining shoulders as they communed with six or seven mariachis on taverna benches, the men ostensibly proficient in Country, as this was the sound. Women and men, they sat together, singing, playing, locking smiles with no amorous suspense. The women's bows sliced at the strings with swift precalculation. The men played concertinas and guitars, which the recording picked up as muted backdrop.

The time to leave was drawing near. "The best of luck with the paste," Adi said.

"Glaze," Neer said. "It's almost there."

"When the product comes out," she said, "the field of assisted living will rush to embrace it."

"There is still the issue with the pigment."

"Particularly in the case of the nonverbal," she said. "Imagine yourself incapable of understanding language. Imagine trying to make sense of an electric toothbrush in your mouth."

"If I can overcome this nonsensical stalling," he said.

"You have no idea how strong Clarence can be," she said. "Amazing upper body strength, hauling himself around all of these years."

For the first time Neer raised his head from the supporting hand. She had alarmed him.

"It could have been available last year," he said.

"Clarence can't conceive of assault," she said. "He just resists. But if I've learned anything in my line of work, it's that I prefer threat to isolation. I should have remained with the mentally ill, working for the state."

"Will you be seeking a new position?" he said.

"I think so," she said. "Yes. I'll keep my eyes open. I receive the daily paper. I pick up the local one when it catches my eye."

The earnings collector returned to his work surface and began to pack up his tote. He put away a cloaked cartridge, and another, and paused, rubbed at his temple, yawned. Bouncing a fist over his widening mouth he looked directly at Adi, as though in working so long alone he had forgotten he was visible, or perhaps he was preparing to weigh in; if so, he soon recalled they weren't speaking the local tongue. When the yawn had worked through him he withdrew again into his business.

Neer leaned his head back on his hand.

"I'm optimistic," he said. "I believe I've got it in me to claim the influential role. What I require now is just the proper phrasing. Already the benefits endure beyond all expectations. The color soon fades. To be concerned more with the temporary looks than the long-term health of a smile, this I can't fathom. We're talking about only two, three days in most cases. It soon goes back to normal."

Acknowledgments

My profound thanks to my parents, Batya Abramson-Goldstein and Yehuda Goldstein, for their example in the world, their unflagging love and reserves of strength; to my groom, Robert Goodman, for his sustenance, faith, and infinite kindness; to my siblings, Hillel, Miri, and Avi, near and far, always here; to my editors at Scribner, Alexis Gargagliano and Rachel Sussman, and my agent, Maria Massie, each a unique and indispensable support and goad; to Robert Earley-wine, Stanley Elkin, Judith Neaman, Peter Genovese, Rabbi James Diamond, Elizabeth Searle, Abby Frucht, Christopher Noël, Yona Plezner, Bracha Lieberman, Mrs. Gretch, every teacher who encouraged and pushed, edified and provoked, incited, cheered and challenged; to Shlomo Bar, Yair Dalal, and Zehava Ben, for musical handholds in the nighttime climbs; and finally, a debt of gratitude to my late grandparents, Channah Abramson, née Tarshish, z"l and Rabbi Avraham Abramson z"l of Jerusalem, and Dorothy Goldstein, née Steinberg, z"l and Benjamin Goldstein z"l of New York, humble citizens of hallowed cities, models of elevating vision and industrious rebirth, in whose honor I do what I can.

NAAMA GOLDSTEIN was born in Boston and grew up in Petakh Tikva, an industrial central Israeli city founded in 1878 as an agricultural village and known as the Mother of Settlements. There, and later in Tel Aviv, she was educated in Orthodox Zionist girls' schools and for several years was a member of the Torah and Labor youth movement, Children of Akiva. At the age of seventeen she returned with her family to the United States and has since resided in Maryland, New York, Missouri, and Massachusetts. She has worked as a bartender, receptionist, Hebrew school teacher, accountant manqué, bakery hand, librarian, pub cook, and behavior coach. She now lives in Boston.